The Call
of the
Triple Spiral

Lisa Saffron

Permissions: Quotes from *A Dream of Angus Oge*, in *The Project Gutenberg EBook of Imaginations and Reveries*, by (A.E.) George William Russell may be re-used under the terms of the Project Gutenberg License at www.gutenberg.org

ISBN 978-1-8383757-0-6

Cover design by Good Cover Design
www.goodcoverdesign.co.uk

OTHER PUBLICATIONS BY LISA SAFFRON

FICTION

Checkpoint, AuthorHouse, 2008.

NON-FICTION

It's a Family Affair: the complete lesbian parenting guide, Diva Books, London, 2001.

What About the Children? Sons and Daughters of Lesbians and Gay Men Speak About their Lives, Cassell, London, 1996.

Challenging Conceptions: Planning a Family by Self Insemination, Cassell, London, 1994.

Risk factors for severe ME/CFS, Derek Pheby, Lisa Saffron, Biology and Medicine, 1(4): 2009.

The human health impact of waste management practices: A review of the literature and evaluation of the evidence, Lisa Saffron; Lorenzo Giusti; Derek Pheby, Environmental Management and Health, 14(2): 2003.

DEDICATION

To Dena, my greatest teacher of the power of love.

I am the sunlight in the heart, the moonlight in the mind; I am the light at the end of every dream, the voice for ever calling to come away; I am the desire beyond you or tears. Come with me, come with me, I will make you immortal; for my palace opens into the Gardens of the Sun, and there are the fire-fountains which quench the heart's desire in rapture.

from *The Dream of Angus Oge* by George William Russell, 1897

Whom shall I send, and who shall go for us?
Here I am. Send me.
Isaiah 6:8

Chapter 1. Ahmtoshtelay

She is alone in the chamber, alone in total darkness. It is nearly time to depart. Her arms hang by her side, her back is straight, her breathing calm and deep. She has prepared for this for many moons. She is as ready as she ever is before a journey into the unknown. She can no longer hear the others chanting. She listens harder, straining her ears. Yes, she can feel the faint throbbing through her feet. The Wise Ones are drumming, the drumbeats carried by Mother Earth through the ground from the chamber in the Grand Palace, more than an hour's walk from the Palace of the Immortals. The monotonous rhythmic beat of the drums travels through her body, merging with her heartbeat and her breathing. She chants in time, excitement building within her.

She reaches out to the stone with the triple spiral carved on its surface. The stone hums and glitters as her fingers pat the spiral. How familiar these stones are to her! How grounding they are, anchoring her to Mother Earth while they send her spiralling out on her journeys. They are always there when she returns, always singing, welcoming her back.

The rest of her circle of ten Wise Ones have walked out the narrow stone passageway, some smiling encouragement, others crying, a few looking nervous and one bursting with excitement. They have taken their burning torches with them. Outside, the full moon is shining brightly in the night sky but none of its cheerful light reaches the inner chamber where she waits.

She runs her hands along her ceremonial garments, comforted by the familiar feel of the knee-length cowhide tunic and the long coarse fibre trousers. With her fingers, she traces the triple spirals and diamond shapes embroidered on the tunic. Reaching up to her head, she pats the beads, shells and feathers she has woven into her coarse, black matted hair. She unwinds the necklace of periwinkle shells wrapped three times around her forehead. She holds the shells to her mouth and kisses each one with loving tenderness. At the last full moon, the ten of them crafted this necklace together. They journeyed by boat down the river to collect the shells at the coast where the shore was covered in shells after the big storm. Carefully, they selected the most beautiful yellow, red, brown, green, purple and black shells, filling sacks for the boat trip home. Working in companionable ceremony, they ground each shell against a stone to create a second opening in the shell. Then they arranged the shells in rows with the domed surfaces to the outside and the largest shells in the middle. Tears come to her eyes, tears of gratefulness for the bond they have for each other.

Suddenly she is overcome by a desire to be back amongst them – chanting, talking, laughing, embracing. For thirty years since she was nine years old, she has never been apart from them, her circle of Wise Ones. Fear and regret blossom in the darkness. How can she bear to leave her sacred circle and her position as Wisdom Keeper? Why did she agree to be the one to make the journey, a journey unlike anything they have ever undertaken, a journey with no guarantee that she will ever return?

She has made many journeys before and is not afraid. Indeed, she loves adventure and is hungry for the new. She has travelled throughout the world, by foot over the land and by boat along the river and across the great ocean. She has travelled by spirit, accompanying the souls of her people as they pass from the world of the living to the Otherworld. As Wisdom Keeper, she has travelled by spirit to the Great Mother's Store Room of All Knowledge and to the realms of the angels. It was no surprise to herself or to her circle of Wise Ones that she would be the one to undertake the journey.

But to travel to another time, not only in spirit but in the body, is beyond anything they have ever done. The instruction had come from Great Mother through Crogan and Charmall, her first teachers, her wise guides. They passed to the Otherworld years before but stayed on in spirit to guide her.

'You are to send one of the Wise Ones to a time far in the future where the people have fallen into a deep sleep,' Crogan had said to the circle of ten. 'These future people have lost their way. They are not in balance with Nature. They have forgotten who they are. They need to be awakened. We want one of you to travel to this time and be with them, not only in spirit but in full body.'

Surprise and fear spread through the circle. She too was frightened and alarmed, even as she stepped forward to be the one who was sent, even as she prepared herself to go on this extraordinary journey. But her spirit of adventure and her curiosity were more powerful than any fear.

'We are here with you throughout your journey,' Crogan says now in her deep, gravelly, reassuring voice. 'Charmall and I are gifting you a new name. From this moment on, your name is Ahmtoshtelay: the One who Travels through Time.'

Ahmtoshtelay. She rolls the name around her lips. It steps lightly into her mind. She embraces her new self.

'I am Ahmtoshtelay, the One who Travels through Time,' she says out loud into the darkness. 'Blessed am I to have you and Charmall with me in spirit. I am ready.'

Ahmtoshtelay lies on her side in the egg-shaped basin in the alcove. She curls herself into a tight ball with her knees by her chest. Beside her is a jug of water from the river and a bowl of berries, seeds, dried meat and cheese. She resumes her chanting, her fingers stroking the periwinkle shells on her necklace. Her voice rises to the roof of the alcove and bounces back, louder and stronger each time she sends it forth. Her chanting, augmented by the stones in the chamber, creates a sound tunnel.

She casts her fears and regret into the tunnel. With one last deep breath, she anchors her body to the stones and leaves it behind in the alcove. Rising up through the roof, she rides the sound tunnel to her spot on the Cosmic Web that encircles the planet. From this spot, she surrenders to Great Mother and is sent along the Web past the Earth, the Moon and the Sun, past planets and stars. She arrives at a future spot on the Web far beyond her own time.

When the drumbeats shift into a faster, more insistent closing rhythm, she follows the tunnel into her body. Returning to her body feels strange. Her ears are buzzing and her whole body is shaking. She feels nauseous. She focusses on her breathing until the nausea passes and she feels more comfortable in her skin. Before she opens her eyes, she scans her body. She wriggles her toes, stretches her arms and legs, twists her head from side to side. Her stomach is rumbling and she is desperately thirsty but her body has survived the journey intact. She smiles with delight.

Chapter 2. Carol

The call has become more insistent, harder to bury among the busy doings of the day. Carol hears it in her dreams, in that moment before full consciousness returns. She hears it when she opens her laptop to start work in those seconds before the file materialises on the screen. She hears it as she comes out of the shower, as she makes coffee for her mother, as she loads the washing machine, as she listens for the hundredth time to Jason explain how the moon orbits the earth.

But the call is elusive, fading too fast for focus. Or is she pushing it away? Carol doesn't have the luxury of pausing to find out. Yet somehow, without knowing what she is doing, she has begun making plans to go away. She discovers these plans when she hears herself divulging the details to her friend, Moira, in her kitchen.

'You must be mad,' Moira says, delicately removing her red "I'm an Artist" beret and patting her short straight hair into place. 'You can't take your mother to Ireland.' She takes another piece of the carrot cake Carol bought that morning and continues speaking with her mouth full. 'Where's my cuppa? Seriously, Carol. What are you thinking of? She's got dementia. Look how long it took to settle her in here. Three years. And she wanders. It doesn't bear thinking about.'

Carol slumps against the kitchen counter, the kettle boiling unnoticed behind her. She can't look her friend in the eye, in case the messy feelings seething just beneath the surface boil over. She doesn't mean to be ungrateful but the kind of help Moira has been offering is not exactly what she needs. It's complicated as Moira has been loyal and generous with her time and with her advice. Ever since their book group read the novel, *Still Alice*, Moira has been coming over each week to eat cake and drink tea around Carol's kitchen table.

'Look, Moira,' she says, her words like bullets. Her whole body is shaking. 'It's easy for you. You dumped your senile mother in a nursing home in Dublin. How often do you visit her? Once every six months? You go off on holiday whenever you want.' Who does Moira think she is, giving advice? She takes a deep ragged breath and tries to calm herself down. 'I'm talking about a short trip to Ireland, less than a week. I have to go. It's not just that I need a holiday, though I do. It's that it's calling me to come. And I don't need your advice.'

She glares at Moira who glares back, then shrugs.

'I couldn't do what you're doing, Carol,' Moira says, shaking her head in that definite way she has that always sets Carol's hackles rising. 'I'm an artist. I need time for my painting.' She pokes at the carrot cake, as if that says it all.

Carol feels like screaming. 'And I don't need time? You have a husband to support you. I don't. I have a full-time job with deadlines to meet which I should be doing right now except that I'm sitting here with you eating carrot cake.' Not that she wants to be working or even enjoys her job as a ghost writer for a pharmaceutical company, but the company does allow her to work from home. And they pay well. So what else can she do?

Moira continues talking and eating, 'So why are you taking your mother to Ireland, Carol? I couldn't do it. And, pardon me for saying so, but I don't think you can either. It's just not doable.'

'Yes, I can' Carol shouts, so loudly and so suddenly that both she and Moira jump. 'I'm sick to death of everyone telling me that I can't do it.' Even as the words shoot out of her mouth, she knows who the "everyone" is, her mother singing the theme tune from her earliest childhood: *You're useless, Carol. You can't even do the dishes properly. You're so clumsy. You're always breaking things. You can't ride a bike as well as your younger brother. You can't get into university with those A level results.* And when she did get into university to study biomedical sciences, her mother said, 'you'll never become a doctor with that degree.' Which was the only comment that didn't hurt as she had never wanted to be a doctor.

Moira is not deterred by Carol's vehemence. 'No, you can't. It's impossible to provide full-time care for someone with dementia while doing a full-time job, both in your home. Not to mention raise two sons. And you can't take your mother on this trip to Ireland. My family come from that part of Ireland. I know what it's like. I can just imagine your mum in her nightie, barefoot, charging down a country road in County Meath with cars racing by. And there are no pavements on those roads you know. And every house has a guard dog. You just walk by and they rush out snarling and barking, ready to tear you to pieces.'

Carol has a sudden image of Moira rushing at her, snarling and barking, about to tear her to pieces for even thinking of asking for help.

'I know. You're right,' she says, suddenly deflated. She lowers her head. From this position, she can see toast crumbs and coffee stains on the kitchen floor, leftovers from breakfast. But which breakfast? She can't remember when she last had time to eat breakfast, and she certainly can't remember when she last washed the floor.

'You're always right. But what choice do I have?' She straightens up and makes herself look Moira in the eye, feigning a confidence she doesn't feel. 'It's, um, it's really important to me to go on this trip. It's like it's calling to me. I haven't felt like this, ever. I want to go. So Mum has got to come with me. I can't leave her on her own and no one has offered to move in and look after her.' She grimaces, hearing the whine in her voice.

'Oh really? You haven't even asked anyone, have you? Where's the milk?' Moira is peering in the fridge which is alarmingly empty. Carol sighs. She forgot to buy milk when she rushed out to buy the carrot cake for Moira's visit. Sometimes she wonders if dementia is catching. There are so many things she is forgetting.

Moira glares as if the thought of tea without milk is a personal insult. She taps the table, a quick drumbeat of irritation and snaps, 'What about your brother? Why can't he move in for a few days?

She's his mother too.' Though she knows he won't. Moira has heard Carol's angry recounting of John's abdication of duty many times over the last three years.

Carol snorts and pours the boiled water into the mug. Does Moira mention John to torment her? Something seems to be missing but she can't think what it is. Watching the steam curl up from the mug, it occurs to Carol that the missing something is practical support, whether from her brother or from Moira or from any of her friends. Her brother has made it clear that he will support her with his money, for which she is grateful, but not with his time, not even to visit more than once or twice a year.

Carol has told the story with increasing bitterness, fuelling her childhood resentment towards her younger brother, the favoured son, now a successful consultant urologist. John lives in London in a house with a recently installed made-to-measure bespoke kitchen from an award-winning flagship collection. John and his wife, Sheila, spent the bulk of their annual visit to Carol poring over the kitchen company's website, trying to choose between "seductive warm cashmere and luxurious dark woodgrains" and "dark pallets complemented by mysterious graphite and fiery copper handles." Not that Carol begrudges John his designer kitchen. She is perfectly happy with her IKEA small kitchen with "its maximised storage and versatile solutions". She has stopped noticing that the cabinet doors hang at an angle and that there are cracks in the lino.

No, it isn't the kitchen - it's the spare en-suite bedrooms with bidets in each bathroom that really rouses her ire. John could easily have accommodated their mother and a live-in care assistant. None of John's three children or Sheila's therapy practice would have had to give up their rooms. Indeed, their mother has made it clear that she would have preferred to live with her darling son in comfort and style than with her fat, unkempt daughter in her grandson's bedroom in a small, cramped house in Bristol.

'Carol, tea bag!' Moira barks. She rakes her hair in exasperation and asks if Carol has considered a respite centre.

'There are such places, you know,' Moira persists. 'In fact, a few months ago, Sue told me she gave you the number of a place that offers residential respite for people with dementia. Did you ever call them?'

Carol feels hysteria rising up from somewhere deep within her belly. She closes her eyes with the effort of keeping it down. Her GP had also suggested residential respite care but seemed to think Francis' dementia had not got to the state where she qualified. In any case, Francis would not co-operate and Carol was alarmed by news reports of abuse in care homes.

'No. I didn't think so,' Moira says. 'Why not? You're impossible, Carol. You're the original Yes But girl. And what about Jason? Are you taking him out of school?'

'No. I'm going to go during half term.' Carol feels a spark of excitement at how much Jason will benefit from this trip. 'Jason is really up for it. Last night we watched a documentary on TV about Newgrange. He's as keen to go as I am.'

Carol tosses the tea bag in the mug of water and slams it on the table.

'So Moira,' she begins forcefully before her voice fizzles out. She pauses and turns to look out the window at the darkening afternoon sky, the heavy clouds threatening more rain. Bristol's October gloom; how depressing. But a trip to Ireland – that would lift her spirits. Carol rallies her failing nerves and says in a rush, 'So Moira, what about you? Would you come over and look after Mum for a few days?'

Moira takes a deep breath and pushes the mug away. Any minute now, Carol thinks, she's going to start barking at me again. She's got that look in her eye.

Moira puts on her red beret and walks briskly out of the kitchen. With a hand on the front doorknob, she turns back to Carol and says firmly, 'I wish I could. But I've got to get my paintings ready for an exhibition next month. It's not going to happen, Carol. You cannot take your mother to Ireland the way she is.'

Seeing Carol's stricken face, she says more gently, 'Someday it will happen. Don't despair, Carol, but you have to be willing to get some professional respite care. I know it's frustrating. I'm sorry but I've done all I can.'

She leaves without another word, without even a goodbye. Carol shakes her head in helpless resignation.

'Moira's right,' she says to the toast crumbs. 'I must be mad.'

'I am the sunlight in the heart, the moonlight in the mind. Come with me. Come with me. Come away.' The call is loud and clear. As loud as her mother's calls are, as clear as her sons' calls had been when they were babies. It is a call that she can't ignore. It is a call that she doesn't want to ignore. Newgrange passage tomb is calling her. She's never been called like this before. It is mad, surreal, out of her comfort zone. Yet, a desire to go with the caller, whoever it is, is growing stronger each time she hears it.

Chapter 3. Carol

The sun is far away behind the darkening rain clouds when Moira put on her red beret and swept out the front door. Carol wants to curl up on the floor and go to sleep. Instead, she marches herself into her study and opens her laptop to the half-finished methodology file. Usually, the discipline of composing a scientific article to a set format has a calming effect but today the words dance on the screen and refuse to come to order. If only she hadn't told Moira about her plans to go to Ireland. If only she hadn't asked Moira to help. If only her mother would sleep for another hour.

Five minutes later she hears her mother calling loudly from the upstairs bedroom. Carol's head jerks upright and she wakes with a jolt. 'Leave me alone,' she mutters under her breath. 'You can walk. Why don't you come downstairs? Why do you make me come to you?' Still muttering, she obediently closes the laptop and leaves her study.

At the bottom of the stairs, Carol's stomach begins to tighten into a dull, grinding ache. It is a familiar ache, one that goes way back to her childhood. When she hears Francis' voice calling her name again, memories of her mother's unpredictable and erratic rages flood her mind. Carol never saw the rages coming, though she had convinced herself that she could prevent them if only she were more sensitive or more observant. She has spent much of her childhood trying to figure out how not to trigger her mother's rages.

Carol opens the door to what she still thinks of as Ben's room though Ben hasn't been in that room since Francis moved in. His posters, music system, piles of clothes, dirty dishes and mouldy pizzas are long gone and not missed. But Carol does miss her son; not the hostile, surly teenage version that he presents to her, but the young man she believes he could be one day.

Francis is standing in front of the open wardrobe, staring blankly at the clothes. The curtains are closed. No lights are on. As soon as she walks in, Carol feels oppressed by the atmosphere of misery and gloom pervading the room.

'How am I supposed to find anything in here?' Francis demands. 'You are such a slob. These aren't even my clothes. It's all in a mess.' She starts yanking clothes out of the wardrobe and throwing them onto the floor.

'Mum, stop that,' Carol cries, turning on the lights. 'Of course they're your clothes. That's your wardrobe. Don't you remember? You and Dad bought that wardrobe from John Lewis thirty years ago. Remember? You chose it because you wanted an oak wardrobe.'

'Don't patronise me. Of course I know it's my wardrobe but where are my clothes? You always make such a mess of everything. I want to go home. I don't want to live here. You ruin everything.'

Carol is picking up the clothes as fast as they are being tossed onto the floor, feeling more and more agitated. 'Mum, stop it. Stop it, please. These are your clothes. See, this is your striped cardigan. Mum, stop.'

'You've always been a disappointment to me, Carol, a complete failure. No wonder Mike left you. Not only a useless daughter but a useless wife. And judging by the way Ben has turned out, you're a useless mother too.'

This isn't a new accusation but the barb hits home, as Francis must have known it would. Carol wonders why her mother's dementia erases some memories and not others. Mike left more than ten years ago leaving Carol on her own with one-year-old Jason and ten-year-old Ben. Carol blames herself for driving Mike away. She nagged him and found fault with him: he saw himself as a free spirit; Carol saw him as irresponsible and afraid of commitment. He left one job after another, moved from one flat to another and finally took up with another woman. The other woman appreciated him for who he was, he told Carol as he packed his belongings. That hurt.

Carol is so caught up in her hurt she doesn't notice the danger signs; Francis' eyes are dilated, her skin pale and her breathing rapid.

Before Carol can register what is happening, Francis has grabbed a wooden hanger and thrown it at Carol's head. It hits her in the eye, causing an explosion of pain. Her first reaction is to duck and shield her head from more blows but there are no more. Francis has turned back to the wardrobe and is yanking a dress off its hanger.

Carol's second reaction is to get as far away as possible. She staggers from the room clutching her eye and runs down the stairs, bumping into the bannister as she flees. Just as she gets through the front door, the clouds that have been threatening rain all afternoon suddenly release a torrent of rain. Within seconds, she is drenched. She stands helplessly on the front step, shivering from the cold and pain, too shocked even to cry. At that moment, the taxi arrives bringing Jason home from school.

The taxi was one of Moira's few practical suggestions. Francis had become less and less willing to get in the car every day to pick up Jason from his primary school. By avoiding the daily battle with her mother, Carol's life had become easier, if considerably poorer. But getting Jason out of the taxi is no easy matter. He is often in mid-flow chatting to the taxi driver and has to finish his story before leaving. Inevitably he forgets his coat or his book bag and has to go back. This time, when he sees Carol standing in the rain, he immediately throws open the taxi door and runs to her, shouting above the deafening rain, 'Mum, Mum, what's the matter? What happened?' Soon, Jason is as wet as Carol, his curly brown hair plastered flat against his head.

'It's your Nan,' Carol moans. 'She hit me in the eye.'

'Jason, my loverly,' calls the taxi driver in her Bristol twang. 'Don't forget your coat.'

Jason runs back to the taxi. Carol can hear him consulting the driver who hands him his coat and some words of sympathy. She then drives off, much to Carol's relief.

'Come inside please,' Jason begs, pulling Carol in through the door. 'You're all wet.'

They stand close together in the front hall at the bottom of the stairs. Puddles form on the floor at their feet. Jason drops his coat and book bag into a puddle and is hopping from foot to foot, wringing his hands. Carol doesn't move, other than to shiver violently. Tears pour down her cheeks. She feels incapable of doing anything.

'Carol,' her mother screeches from the top of the stairs. Francis is standing on the top landing, her arms full of coat hangers. This time, Carol recognises the warning signals. Francis is like a volcano about to erupt.

'Let's go,' Carol whispers to Jason and guides him into the kitchen, squelching soggily as they go. Just as she shuts the door behind them, they can hear Francis shout, 'Stop that weeping and wailing, you crybaby. I'll show you what happens if you walk away when I'm talking to you.'

There is the sound of a dozen coat hangers clanging against the bannisters and crashing into the puddles on the floor below. They can hear Francis walking back and forth from her bedroom to the landing collecting an arsenal of items to hurl down the stairs should they reappear in the hallway.

'What should we do, Mum?' Jason says, squelching anxiously from foot to foot. 'Maybe we could call Sue and Alison?'

'No, they'll just lecture me about putting Nan in a home. I can deal with this. It's my fault. I didn't handle Nan very well. I guess I provoked her. She'll calm down soon. I'm sorry, Jason. This isn't fair on you.'

'You're bleeding, Mum. Your eye looks bad,' Jason says, peering at Carol's eye.

Carol's phone rings. It's her friend, Alison. Carol scowls and is about to reject the call but Jason grabs the phone. Before he can speak, Alison says in a severe voice, 'Carol, what's going on? Moira just called me. She's worried about you or angry at you or something. She wouldn't stop talking about how unreasonable you are. Are you seriously thinking of taking your mother to Ireland with you?'

Carol groans. Jason interrupts, 'Alison, it's me, Jason. Come over please. Nan's gone crazy. She hit Mum in the eye and she's throwing things at us.'

'Oh my God! I'll get Sue and we'll be right over,' Alison says and hangs up.

In the half an hour it takes them to arrive, Francis has retired to her bedroom, Jason has tiptoed upstairs to retrieve dry clothes, and Carol has filled her Francis Bubble. This is a space at the back of her mind where she shoves her thoughts and feelings about her mother.

The Francis Bubble is already full but is able to accommodate slight variations on previous thoughts, including: *I shouldn't have turned the lights on when I went into Francis' bedroom. I shouldn't have contradicted what Mum said. I shouldn't have told her to stop throwing her clothes on the floor. I shouldn't have patronised Mum. I shouldn't have spoken to her as if she were a child. I should have known Mum is sensitive to being slighted. No wonder she exploded.*

With Alison by her side, Carol cautiously knocks on Francis' door and looks in. Francis sits slumped on the bed, surrounded by the contents of her wardrobe. Although no longer in the active throwing stage, she is muttering angrily to herself. From experience, Carol knows that it is best to wait until the muttering stage is over and the sulking stage has ended. If she goes in too soon, there is a high likelihood of triggering another violent eruption.

Sue makes hot chocolate and helps Jason finish off the carrot cake. Carol holds a bag of frozen peas against her eye and watches Alison warily. She does not want her friends to pity her or judge her or step in and sort her life out. She does not want to divulge shameful secrets from her childhood in front of Jason. Nor does she want to lie and pretend that her mother's violence is a symptom of the dementia. But Alison is a social worker and Sue a counsellor. They believe that every problem has a solution and if they can't fix it, they will signpost you to some professional or some agency who can. And they are very good at making you talk.

'How often does this happen?' Alison asks in her brisk and

purposeful professional voice.

'She gets so frustrated,' Carol replies, thinking that her mother is not the only one who gets frustrated. 'She can't help it. I over-reacted. Please, let's not make a mountain out of a molehill.'

Undeterred, Alison asks again. When Carol doesn't reply, Sue says softly, 'She's done this before, hasn't she? God, Carol, we've known you for twelve years, since before Jason was born. Yet you've never talked about your childhood. I've often wondered what she was like. You seem so scared of her, always trying to appease her.'

Carol blinks. Sue's kind smile disarms her. She yearns to spill all and get this impossible burden out in the open where she might get some perspective. 'My mother is complicated,' she says slowly. Sue nods encouragingly. 'She's never been diagnosed with anything.'

Carol pauses, lost in thought. When she first left home, she went through a phase of trying to figure out what was wrong with her mother. Was it borderline personality disorder, ADHD, bipolar? Whatever label it might have been, Francis never thought there was anything wrong with her behaviour. As far as Carol knew, she didn't seek professional help and never took medication.

'All I can say is that from as long as I can remember, she's had mood swings and violent episodes always directed at me. Only me. Not my brother. Why me? I guess I triggered something in her. I really don't know.'

Jason is staring at her wide-eyed. 'Nan hit you when you were little?'

'I don't want you to get the wrong impression of your Nan, Jason. It wasn't that often. And I probably deserved it most of the time. I was clumsy. I broke things. I didn't do what she said. She was frustrated. She couldn't help it. It wasn't that bad.' Carol's stomach hurts. Even as the words come out of her mouth, Carol knows they're not true. It was that bad.

Jason shakes his head, his wet curls swinging from side to side, sending drips flying in all directions. Sue and Alison are frowning.

Out of the side of her eye, Carol sees Alison exchange a glance with Sue. *Now what?* she thinks resentfully. Alison takes a breath and says gently, 'Carol, we need to talk. You can't carry on like this. It's not humanly possible for one person to do all the caring of someone as, um, as challenging as your mother. It's not fair on you. It's not fair on Jason. You've done amazingly well for the last three years. You have done your duty by your mother. But it's too much. Surely you can see that it's time ...'

'No,' Carol says. 'I'm not putting her in a home. Never.' Can't they leave her alone? First Moira, now Sue and Alison in tandem. How is this supportive!

'Not all residential care facilities for dementia are bad places,' Alison pleads. 'You hear about the worst places on the news but they're not all like that.'

'No, I just can't,' Carol says. 'I'm planning a trip to Ireland to visit Newgrange. I don't want to but I think I'm going to have to take Mum with me.'

'Yes, that's what Moira was going on about when she called earlier,' Alison says. 'Even after this episode, you still want to take your mother? It doesn't seem like such a good idea.' She speaks in a careful tone of voice that Carol assumes she uses with her social work clients when they are up to something crazy.

'What is Newgrange anyway?' Sue asks. 'And why is it so important for you to go there in particular?'

'It's a Neolithic passage tomb built before Stonehenge.' Jason is ready to launch into a lengthy explanation when Alison interrupts impatiently. 'OK, but aren't there plenty of places like that here in England? Why don't you go to Stonehenge? It's an hour and a half away.'

'There's something like that at Stanton Drew. It's only half an hour from here,' Sue says. 'I didn't know you were interested in Neolithic stuff.'

'Those are stone circles,' Jason objects. 'Not passage tombs.'

Alison rolls her eyes dismissively. 'Whatever! The real question is why do you have to take your mother?'

'I have to because there's no one to look after her but me,' Carol sighs and closes her eyes wearily. The real question, which she can't answer, is why this trip is so important to her. She can't explain to herself, let alone to her friends, about the call she so distinctly hears to come away. Who is it who is calling her? Perhaps she's imagined it. She hasn't actually heard a voice speaking. The call is only in her mind. Would Sue and Alison think she is crazy, or worse - would they think she'd become religious? How could she describe this ethereal call? She has no language for such an experience. When she thinks about describing it to her friends, her mind goes blank.

Instead, she says, 'I haven't been away on holiday since Mum moved in three years ago.'

This hits home. Both Sue and Alison have the grace to look uncomfortable. Only a week ago, they booked a three-week holiday to Thailand in the new year.

'Please don't go through the list of people who should help,' Carol says, feeling weary. 'Moira already did that. There's no point asking my brother, or Ben or Moira.'

A mad reckless voice suddenly pipes up in the back of her mind. Before she can censor it, she hears herself saying, 'What about you two? Mum wouldn't get violent with you. She only does that for me. I know you both work full-time but you could take time off. It's only for a few days.'

There is an awkward pause until Sue says, 'The thing is,   Carol ...' but the words fade away and she looks pleadingly at Alison. Carol feels a flash of irritation at the dynamic between the two women. Or does she resent their coupledom? They do everything together from the book group where she first met them to socialising to giving advice. Her stomach tightens into an even tighter knot. It's not fair that they have each other and there's only one of her.

Alison clears her throat, 'We've been talking about what we

can offer and we decided that the best way we can support you is to encourage you to find a good residential care facility for your mother.' She pauses and shifts in her chair, her professional manner wilting under Carol's stony glare.

'The thing is, Alison, I want to go to Ireland in two weeks. I've already been to the GP to talk about respite care but it takes time to arrange these things. The GP said this isn't an emergency. You know more about this than I do. I promise to look into it when I get back. But it's not what I need right now.'

'Can't you go later when you have sorted something out?' Sue asks. 'What do you need right now?'

'What I need right now is ...' She doesn't know where to start. She can think of dozens of things she needs, like a loving partner, like someone to look after her, someone to share the responsibility with, an uninterrupted night's sleep, a cleaner, a bit more money, freedom from constant worry and dread. The more she thinks about it, the more things she realises are missing from her life. Like fun. Like sex. But what's the point of spelling it out?

'So what are you going to do, Carol?' Alison is looking at her unsympathetically, tapping her foot. 'If it's so important for you to go to this Neolithic whatever, as you said it is, why sabotage it by taking your mother with you? A respite centre is not an option. Moira won't do it. We won't do it. It has to be your brother. Why are you resisting? It's obvious.'

Carol stares at Alison, dumbfounded. Her heart is beating fast. She can hear her mother's voice in her head berating her for being so weak, but it's fading. Alison's voice is louder. And Sue's. And Moira's. They're making a lot more sense than anything her mother has ever said.

'What's for dinner, Mum?' Jason interrupts the conversation. 'Can you give me some money for fish and chips? Will you take me, Sue? You too, Alison.'

'Think about it, Carol,' Sue says as they gather coats and bags and head out the door with Jason.

Carol stands at the bottom of the stairs, straining to hear if her mother is awake. The house seems unnaturally quiet. She knows she should make use of this opportunity to dash into her study and finish the methodology section. But an invisible force roots her to the spot. She hears a clock ticking, the fridge humming, her heart pounding. She feels her eye throbbing, her stomach rumbling, her breath inhaling and exhaling. She notices coat hangers on the stairs, water puddles on the floor, an unopened letter by the door, the dim overhead light barely lifting the gloom. Imperceptibly at first and then more clearly, she senses a presence filling the space, a light dawning around her, a stillness flowing through her.

She hardly dares to take a breath in case it vanishes. This is the source of the call, she realises. It seems to her to be more real and more tangible than the physical objects around her in the hallway. It is calling her to awaken, to come away. Every cell in her body tingles in response. Overcome by yearning, she closes her eyes and throws her arms out, opening herself to the presence.

A tremulous voice penetrates her consciousness, calling her back to the present time. 'Carol? What are you doing there? Are you going to cook dinner? I'm hungry.' Francis comes slowly down the stairs, holding onto the bannister for support. Opening her eyes, Carol sees her mother glowing with light. She feels a rush of love for this vulnerable, suffering woman.

'You've got a black eye,' Francis says, peering closely at Carol's eye. Carol sighs. She waits for a moment, wondering if she might get an apology or at least an acknowledgement. Though that is not her mother's style and has never been.

'How did you get that black eye? You should put some frozen peas on it,' Francis says, walking purposefully into the kitchen and opening the freezer. She stares blankly inside, then shuts the freezer door and sits at the table.

'It's okay,' Carol says, smiling at her mother, the rush of love still flowing between them. 'Jason and I are going on a trip to Ireland to see the Newgrange Monument. And you're going to stay with John and Sheila.'

'I'd like that,' Francis says. Her whole body relaxes, her face is smooth, her hands lie still in her lap; even her blue eyes sparkle. 'I haven't seen John for years. Why doesn't he come to visit me?'

'Let's call him right now and ask him. Come on.' She gives her mother a kiss on the top of her curly white hair and pulls her phone out of her pocket.

'What are you doing on that phone?' Francis demands, her usual cross tone restored. 'You're always on that thing, day and night. Anyway, what trip? Where are we going?'

'You're going to London to stay with John and Sheila while Jason and I go to Ireland.' She isn't sure if it is wise to make such a promise to her mother before she's even got through to John. But, to her surprise, John answers. More surprising, he agrees, immediately.

Maybe it is her determined tone of voice or her absolute certainty that she really, really cannot take her mother on a trip to Ireland, but whatever it is, John makes no objection. By some strange fluke, John and Sheila have not made plans to go away during half term, as they usually do. In a voice of certain authority, John volunteers Sheila to look after Francis as well as their three children for the week. He even sees the advantage for his kids. They will have a chance to get to know their grandmother.

Long after John says 'yes, fine, no problem,' she keeps on talking, persuading, pleading. When she runs out of breath and stops presenting one argument after another, she stands in the middle of the kitchen, stunned, unbelieving, as John repeats his offer to drive to Bristol and pick Francis up.

John's willingness to take their mother for the week is so sudden and unexpected that Carol doesn't know what to think. She wonders whether she has misjudged her brother. She's only seen him as self-centred and irresponsible, unconcerned about leaving Francis' care to her. Of course, he won't be inconvenienced, she thinks sourly. It is Sheila who will be doing the day-to-day care. But that is irrelevant.

She feels as if someone has abruptly turned the heat off a pressure cooker that was seconds away from exploding. In the calm that follows, she feels an almost imperceptible shift, a gentle breath, but one promising more than she could ever imagine. She recognises it as the call and knows it has everything to do with what just happened.

Chapter 4. Carol

In the dark, cold October morning on the day of departure, Carol is alone in the kitchen slumped at the table, still in her dressing gown. Her breathing is ragged and shallow. A carton of orange juice, a box of Shreddies, and a bag of pasta bows are waiting by a large cardboard box on the counter. Her half-completed To Do list has mysteriously disappeared, probably hiding with the pens that are never around when she needs one. The sight of Jason's backpack stuffed with summer beach clothes and her empty suitcase fill her with panic.

Jason runs into the kitchen. 'Mum, shall I bring these books about Newgrange? We can read them on the way. I can't believe we're really going. I'm so excited.' He dances around the room. 'What's for breakfast? Can I have those Shreddies?'

Carol pulls her bathrobe tighter around her waist and sits up straight. Jason is moving around so fast, she feels dizzy. She realises that he is asking for something but there are so many other things in her head, clamouring for her attention, making her anxious, that she can't focus on him. At least Francis is not taking up much space in her mind now that John has whisked her away.

Carol shakes her head to dislodge the many things cluttering her mind – worry about the long drive on her own, worry about what clothes to take, worry about missing the deadline for the article she's been working on for work, worry about Ben's latest aggressive demand for money, and worry about the call which she hasn't heard for several days. She's beginning to doubt it ever happened. Maybe she made it up. Why has she gone to all this trouble to visit a Neolithic monument? She's not even interested in the Neolithic period.

But Jason, himself, is not one of the things in her head and never has been. This is her chance, she knows, to change that. If only she could unload her worries for the duration of the trip. Maybe being away from home will give her the space to do just that.

Making a supreme effort, Carol concentrates on Jason. 'Yes, bring the books and yes, have some Shreddies. But no to your swimsuit and goggles. Go get some winter clothes.'

As the sun lights up the eastern sky, they are finally packed and ready to go. 'We're off to see the wizard, the wonderful wizard of Oz,' Carol sings as she starts the car and sets off down the road. Jason joins in.

'Mum, can I tell you the Ninjago story?' Jason says as they merge onto the M5 motorway. Without waiting for her answer, he launches eagerly into his explanation. 'There's these two Ninjas. There's a master who teaches them all the things. But then there's this guy who's got a bad guy dad who's also kind of ...'

Bad guy dad? Is this his way of telling her that he misses having a dad? Carol shoots a quick look at Jason. His hair hasn't been brushed. It's sticking up in all directions and his jacket sleeves don't reach his wrists. He must have had a growth spurt. She'll have to get him another winter jacket when they get back from Ireland.

'But then the master tells him a story of his dad and him but first of all his dad was actually bad but then he was good. His dad was the Golden Ninja who could do all the powers.'

He's still going on about the dad. Carol's stomach lurches. Guilt and worry stand on the sidelines, ready to rush in. Clearly Jason is hoping Mike will develop special powers and turn into a good dad. She hasn't done enough to nurture Mike's relationship with Jason. She should have done ... what? Her mind goes blank. Trying to get Mike to do anything he didn't want to do has never worked.

'And then the skeletons. Mum, are you listening?'

'Jason, honey, I have an idea,' Carol says brightly, though with a touch of desperation. 'Instead of telling me the Ninja story, why don't you read to me from that book we bought about Newgrange? It's in my bag there by your feet. *First Light: The Origins of Newgrange* by Robert Hensey.'

'Okay,' Jason says, his brown curls flopping up and down as he nods enthusiastically. 'As soon as I finish the Ninjago story. Where was I? And then the Golden Ninja ...'

'Jason, stop with the Ninjas please. I need to concentrate on the driving.'

It isn't the driving that requires her attention. She just needs some unoccupied space in her head, away from Golden Ninja dads and guilt about Mike. Space to allow in something unknown, something wonderful. The bright blue sky and the traffic-free motorway hint at that something. She feels an almost audible buzz of excitement.

'I just need to tell you what happened ...'

The buzz of excitement evaporates. Carol slumps forward and opens her mouth to scream.

'Okay. Okay. I'll read the book.' Reluctantly, Jason opens the book at random and begins reading in a monotone. 'The construction of passage tombs with recesses large enough for a person to occupy, where a covered passage could easily block out daylight, would have been ideal to facilitate such an experience.'

'Facilitate what experience? Don't just start reading in the middle,' she snaps, barely aware of the real cause of her irritation. 'Go to the beginning of the chapter. Come on, Jason. I need your co-operation.'

Jason sighs but complies without further argument. Carol smiles with relief, thinking what a sweetheart he is. Even as a baby, he had a bubbly, good-natured personality. It took a lot to dampen his spirits. He cheerfully reads the chapter out loud, adding his own observations and questions.

Carol tries to pay attention but after a few minutes, all she can hear is Jason's voice droning on in the background. Her thoughts are swirling relentlessly around the unanswerable questions: has he been harmed by not having a dad around? Should she have done something to foster their relationship?

Carol has the sense that an unseen hand is choreographing the trip into one seamless dance. They are blessed with five hours of perfect driving weather and traffic-free motorways, a calm Irish Sea, and clear road markings for the short drive from the Dublin ferry port to Newgrange. She finds the lodge without trouble and is delighted with the room and the tiny self-catering kitchen. It doesn't even phase her that their food won't fit in the one cupboard shelf they've been allocated.

Before she falls asleep, Carol allows herself a brief moment of congratulations. She did it! She made it to Newgrange without losing her way or having an accident or a panic attack. Maybe she's not as incompetent as her mother has led her to believe. However, she doesn't feel the buzz of excitement again until the next morning when they join the first tour of the day to the Newgrange monument.

Chapter 5. Carol

As they cross the footbridge over the River Boyne, Carol feels a fluttering in her belly. The river is lively and exuberant. It seems to be waving to her, greeting her. She smiles at Jason who smiles back in a moment of connection that seems to go on forever. She reaches out to hold his hand, feeling the aliveness flow between them. They follow the herd of tourists onto the bus to the Newgrange monument, still holding hands. After a short ride, they are off the bus and facing the entrance to the monument.

Carol blinks and focusses on the imposing wall of white quartz that towers over them and spreads out to either side. It is capped by a domed roof of green grass. An enormous stone with a triple spiral pattern on it lies directly in front of them. Overcome by awe, Carol squeezes Jason's hand.

'How could people without our modern-day technology build such an incredible monument?' she says under her breath, so as not to disturb the spirit of the place. 'It must have been very important to go to all that trouble.'

Jason whistles appreciatively and gazes at the monument wide-eyed. Carol glances at her son. She is about to turn back to take a closer look at the triple spiral when her attention is caught by Jason. He is totally absorbed in the sight. She notices, as if for the first time, his shining eyes, the freckles splattered across his nose, the wild brown curls bursting out of his woollen hat and an almost imperceptible glow. Her heart fills with love. When was the last time she looked at him this way, when she really saw him? Probably not since he was a newborn. Her stomach clenches with regret. She pulls him close in a fierce hug but Jason wriggles free.

'C'mon, Mum. The guide is taking us inside.'

They climb the wooden steps over the entrance stone and enter a five-thousand-year-old passage to the centre of the monument.

Ahmtoshtelay

Ahmtoshtelay opens her eyes and cautiously looks around. She is still inside the Palace of the Immortals. But it is as different from the Palace she knows as night is from day. The chamber is lit by a harsh light. It does not sparkle and glow like the sunlight that enters from the window above the passage entrance at the winter solstice. It does not flicker and warm like the light from their burning torches.

In that strange light, Ahmtoshtelay is reassured to see the spirals etched on the stones as well as the diamonds and zigzags. There are unfamiliar markings as well that she cannot decipher. The overlapping stones making up the top of the chamber have not changed; nor have the three alcoves. Wooden boards have been placed between the two leaning stones at the start of the chamber.

Yet there is something missing, something disturbing. It takes her but a short time to discern what that something is. Gone is the wild exuberance of song and laughter, the shimmering life-force that radiates from the surface of every stone. There is nothing but emptiness. It is indeed a desolate place. In this future time, the stones themselves, the Beings of song and life, are silent and blank.

'How has this tragedy come to pass?' she calls out in an agony of grief. 'Crogan, Charmall. What is my task?'

Crogan replies instantly in song, her voice tuned to a soothing melody. 'Welcome Ahmtoshtelay. You have arrived. Your task is to awaken the stones.'

Ahmtoshtelay is stunned. She had no idea that it was even possible for the stones to lose their life-force. She is not sure how to awaken them, but she knows she can draw on a wealth of skills, experience and confidence. She reaches out with both hands and touches the stone nearest to her in the alcove. It is cold and lifeless, like ice. Shocked, she pulls her hands back and rubs them together. She takes a deep breath and begins. With songs of yearning, she entreats the stones to awaken. With her tears, she bathes them. She sings of her love for them. She reminds them of who they really are. She calls them back to the present.

Carol

Packed tightly with the rest of the tourists, Carol and Jason stand within the lofty, cross-shaped chamber, the heart of the Newgrange passage tomb. Carol's heart is beating in anticipation. *Any moment now, the call will come*, she thinks. *Something wonderful might happen.* Maybe she'll be transported to a different reality. Maybe she'll meet the caller. Maybe something unimaginable will happen. Then again, with her luck, maybe nothing will happen.

In the meantime, she looks around and listens half-heartedly to the guide, a young woman who speaks briskly and authoritatively about the monument. Carol notes her soft Irish accent and her smart uniform. She must have given the same talk a thousand times, leading small groups of tourists into the chamber. Yet she manages to convey a genuine enthusiasm and interest in this extraordinary site.

Ahmtoshtelay

Only when she hears voices outside does Ahmtoshtelay stop her entreaties to the stones. A crowd of over-sized people enter the passageway. They have to stoop and turn sideways as they walk between the stones that line the passage. Ahmtoshtelay has to tilt her head back to see their faces. Are they giants? She is tempted to touch them, to feel their strange garments, to sniff their unusual odours, but she doesn't dare.

Without ceremony or ritual, they walk boldly into the sacred chamber. There they stand, listening and looking around, as a tall woman talks to them in an unfamiliar language, a language that sounds like a stream crashing over rocks. Only to the woman do they listen, not to the stones. Ahmtoshtelay bristles with indignation. How dare they treat the holy stones with such disrespect.

Carol

'... built around 3,200 BCE ... older than Stonehenge and the Great Pyramids of Giza ...'

The guide reels off one fact after another. But Carol is finding it hard to concentrate. When will she hear the call?

'... white quartz stones from County Wicklow 70 km south ...' '... cremated remains found in the recesses ....' '... polished stone balls placed with the dead ...'

Jason is listening, spell-bound to the guide, hanging on every word. Carol is only half-listening. She's waiting for the call. The wait is beginning to drive her crazy. There is nothing in her experience to compare it to. She can't make sense of it. She is certain it isn't the voice of Jesus, for which she is grateful. That would be embarrassing. Religion is not part of her vocabulary, her world view. She has never even been to church.

'... the world-famous tri-spiral design ...'

'... a corbelled roof constructed of overlapping layers of rocks ... still waterproof after 5000 years ....'

'Mum, what's a corbelled roof?' Jason whispers, tugging at Carol's arm.

'Shush Jason. I'm trying to listen,' Carol mutters, struck by a sudden change of tone in the guide's voice.

'From my research into this monument,' the guide is saying, 'it isn't correct to call this merely a passage tomb. That's like saying Westminster Cathedral is just a mausoleum. Yes, remains of the dead are found in both, but both are sacred sites where people worship their version of the divine.' Here she pauses, her voice choking with emotion. 'We are standing in the Holy of Holies, the hallowed cathedral of the Neolithic people.'

Carol feels the hair on the back of her neck rise. The Holy of Holies! Of course, this must be where the call will come from. She looks around, as if she can see the call itself. But all she sees are tourists with their cameras and mobile phones, surreptitiously taking photos behind the guide's back.

Ahmtoshtelay

Although Ahmtoshtelay is intensely aware of the over-sized people, they pay her no attention. This is unsettling. She wonders if she is invisible to them. Perhaps she didn't manage to bring her body after all. Perhaps only she can see herself. But a boy about her height looks her in the eye, smiles and nods before looking around again. She has been seen. But what are they doing here? She moves among them, chanting quietly under her breath, her voice no louder than a gentle breeze.

'I have been here since the beginning.
I am the dance and I am the dancer.
I am the song and I am the singer.
Why are you here?
You enter this sacred space to look.
Yet your eyes are closed. You see nothing but
a narrow passageway, stone walls,
a domed chamber, alcoves for bones.
Stop. Send away the storyteller.
Be here now.
Just breathe.
Are you here yet?
What do you hear?
The Wise Ones are ready.
We chant and sway.
We beat our drums.
What do you see?
The bones of the dead,
flesh picked clean by animals,
we gather.
Slowly, steadily, reverently,
we carry the bones inside.

What do you smell?
Sound and smoke swamp the inner space.
Torches cast flickering light on the stone walls.
Living bodies and bare bones fill the chamber.
On winter solstice day, the sun drops from the sky,
the chanting stops, the drums are mute,
the dancers dance no more.
In the throbbing, pulsating silence,
the sun's rays pierce the chamber
and burst into flame on the stone.
Does your heart crack open with the beauty of the moment?
Do you float out of your body into the Light?
Do you become one with the dance of the universe?
Do you become one with the song of all creation?
Now do you know why you are here?'

Ahmtoshtelay remembers Crogan's words. These people are clearly not from her time. Are they the ones who have fallen into a deep sleep? How many solstice suns have cast their radiant light into the chamber since she began her journey? She has no idea. She senses that these people live in a time that even her great great grandchildren's great great grandchildren would not live to see. Excitement runs through her like a bolt of lightning. Her toes and fingers tingle. She closes her eyes and tries to calm her breathing.

'Crogan, Charmall,' she calls inwardly. 'We have succeeded. I am indeed Ahmtoshtelay, the One who Travels through Time.'

Carol

'... give you an idea of what happens at dawn on the winter solstice ... roof box above the passage entrance ... turn the lights off ...'

Carol scowls in the sudden darkness. If this is where the call comes from, shouldn't she be hearing it by now? She's done what she was asked to do, at great expense and effort. Maybe she got it all wrong. Maybe she misinterpreted the call. Maybe she just imagined it. Disappointment washes over her. She hardly notices the light show simulating the dawn sun's entrance through the passage at the winter solstice.

'Look, Mum,' Jason gasps. 'Isn't it amazing! See the way the light comes in all the way to the back of the chamber! Look at the level of the roof box. Mum! You're not looking. We actually climbed up a slope when we walked along the passage and we didn't even notice. I didn't notice. Did you Mum?'

'Notice what? What are you going on about?' Carol says more sharply than she intended, snapping out of her preoccupation with the call. Jason shrugs and Carol moans. She shouldn't have snapped at him, she berates herself. He didn't do anything that warranted a telling off. Yet she doesn't apologise and she consoles herself with the thought that Jason doesn't appear to be crushed.

Ahmtoshtelay

Suddenly the crowd of people file out down the passage, leaving her alone in the chamber. Ahmtoshtelay breathes a sigh of relief. Now she can get back to her task of awakening the stones. But Charmall stops her and instructs her to follow the boy. Without a moment's hesitation, Ahmtoshtelay leaves the chamber, climbs over the wooden steps and catches up with the boy by an unfamiliar standing stone not far from the entrance.

The stone is new. To reach the top one person would need to stand on top of another. Four such stones are around the entrance. They look like part of a stone circle that has been built around the Palace of the Immortals after her time. Ahmtoshtelay is curious. She would like to investigate further and only reluctantly returns her attention to the boy.

Carol

Carol blinks as the lights come back on in the chamber. 'Please call,' she cries out inwardly. 'I don't know who or what you are. I don't know what I'm doing here. Please help me.'

Chapter 6. Carol

Carol isn't ready to leave the chamber and hangs back as the tightly packed crowd of tourists shuffles down the narrow passage to the entrance. Jason has gone on ahead. The guide shoos her out. She's got a schedule and another group of tourists are already assembled outside. Carol complies, slowly and reluctantly. If only she could stay here on her own. Clambering over the steps, she sees Jason in the distance, talking to a petite, Black woman by a large standing stone.

Ahmtoshtelay

Ahmtoshtelay looks at the boy, unsure how to approach him. He's looking at her with undisguised curiosity. She catches his eye and smiles at him. He smiles back, a smile of such genuine delight that her heart warms to him instantly. Just as she's about to say something, a woman rushes out of the passage and hurries over.

Glancing behind her, Ahmtoshtelay is stunned by another major change to the Palace of the Immortals. Around the outer entrance and extending along the front, white quartz crystals have somehow been attached to a vertical wall. It is a striking display but, for what purpose, she cannot guess. Surely the crystals would lose their potency spread out on the outside wall instead of concentrated inside with the stones. But she has no time to investigate this strange phenomenon as the woman has arrived by the standing stone.

The woman is like a robin hopping closer and closer, keeping an eye on Ahmtoshtelay and chattering. Ahmtoshtelay is fascinated by her liveliness, the way her face displays one emotion after another, her short brown hair, her enormous shoes that look like she has bear claws for feet. Smiling at both of them, she sends them loving energy.

The boy says something and thrusts his hand towards her. Like Robin Woman, he also speaks quickly. Looking into the boy's bright hazel eyes, she feels a rush of warm affection towards him. She sees herself in his open-faced curiosity and eagerness. If she had had a son, he would be just like this boy. She pauses to consider how different her life would have been if she had not become a Wisdom Keeper; if she had had her own children.

Carol

She's even shorter than me, Carol marvels. At five foot two, Carol rarely meets adults shorter than herself. But it isn't her size that hooks Carol's attention. It is her eyes. They are a deep vibrant blue. Yet, her skin is a dark brown colour, as dark as Carol's Afro-Caribbean friend, Alison. Carol stares intently at the woman's face. There is something incongruous about the combination of blue eyes and brown skin.

Their eyes meet. Carol's cheeks burn and she looks away, then glances back only to meet those blue eyes again. Her heartbeat quickens. *I am being rude*, she thinks. But she can't break her gaze. The woman is looking directly into her eyes as if she can see right into her soul.

Carol begins talking rapidly, asking questions. *I'm babbling*, she thinks. Why is she so unhinged? But she can't stop herself.

Ahmtoshtelay

Robin Woman introduces herself and the boy with exaggerated gestures which Ahmtoshtelay copies. Each of their names are made up of two claps, the first strong, the second soft: KAR-ul, JAY-zon. She tells them her name in four claps – ahm-TOSH-te-Lay. They try to repeat this back to her but to her surprise, they cannot say her name. After many unsuccessful attempts, JAY-zon looks her in the eye and says, 'TIL-da.'

Ahmtoshtelay bows and makes a goodbye gesture. As she steps away from the standing stone, Jason clutches her arm and looks pleadingly at her. She tries gently to release herself but he grips harder and sends forth a volley of words, all the time peering earnestly into her face. The Robin Woman seems alarmed by the boy's behaviour and tries to make him let her go. Finally he does, but Tilda notices there are tears in his eyes. Carol waves to her, turns her back and leads the boy away.

Upset by the boy's obvious distress, Ahmtoshtelay calls on Crogan. 'What shall I do?'

'Stay with them,' Crogan replies.

Ahmtoshtelay runs down the hill through a gate where she joins a crowd of people standing on a path. The boy and Robin Woman are hovering at the back of the crowd. When the boy sees her, he throws his arms around her. His face is stained with tears. Robin Woman looks uncertain but Ahmtoshtelay detects a spark of relief or happiness in her eyes.

They are on a path made of a hard material that covers the ground like a skin of rock and stretches out before them like a lifeless, dark, unmoving river. Ahmtoshtelay cannot feel the earth through the skin. She prods it with her foot but it is solid and unyielding. She takes a few deep breaths to still the dread that consumes her at being separated so alarmingly from Mother Earth.

She can see the river in the distance still flowing around the bend in the same direction but much farther away than in her time. Individual trees are dotted around the landscape like arms detached from their bodies. There is no forest. There are only fields of grass where cows graze. She catches her breath in shock. Her pain is visceral, as devastating as if her own body had been violated. The forests have been murdered. This is what happens when all the trees are cut down, she thinks. She vows to warn the farmers when she returns home to her time that they must be more respectful of the forests.

She wants to greet the trees by touching their trunks but the nearest is out of reach. In any case, she is held tightly by the boy. She calls to the tree but the tree is lethargic. Although surprised to be addressed, the tree does not return her greeting. Ahmtoshtelay sighs heavily.

Carol

'What has got into you, Jason?' Carol mutters beneath her breath so as not to be overheard by the other tourists on the bus. 'You can't pick up a woman like you would a stray dog. Who's she with? What's she doing here?'

But Jason is clinging to the woman's arm and ignoring Carol altogether. Carol is squirming in her seat. She has never seen Jason do anything like this before. He has attached himself to a complete stranger. What does Tilda, or whatever her name is, want? She clearly said goodbye and then a few minutes later, ran over to join them. But what else could she do? The only way to leave the monument is by bus.

More unnerving than Jason's strange behaviour is her own visceral reaction. The relief she felt when Tilda ran through the gate took her by surprise. She has the sense that she knows this woman, which is impossible. She has never in her life met anyone remotely like Tilda.

Ahmtoshtelay

Along the path glides a long yellow boat. It stops in front of the crowd of people. The boat has a roof like a house and holes in the walls that are filled with a flat, see-through substance like ice but not cold to the touch. It is sitting on top of full-moon shaped plates that enable it to roll but she cannot understand how it moves. It roars like an angry wounded bear as it approaches but when its door opens, everyone climbs in still chattering, obviously unafraid. As it rolls away, the yellow boat vibrates fiercely causing her head to ache. The boy is still holding her arm as they get off the yellow boat and cross a bridge. Beneath them, the river calls out a song of greeting but the boy does not notice. Ahmtoshtelay pauses to reply and is overjoyed to hear the salmon, on their way to spawn, join in the greeting.

The salmon welcome her with love. They call to her, saying, 'We are thankful for your safe arrival. These people are the ones you have been sent to awaken. Stay with them.' Her heart overflows with joy. She calls Great Mother, chanting a song of thanksgiving.

Beaming with delight, she embraces the boy and Robin Woman. She speaks to them in her language, knowing they will not understand. 'I am honoured to be working with you in service to Great Mother. I dedicate myself to my mission. I gift you with all the wisdom and knowledge I have gained over my many years of training.'

She is not deterred by their blank, puzzled expressions. When she finishes, she follows them willingly, open to whatever challenges Great Mother will place before her, vowing yes to the unfolding mystery, deliberately ignoring the small nugget of fear coiled in her belly.

Carol

'Right,' Carol says firmly as they leave the bridge and come to the car park. 'It's been a pleasure to meet you. Now we've got to go. Goodbye.'

Jason grips Tilda's arm and glares at Carol.

'Tilda, nod your head like this and say yes,' Jason says, nodding his own head vigorously up and down. 'YES. Say it after me. YES. Do you want to stay with us?'

He points to her and then to Carol. Tilda nods and says yes, smiling broadly. *She looks so happy*, Carol thinks, wondering why.

'See,' Jason says triumphantly. 'She wants to be with us.'

'Tilda or Ahmdosheleshy or whatever your real name is.' Carol puts both hands on the woman's shoulders and looks into her smiling blue eyes. 'You can say no. Shake your head from side to side and say no. Do you want to stay with us?'

The woman rolls her head in a circle, back and forth, side to side, up and down, the beads and feathers in her hair flopping with each movement of her head. 'Yes, no, yes, no,' she says, laughing. Then with a serious expression, she points to the river, to herself and back to the river. She moves her hands in a waving motion.

'She's thirsty,' Jason says. 'No, she's hungry. She wants to eat fish.'

What does she want? Carol wonders. This is impossible. How can they communicate with someone who doesn't speak any English? Maybe she's hungry. Maybse she's not. Carol taps her feet impatiently. Then her eyes lock onto Tilda's and she feels a jolt pass through her body. Confused, Carol looks away. What is going on? Cautiously, she looks at Tilda again. Those deep blue eyes are smiling at her. Shyly, Carol smiles back. Maybe they can hang out with this strange woman for a little bit longer. Jason seems very keen on her.

'Jason, what do you say?' Carol asks. 'Shall we invite her to lunch with us? I'm sure we can find a cafe nearby.'

'Anywhere,' Jason said, 'as long as it has fish and chips. And chocolate cake.'

Ahmtoshtelay

'Ahmtoshtelay, dear one,' calls Crogan. 'Thus begins your mission. We are here with you, watching you with admiration and love. We have confidence in you. It is our honour to work with you.' Ahmtoshtelay can feel their love spreading through her entire body like sunlight.

Chapter 7. Ahmtoshtelay / Tilda

My name has been taken from me. I am no longer Ahmtoshtelay, the One who Travels Through Time,' she says to Charmall as she is ushered into a blue boat by her new companions. The boat is similar to the yellow boat that carried them from the Palace but much smaller. 'Tell me, Wise One, what is the meaning of this name I have been gifted?'

'Dear Wise One, you are now Tilda, the One Who Awakens,' Charmall replies. 'We bow to you in awe. We bestow on you our highest appreciation. You are a Being of great courage.'

The blue boat appears to move of its own accord though Tilda notices that it sometimes communicates with Carol in a language that sounds like a continuous roar. Sights and colours and shapes flash by her at a breath-taking speed, faster than she has ever travelled on land. The seats are soft but she is not comfortable. Her body is shaken by violent vibrations and the smell curdles her stomach. She aches all over. She feels sluggish as there is no fresh air inside the blue boat.

She is relieved when they stop and leave the blue boat to enter a large palace, even larger than the Palace of the Immortals. It is not made of wood like their rectangular dwelling places. Nor is it made of stone, like their monuments. She is ushered inside before she has a chance to study it further.

They have come to feast in a place crowded with people and objects pulling her attention in all directions at once. She feels faint and dizzy. The smell of food cooking, the noise of people talking, of music, of chairs scraping the floor, the flashing lights, the bright, harsh lights; being surrounded by unfamiliar objects is too much. As they sit round a table, her head feels as if it will explode.

Judging by their lively chatter and friendly smiles, they do not seem to be suffering the way she is. She wonders if their bodies are shielded from the toxic bombardment in some way. Perhaps they have been trained, like she was, to screen out anything from their environment that does not serve them. Perhaps their bodies are better able to cast out anything harmful.

They ignore and are ignored by the people in the house of feasting except for one woman who brings them food. The objects Tilda touches seem to be asleep or lifeless, like the stones had been. The water tastes sour and sad. She expects the food to be unfamiliar, though she does find fish hidden under a brown coat of something inedible on the enormous platter put in front of her. Her stomach sends frantic signals not to take more than one bite of anything. When she bites into a piece of what they call "chock lit kayk", her tongue tingles violently. Enough food is brought to the table to feed her entire village. She cannot eat the quantities that they consume. They devour the food, dispatching every morsel very quickly, without pause.

Carol

'Go on Tilda,' Carol urges. 'Eat. Drink.' She mimes the actions. Tilda picks up a glass of water and passes it to Carol.

'That's for you,' Carol says, passing it back. 'You drink it.'

Tilda passes it to Jason. When he too refuses, she carefully places it on the table and bows her head.

'I think she wants us to say grace,' Carol says. 'Sorry, love. We're not the religious types. We're uncouth barbarians from the stone age. Put those chips down, Jason. We're going to say grace.'

Reluctantly, Jason obeys. Tilda reaches out to hold their hands and indicates they should all hold hands in a circle. There in the noisy pub surrounded by people, Tilda sings. She sings to the food and to each of them, a song of such sweetness that tears come to Carol's eyes. She wishes it would never end. *This is what I need,* she thinks. *I need Tilda in my life.*

Tilda passes the glass of water to Carol and watches her until she takes a sip, then to Jason who takes a big gulp and hands the glass back to Tilda with a flourish. Tilda drinks slowly with her eyes shut as if that glass of ordinary tap water is the most sacred drink on the planet. She does the same with a chip and a piece of fish.

Jason breaks the spell by shouting, 'Thanks for the grub. Let's tuck in.' They all laugh, including Tilda.

'These are the best fish and chips I've ever tasted,' Jason declares. Carol agrees. Tilda nods her head and says yes.

Carol leans back against the plaid cushioned seat and closes her eyes. Her heart feels full. Tears hover behind her eyelids. Something is missing and that something is the grinding tension, the constant worry and the heavy burden of responsibility. For a brief moment, Carol has a vision of how her life could be.

In the space of a few hours with this stranger, Carol has relaxed her guard and allowed Tilda in, past all her defences. She smiles shyly at Tilda, overwhelmed with gratitude. Tilda puts down her glass of water and smiles back, her blue eyes twinkling. Carol flushes; her face is hot and her heartbeat quickens. She quickly looks away.

Tilda gets up from the table and walks round the pub, looking carefully at everything in sight. Carol and Jason watch her, interested. She is so out of place in this environment. Carol turns to Jason and says quietly, 'You know who Tilda reminds me of? That boy in your class last year, the autistic boy. Can't remember his name. He came to your birthday party and couldn't cope with all the noise.'

'I don't get it. How is Tilda like him?' Jason asks, dipping a chip in ketchup and licking the ketchup off before eating it.

'She covered her ears in the bus to the visitor centre. The noise was too much for her. But it's not that exactly. That boy, Robert, wasn't it? He walked into our house, the first time he'd ever been there, and he greeted every object as if each one was equally important. Like the lamp was as worthy of his attention as a human being. Tilda does that.'

'I don't think she's autistic,' Jason says thoughtfully, dunking another chip in ketchup. 'But there is something different about her.'

'Yes, there is. I can't figure her out,' Carol says. 'How did she get to Ireland, not speaking a word of English? I wish I knew where she was from and what she's doing here.'

It is dark when they finish their meal. Carol knows she should take Tilda somewhere, to her people or to her hotel, but she can't bring herself to say goodbye and Tilda isn't making any moves to leave. There is a spare bed in the dormitory where they are staying. Just one night, she reckons, and then they can go their separate ways.

Tilda

Tilda is standing by the blue boat outside the lodge, shivering in the October evening cold. The others have gone into the lodge. She needs to consult Crogan and Charmall before sleeping.

'They are teaching me their language,' she says. She is proud of her ability to learn this new language and has committed to memory an impressive number of words in just one day. 'But I don't need their words to understand them or to be with them.'

Crogan's gruff voice is warm and admiring. 'No, you don't. You remember, Oh Wise One, when you first began your training and I sent you to learn the language of the bumble bees.'

Tilda laughs out loud. 'I sat by the flowers watching the bumble bees throughout the day and throughout the night. I learned that they don't visit flowers in the dark. It was a good lesson but I was sore from sitting for so long. And very thirsty.'

'What have you learned about Jason?' Charmall asks.

Tilda smiles. She likes Jason and knows that he likes her.

'Jason is like a sapling, a pure being of love,
growing strong towards the light.
Straight up from the ground,
his crown a wild tangle of possibilities,
bending and waving with the wind.
His roots spread out, reaching to others,
trusting, connecting, hungry for love.
Jason is ready to awaken.'

'What does Carol show you about herself?' Charmall asks, and listens attentively.

'Carol hides behind layers of bramble vines,
tangled vines thick with thorns,
woven with the stinging nettles.
Blackberries grow on the bramble,
mouldy, musty berries,
red, unripe berries,
and beautiful vibrant black berries
calling out for love.
Many vines must be cut before I reach the berries.'

She finds Carol interesting and complicated. She wonders how best to awaken her.

Carol

In the dorm, Jason makes a determined effort to find out about Tilda – where she's from, what language she speaks, where her luggage is, how she got to Ireland and why she doesn't have any money. Elaborate gestures and slow speaking in English do not produce any answers. He draws a map of England and Ireland with arrows from their home in Bristol to Newgrange, then a question mark pointing to Tilda. Tilda studies his drawing and smiles appreciatively but clearly doesn't understand what he means.

Pointing to his backpack, Jason says 'backpack', pulls out his fleece and says 'fleece'. Tilda strokes the soft material, rubs it against her cheek and peers intently at the almost invisible stitching. She points to her baggy trousers and long tunic, made of animal hide sewn roughly with sinew. She shivers dramatically and rubs her arms. Then she nods her head, says 'fleece', and puts it on over her tunic. Next she pulls a pair of blue jeans out of Jason's backpack.

'Mu-um,' Jason cries. He turns to Carol, distressed. 'Mum, I'm not giving my clothes to her. I just wanted to ask her where her clothes are.'

Carol looks up. She's been observing Tilda closely while trying to read Hensey's book. 'That was nice of you to offer Tilda your fleece, Jason. She's not dressed for winter, is she?'

'Mu-um, get it off her.'

Carol puts her book down and focusses on Tilda, noticing for the first time the unusual clothes and the shell necklace Tilda is wearing.

'You're a hippie, aren't you Tilda? All natural, homemade stuff. Those moccasins, they're beautiful but they're not proper shoes. No wonder you're cold.'

Curious now, Carol takes a closer look at the pattern on Tilda's tunic. It is the same triple spiral design she's seen on the stones at Newgrange earlier that day. On the trousers, there is a diamond pattern, the same as on the stones in the chamber.

'I've got an extra pair of corduroy trousers you can borrow and some woollen socks and boots. Here, Tilda, you can wear my jumper. Take Jason's fleece off.'

Tilda

Tilda gratefully accepts everything. She is smaller than Carol by at least a hand's length. The sleeves of Carol's jumper dangle past the tips of her fingers, the trousers have to be rolled up; but she is warm and happy. When she is fully dressed, she dances around the room, laughing, singing and clapping. Will they play with her? Jason does, shyly at first. Carol laughs and claps her hands.

Tilda kicks off the boots and stands face to face with Carol. Holding Carol's shoulders, she touches her forehead to Carol's forehead and then her nose to Carol's nose. She says a short blessing in her own language and then climbs into the bottom bunk without taking any of her own or the borrowed clothes off.

Carol

Carol purses her lips at Tilda's strange attire. Just as she is about to say something, Jason says, 'Maybe that's her way of saying thank you. Hey Tilda, here's a word for you to learn. Thank you. Say it after me. Thank you.'

'Fhank you. Fhank you,' Tilda says sleepily.

'Good night,' Carol calls. It seems such a natural thing to do that Carol doesn't even reflect how seldom they say either thank you or good night to each other at home.

For the next two days, there never seems to be the right time to ask Tilda to leave. Nor does Tilda show any signs of wanting to leave. Somehow, in the space of three short days, she has become part of the family. Carol sees Jason's face come alive as he chats to Tilda and feels her own heart opening as they spend time together outside, walking, exploring, being curious. Carol notices things she wouldn't normally see: the River Boyne's lively flow, shafts of sunlight through the clouds, the low-lying mist in the morning.

She doesn't think twice about paying for Tilda to stay extra nights in the lodge or for her meals. She even takes Tilda to a department store in Drogheda and buys her clothes and shoes from the children's section. It feels like the right thing to do. Carol has never had a holiday romance but she imagines it would feel just like she is feeling on this holiday. She knows it has to come to an end but the thought of going back home without Tilda fills Carol with panic. *What if*, Carol thinks, *she comes back to stay with us in Bristol? She's so good with Jason. She probably would know how to handle Francis.* A warm glow seeps through Carol as the thought takes root.

She hasn't heard the call but she has heard a voice saying very clearly, 'This is meant to be. Tilda belongs with you.'

Love is the emotion;
sound is the vehicle;
healing is the intention.

(in *Voices Out of Stone, Magic and Mystery in Megalithic*
***Brittany* by Carolyn North and Natasha Hoffman)**

Chapter 8. Tilda

A wild beast rushes by on the hard, unmoving river in front of the sleeping house. Its roar is deafening and its smell is offensive. Close behind is another beast. And another. Are they being pursued by demons? Or perhaps they are demons. Tilda stands at the edge of the hard river, watching them cautiously. Beasts such as these are unknown in her time. In the three days since her arrival, she has observed the beasts carefully. They are everywhere. A blue one guards Carol day and night, waiting outside while she sleeps. They live amongst people as cows do in her world but unlike cows, the beasts do not share their gifts with love. They provide neither meat nor milk nor manure. Indeed, they are selfish, aggressive and insensitive. Yet the people serve them. They cover Mother Earth with a hard, unmoving river so the beasts may travel wherever they please. They feed them with foul smelling drink.

'Charmall, hear me,' Tilda cries out as several more wild beasts pass without stopping to greet her. 'These wild beasts appear to rule this world. Are they the masters here? I am greatly fearful and confused. What is my task with these beasts? How am I to awaken them?'

'Dear One. Be not afraid. It is not your task to awaken the beasts,' Charmall says. 'Your task is to make peace with them and to accept what they have to offer. Be mindful. Be awake.'

Make peace with them! Tilda frowns. How is she going to do that?

Later that night, Tilda is lying on her bunk, restless and hot. Carol and Jason are asleep in their bunk beds. Tilda pulls the blanket off the bed and tries to settle to sleep on the floor. But the floor is heated, as if a fire is blazing beneath. She shakes her head in amazement, wondering how they can sleep in this heat. She yearns to be home in her familiar wood house, lying on rush mats on the ground, fresh air flowing through. Abandoning the attempt to sleep, she decides to walk to the Palace of the Immortals and see how the stones are doing. No one else will be there. She'll have the place to herself.

Quietly, so as not to disturb Carol and Jason, she puts on her moccasins and tiptoes out of the sleeping house. As the door shuts behind her, she runs through the route in her mind. She is confident she can find the bridge over the river but is less sure about the way from the river to the Palace. She has only travelled this way in the yellow boat and the landscape is very different from her time. Now the land is divided up by fences and hedges and the paths that the beasts use. One step at a time, she tells herself, and sets off to the bridge.

So focussed is she on her destination that she does not hear the roar of the beast, nor does she see his blazing eyes until he hits her with the force of a lightning bolt. She is thrown into the air to land on the hard unforgiving river. The blow knocks her spirit out of her body and breaks many bones. The Otherworld beckons her to leave her body forever.

While her body lies unmoving on the ground, her spirit flies to her spot on the Cosmic Web.

'Great Mother, O wondrous Healer of all flesh,' she calls inwardly. 'I turn to You and seek Your help. I thank You for the gift of life and for the healing powers that You have planted within me. Grant me courage and strength to endure pain. May it be Your will, Great Mother, to speedily grant a perfect healing of my body and mind. Crogan, Charmall, my circle of Wise Ones, hear my call. Chant with me.'

From five thousand years in the past, the nine in Tilda's circle of Wise Ones back home stop whatever they are doing and join in the healing chant. Tilda feels their presence, as they chant her back to life, as their spirits dance around hers, as they shower her with petals of fragrant flowers.

Soon after they join her, Tilda awakens. She is shocked to discover that she is lying on a raised platform inside a brightly lit building assaulted by strange smells, loud clanging noises and streams of over-sized people moving about and speaking to her in their incomprehensible language. She can no longer hear the Wise Ones chanting. In panic, she tries to sit up. The pain is intense. Her breaths come in shallow gulps. A face appears in front of hers, its mouth opens and shuts, unseen hands guide her back down.

'Charmall, Crogan. Help me,' she gasps as strange sensations flow chaotically around her.

Charmall's voice is soothing. 'Breathe deeply. Tune out everything but the chanting. As soon as you can, go to the Palace of the Immortals.'

Soon Carol and Jason arrive, peering at her with wide, frightened eyes. Tilda does her best to explain that she wants to be taken to the Palace of the Immortals. They appear to understand but refuse to take her. She breathes deeply to dispel the panic that blooms in her gut at this setback. *Tune out everything but the chant*ing, she reminds herself. That's all she has to do.

She starts chanting. At first she can only hear her own voice, but within minutes she has tuned in to the chanting of the Wise Ones. Still it takes a few hours of communal chanting before she is able to tune out everything else and focus only on the complete healing of her body. The chanters are assisted by a powerful Being of Light. She summons Tilda to her chamber and introduces herself as the Blessed Virgin Mary of Our Lady of Lourdes. She stands silent and still, dressed in long white robes and a white head covering with a flowing blue scarf around her waist. With her hands pressed together in front of her, she steadily radiates a healing Light until the entire chamber is vibrating.

The next day, after fourteen hours of continuous chanting, Tilda signals to the others that her body is healed and the chanting can cease. Her broken bones are mended. The bruising has cleared up. She is no longer in pain. She feels well enough to make her own way to the Palace of the Immortals.

It is but an hour's walk along the river from the Lady of Lourdes' chamber to the Palace of the Immortals. On the way, she meets

Carol and Jason, travelling with their blue beast. Tilda is delighted to see them and invites them to walk with her. But the beast forbids them to leave him. Tilda is not ready to forgive the beast nor to make peace with him. The best she can do is accept his hold on her friends. She wishes she could explain to them that she will join them as soon as she's been to the Palace of the Immortals. Frustrated at her limited knowledge of English, she speaks rapidly to them in her own language, gesturing with her arms. She fervently hopes that they understand something, but their downcast faces tell her that they don't. She can't afford to wait any longer and leaves them with their beast.

Night has fallen and a full moon blazes in the clear night sky, but it is still dark enough to see the meteor shower. At the Palace of the Immortals, Tilda finds a gate has been attached to the entrance, sealing it closed. She detaches the gate with a little focussed effort and walks in.

Once in the chamber, Tilda sings songs of praise and thanksgiving to Great Mother and to the stones. Where they had been lifeless and unresponsive a few days earlier, they have finally awakened and burst into songs of joy. After the celebration, Crogan and Charmall appear with a question for Tilda.

'What have you learned, Wise One, from this experience?' Charmall asks.

Tilda reflects for some time. 'I have learned to be afraid of the beasts,' she says, feeling a heaviness descend upon her.

'What else?' Crogan insists, not willing to let this be all.

Hesitantly, Tilda replies, 'When I come to the edges of the paths where the beasts roam, I must stop, listen, and look both ways.'

Crogan and Charmall are satisfied. 'Be cautious. Be mindful. Be awake. But do not be afraid. You are doing well.'

Carol

It is late at night on the third night since Tilda's arrival. Carol is sound asleep and has no idea that Tilda slipped out of the lodge. Shortly after midnight, Roisin, the manager of the lodge, knocks frantically on the door. 'Are any of you missing?' she calls through the door. 'There's an ambulance outside. There's been an accident on the road. A lady's badly hurt.'

Carol leaps to her feet and turns on the light. Shocked, she sees that Tilda is indeed missing. With her heart racing and panic blinding her, she rummages under the bed for her shoes and in her backpack for a jumper and rushes out of the room. Roisin, her white curly hair in chaotic disarray, is hovering by the door. She runs with Carol to the front door and calls after her, 'Don't worry about your boy. I'll look after him.' Carol hesitates. She hadn't even thought about Jason left alone in the dorm on his own. But she decides to trust Roisin.

On the road in front of the lodge, Carol sees Tilda strapped onto a stretcher, not moving. Two paramedics are trying to load her into an ambulance, its blue light flashing ominously. A pair of policemen are interrogating a young man who is answering their questions in a wobbly voice, his hands shaking and close to tears.

'I didn't see her,' the young man is saying to the police, his voice a high, tight wheeze. 'Please believe me. She stepped into the road right in front of me. I didn't have time to swerve or stop. She just came out so suddenly. She didn't look.' He looks around at the paramedics as if they can corroborate his story.

The older paramedic approaches Carol. 'We've got to get this lady to hospital right now. We're taking her to Our Lady of Lourdes Hospital in Drogheda. Can you follow in your car?'

'I ... I don't know. My son ... he's in the lodge. I don't know if I can find it.' Carol's heart is racing. Just then, Roisin, in a blue anorak over her nightie, rushes out of the lodge with a wild-eyed, half-dressed Jason.

'You head on,' she says to the paramedics. To Carol, she says, 'Here, put these on. I'll drive you in my car.'

At the hospital, Carol's inability to answer any questions about Tilda or to explain how she knows her sound more and more peculiar. All she can say with any certainty is that she feels unbearably dreadful. Tilda has been injured while Carol slept. Jason is struck dumb, his eyes like saucers, holding onto Carol's hand. Roisin brings them tea in plastic cups from a machine in the corridor. The emergency department is not crowded and they wait less than an hour before a young doctor appears with news of Tilda.

'I'm Dr Carew,' she says, looking down at her notes with a puzzled expression. 'Um, Miss Tilda is conscious and somewhat comfortable. We've done X-rays and she has a fracture in her right arm. She's badly bruised and we're concerned about internal bleeding. We'll need to keep her in for observation for a few days at least. Tomorrow we'll put her arm in plaster. It's a compound fracture and will take six to eight weeks to heal.'

'Oh no. Oh no. Poor Tilda. Can we see her?' Jason cries.

Dr Carew hesitates. 'She's just had a major trauma. She's badly injured and needs calm.'

'Please,' Carol says. 'We'll go as soon as we've seen she's okay. Calm down, Jason.'

The doctor nods and shows them to the cubicle where Tilda is lying very still, drenched in sweat. She is pale, breathing steadily and slowly. When she sees them, her whole face beams. She tries to explain what happened, saying 'car' several times. Then she points to Carol's purse and mimes drawing. When Carol produces a pen and a notebook, she uses her left hand to laboriously draw a sketch of the triple spiral design on the entrance stone to the Newgrange mound. Pointing to Carol, to herself and to the drawing, Tilda makes it clear that she wants them to take her to the monument.

'No, no, you can't leave the hospital,' Carol explains firmly, shaking her head emphatically. She's puzzled by this odd request. 'Anyway, you can't go to Newgrange at night. It's all locked up.'

Tilda closes her eyes and nods acceptance. Just then a nurse appears to take her to a ward. Carol and Jason leave, promising to come back later. The next day, slightly more rested, Carol manages to find the hospital without Roisin's help. It takes them a while to track Tilda down.

'She's been making a lot of noise,' a nurse informs Carol as she leads them rapidly down the corridor. 'It was disturbing the other patients. And the staff. It was weird, made my heart beat faster. We couldn't think. We moved her out of the way. Into the chapel. Here she is. See, she's still at it.'

Tilda is sitting up, chanting loud, repetitive tuneless notes and banging the metal bars on the side of the bed in a steady, monotonous rhythm. She stops when they walk in and smiles with delight. Her colour is good. She shows no signs of being in pain. She doesn't look like she'd been hit by a car the night before.

'What did you give her?' Carol asks the nurse. 'She's high as a kite.'

'Nothing,' says the nurse wearily. 'She won't let us do anything or give her anything. She hasn't slept or eaten. All she's done is drink water and make a racket with that singing and banging. She's been at it for ten hours solid. I've never seen anything like it.'

Another doctor, not the lovely Dr Carew of the night before, appears in the chapel. He walks up to Tilda's bed and consults the notes hanging from a clipboard at the end of the bed.

'Nurse,' he says, in a voice that makes Carol think of a sergeant major commanding his troops. 'This patient needs to be taken to the plaster room. It should have been done hours ago. Call the porter.'

He would have marched out again if Tilda hadn't said no in a voice as commanding as his. She then raises her right arm, touches her right shoulder with her right hand, rotates her shoulder and stretches it above her head. She does the same with her left arm.

'Arm good,' she says. She hops off the bed, gets her balance after a brief wobble and stands face to face with the doctor. Holding his shoulders with both hands, she stands on tiptoes and touches her forehead to his much taller forehead, then her nose to his nose. The doctor takes a step back, not at all pleased to be nose-to-nose with this strange woman.

'Fhank you. G'night,' she says, and moves to do the same to the nurse. Surprised, the nurse taps forehead and nose with Tilda.

'Nurse, I'm going down to radiology to have a look at the X-rays.' The doctor studies the notes again, frowning and tutting. 'Who saw her in ER? Carew, huh. There must have been a mix-up. This woman clearly hasn't been hit by a car.'

'Dr Walsh,' Carol says, reading his name tag. 'Tilda was hit by a car last night, knocked unconscious, broken bones, internal bleeding. Now she seems fine. What is going on?'

'There's been some mistake,' Dr Walsh says shortly. 'I'm going to radiology.' He exits abruptly.

A porter arrives and wheels Tilda out of the chapel. Carol and Jason wander out of the chapel, not sure what to do with themselves.

'Tilda could be here for hours,' Carol says. 'Let's do more sightseeing and come back later. They've got my mobile number so they can always call me.'

They spend a few satisfying hours at the Battle of the Boyne museum at Oldbridge House. Carol's phone rings as they are sampling the cakes in the cafe.

'Hello, Mrs Williams. This is Dr Carew from the hospital. We did another Xray on Tilda's arm and I don't know how to explain this, but it's not broken anymore. It's completely healed. We checked her over and she's fine.'

'Really?' Carol exclaims, gesturing to Jason to come closer and listen. 'What do you mean, she's fine? You mean, like a miracle? Like your lady of Lourdes healed her? Is that why she was moved to the chapel?'

'No, um, of course not. No, I'm not saying that.' Dr Carew sounds flustered.

'What are you saying?' Carol snaps.

'We're very confused as to how we got it so wrong last night. I'm terribly sorry. We made a dreadful mistake, it seems. I can't explain it.'

Carol rolls her eyes. 'Shall we come over and pick her up?'

'Well, no,' Dr Carew says hesitantly. 'The thing is ... well, she's not here. She left of her own volition. We actually don't know where she is.'

'What do you mean, she left? What if she gets run over again? Anyway, how do you know she's fine? She wasn't fine last night. How could she be fine today?'

'I'm sorry. We couldn't keep her against her will and she was very determined to leave. The guards have been here. They want a statement from Tilda.'

Carol stares at the phone blankly.

'I know where Tilda would go,' Jason asserts eagerly. 'She'd go to Newgrange. I'm sure of it, Mum.' He jumps up and down in excitement.

Leaving their half-eaten cakes, they rush to the car and head out of the estate. But they don't have to drive all the way to Newgrange. Just before the turnoff to Donore, they see Tilda striding along the footpath by the River Boyne. She is travelling west, her matted hair bouncing up and down as she walks along, singing. When Carol screeches to a stop and beckons her into the car, Tilda does not seem surprised to see them. However, she refuses to join them, instead beckoning them to get out of the car and walk with her. When they don't budge, Tilda nods agreeably and resumes her walk along the river, leaving them staring after her. Carol's thoughts are churning. She can't believe Tilda is really as fit and hearty as she appears. Surely there will be a delayed reaction. The thought that pierces her heart the most is that they may never see Tilda again. Perhaps she's finally gone without even saying goodbye, disappearing from their lives as mysteriously as she had appeared.

They drive back to the lodge, a cloud of uncertainty hanging over them. They wander into the lounge and sit next to each other on a sofa, both gazing at the floor.

'Mum, I miss Tilda,' Jason says suddenly. 'I want her to come live with us in Bristol. Let's ask her. I bet she'll come. She likes us. Can we, Mum? Please.'

A hurricane of emotions sweeps through Carol's exhausted mind. Of course she wants Tilda to come back with them. She admits it. She can't imagine life without Tilda. The thought of going back home to the tension and drudgery of her life fills her with dread. But it doesn't make sense. She only met Tilda a few days before. She grunts in frustration, dangerously close to tears.

Roisin passes them on her way to the kitchen and hurries over. 'How's your friend?' she asks breathlessly, ready to commiserate. 'You found your way to Our Lady of Lourdes by yourself this morning?'

Carol nods and is about to speak when Roisin says, 'What a drama what with the ambulance and the guards here in the middle of the night. I was so shocked. How is she? How long will they keep her in? My mother was there for six weeks when she broke her hip. It's a grand place but you'd always rather be at home, wouldn't you?'

'She wasn't hurt as badly as everyone thought when it happened,' Carol mutters. 'She discharged herself this afternoon and is walking by the river. She seems fine.' She shakes her head and shrugs. She knows Tilda isn't fine but she has no idea what she can do. Somewhere out there, Tilda is wandering about, in mortal danger of getting hit by another car.

Roisin gapes at Carol. 'That's not possible. She was unconscious. She was badly injured. She couldn't have recovered that quickly. No, it can't be true.'

Jason shakes his head. 'She's gone to Newgrange. I'm sure she has. I'm going over to find her.' Abruptly he stands up and starts walking to the front door.

Roisin stops him. 'It's after five. It will be locked up and, anyway, you can't just go in. You have to go on the tour bus.'

'Tilda can,' Jason asserts proudly. 'She does whatever she wants to do. I'm going to get her.'

'I'll drive you there,' Roisin says. 'It's a long way round by car and we'll have to climb over the gate. And we won't be able to get into the passage. But neither will Tilda so if she has gone there, we'll meet her just outside the mound. Are you coming, Carol? Grand. Let's go.'

The gate is easy to climb but as they run up the path, there is no sign of Tilda. They walk around the mound and come to a stop by the entrance stone. The sun has set and the quartz-covered outer wall is gleaming in the light of the full moon and the spotlights.

'In two months, it will be the winter solstice,' Roisin murmurs, shining her torch on the triple spiral carving. 'It's magical to be in the chamber when the sun rises. I won a place on the lottery a few years back.'

'Listen,' Jason says suddenly. 'Can you hear that singing? It's coming from inside the chamber.'

Tentatively, they climb up the wooden steps over the entrance stone and down towards the entrance. They can clearly hear the sound of many voices chanting. Approaching nearer, they see that the metal gate is hanging from its hinges at an angle. Jason reaches for Carol's hand and they follow Roisin into the narrow passage. They move slowly until they arrive in the heart of the chamber.

By the light of Roisin's torch, they can see that there is only one person in the chamber and that person is Tilda. She is lying in the egg-shaped bowl with her eyes shut, chanting. Her voice bounces back and forth and up and down against the stones. With each bounce, the sound becomes louder and louder until Carol feels her body vibrating in resonance. The sensation is overpowering. Jason runs down the passage, Roisin and Carol following. They grip their heads and lie on the ground, panting. They can still hear the chanting but it doesn't disturb them outdoors.

They lie there for an hour in perfect contentment watching the stars in the cloudless night sky. Lying on the cold ground outside, listening to Tilda chanting inside the Newgrange chamber, Carol realises she's never felt such peace in her life.

Tilda emerges soon after. She sits down beside Carol and holds her hand. Looking deep into Tilda's blue eyes, Carol feels a wild hope well up from within.

'Come wivh you,' Tilda says, pointing to herself. Slowly, she counts six of her fingers and then raises her hand to the moon.

I am the sunlight in the heart, the moonlight in the mind; I am the light at the end of every dream, the voice for ever calling to come away.'

Carol gasps. Finally, she's heard the call. She looks around wildly, half expecting to see something or someone. Tilda is still holding her hand and looking up at the moon. Jason and Roisin are lying on the ground without showing any signs of having heard anything. She looks suspiciously at the stones who shimmer sweetly at her but don't appear to have spoken. She glances up at the moon. Did it wink? Confused, she closes her eyes and listens for more.

She hears it: '*Light and peace and joy reside in you. There is nothing to fear. Everything is all right. You are Home.*'

Chapter 9. Carol

It has been ten days since she and Jason left Ireland and returned to Bristol, bringing Tilda with them. Carol pinches herself every day just to make sure she's not dreaming. What started as a vague fantasy, an unattainable wish, has come true. Not only is Tilda staying with them but she has bonded with Francis. Peace reigns in Carol's heart and household for the first time since Francis moved in.

This night, Carol has invited Sue and Alison over to thank them for convincing her not to take her mother to Newgrange. She has made her classic lasagne. It's the first dinner party she's hosted since her mother moved in with her.

'See that stone with the triple spiral carved on it? There are more like that inside as well. The carvings are just amazing.' Carol passes her phone over the kitchen table to Sue who swipes through the photos without much interest. Alison leans closer to look, her braids hanging down from her short Afro alongside Sue's straight blonde hair. One arm rests lightly on Sue's shoulder.

Carol notices the loving squeeze Alison gives Sue and feels a pang of jealousy. Not for a woman lover; no, she definitely isn't a lesbian. What she wants, and what she's never had, is a man who would touch her with the same casual, taken-for-granted loving tenderness that Sue and Alison show each other. She never had that with Mike. In the eleven years they'd been married, he'd never touched her tenderly. Although he wasn't physically abusive, he had constantly criticised her body, pointing out how fat and ugly she was.

She knows she's fat. Mike was right. Not as fat as Moira but considerably fatter than either Alison or Sue. Moira doesn't appear to mind being fat but she has a husband who appreciates a buxom, full figured female form. At least Sue and Alison are discreet around her, aware that Carol minds her lover-less status very much. Carol feels more than a pang of jealousy when Moira's husband pats Moira on the bum and kisses her on the lips in Carol's presence. Which is why she has not invited Moira and her husband to dinner, though she is equally grateful to Moira for her wise advice.

Sue glances up from looking at the photos. 'We haven't been over for a dinner party since your mother moved in. How long ago is that? Two, three years?'

It has been three years but Carol had stopped inviting friends over long before dementia was diagnosed. Carol had become ill from the stress of dealing with Francis living on her own. There were too many odd situations that made Carol worry about her mother's safety, like putting a bottle of milk in the washing machine or burning garlic bread in the microwave, setting the smoke alarm off. Too many times Carol had had to drop everything and rush over to deal with another calamity, each one more bizarre and serious than the last. Even if Francis had lived next door, it would not have been sustainable. But Francis lived on the other side of Bristol.

Carol decided there was no option but to move her mother in to Ben's room. Ben, unsurprisingly, objected even though he was due to start at the university of Reading. Francis also did not want to be bossed around by her daughter and made the move more stressful than it needed to be. Once she was settled in, she went out of her way to make Carol's life difficult. Carol gave up having dinner parties. She gave up going out with her friends. She gave up her lifeline, the monthly book group that she went to with Moira, Alison and Sue. She resigned herself to looking after her bitter, angry mother who vented her frustration on her daughter.

'Who's that weird hippie in front of the tall stone?' Alison asks, turning the phone around to make the image bigger. 'What is she wearing? It looks like the hide of a cow. And what's that on her head? Is that her hair?'

'Oh, her. Yeah, that's Tilda. She's quite distinctive looking, isn't she?' Carol picks at the lasagne, suddenly feeling too nervous to eat. 'We met her at Newgrange, on a guided tour. She doesn't speak any English. We became good friends.'

'How do you become good friends with someone who doesn't

speak English?' Sue asks, squinting her eyes to see the weird hippie in the photo.

'We just did,' Carol says thoughtfully. 'It made me realise how few words you need to communicate. We had fun together. We went on hikes and explored the area. Jason completely bonded with her, like from the minute he laid eyes on her. It was uncanny. I can't explain it.'

Sue and Alison fall silent, though Carol can sense more questions are coming. She fiddles with her lasagne, takes a deep breath and says, 'I invited Tilda to live with us. She's looking after my mother in exchange for English lessons.'

'The hippie in the cow hide is living with you?' Sue gasps. She reaches for the phone to have another look.

'You are trusting a complete stranger to look after your mother in your home?' Alison keeps shaking her head. 'What does she know about caring for someone with dementia?'

'Can you stop being a social worker for one minute, Alison?' Carol feels annoyed. 'I followed my intuition and I did what I needed to do. And it's working out brilliantly. My Mum's getting better care from Tilda than she ever would get in one of those warehouses for the unwanted elderly you want me to incarcerate Mum in. And don't worry. I have been to my GP and got a proper dementia care plan sorted out, just like you suggested.'

She pauses, regretting the automatic feelings of annoyance that pop up whenever someone challenges her.

'We don't want to incarcerate your mother in a warehouse, Carol. God, you are so closed-minded.'

'Be quiet, Alison,' Sue says. 'Go on, Carol. How did Tilda get into the picture?'

'I somehow just knew that she would be a big help to me, especially looking after Mum. And she is. She's a godsend.'

'Do we get to meet her, Carol?' Alison asks.

Carol scowls. A part of her does not want to expose Tilda to Alison's scrutiny. Not for Tilda's sake but for her own. It does sound rather strange that she would trust this complete stranger after knowing her for only a few days. But deep inside, Carol has no doubt at all.

'Yes, of course. She's out now with Mum and Jason.' Carol doesn't feel comfortable with the thought of her mother and son wandering around Bristol at night. But she isn't going to admit it to Sue and Alison.

'What, at nine at night?' Alison is outraged. 'Where did they go? To the pub?'

'Alison, stop it! Why not at nine at night? Why not the pub?' Carol can't answer those questions herself. It seems just as weird to her as it does to Alison.

'Well, I don't know,' Alison says, putting her elbows on the table and looking directly at Carol. 'Shouldn't your mother be tucked up in bed by now? And Jason's only ten.'

Carol shrugs. 'Mum has never been the pub type. And Tilda's definitely not. We took her for a meal in a pub in Drogheda and she really didn't like the atmosphere. No, I think they've gone for a walk by the River Frome over by Snuff Mills. And I am going to a film with Moira tomorrow night.'

Alison is even more scandalised. 'They're walking by the river at nine at night?' she cries. 'In the dark? You have really changed, Carol. All these years, you've been so protective of your mother and of Jason. And now you've known this stranger five minutes and you're trusting her to look after an elderly woman with dementia and a ten-year-old boy. How does that fit in with your GP's dementia care plan?'

Sue is shaking her head. 'If Tilda doesn't speak English, how can she, um, how can she manage? Where is she from, anyway? She looks like she is from Afghanistan or somewhere like that. Is she a refugee?'

Carol takes a deep breath. 'Actually, I don't know where Tilda is from. I don't know how she got to Ireland. I don't even know her name. Jason named her Tilda.'

'Maybe she was trafficked,' Alison says. 'I've worked with people who've been brought here illegally for sex work or to work in nail salons. Do you think that she escaped from her controllers and that's why she was so eager to come with you?'

'I don't know. Maybe you're right,' Carol says, thinking that does make more sense than any explanation she'd come up with.

'That means she's here illegally,' Alison continues, twirling her braids. 'How did you get her into England?'

Carol stands up and starts clearing the table. She badly wants to change the subject. This is not going in a direction she likes.

'What would you like for dessert?' she asks, stacking the plates and moving them to the sink. 'I've got peanut butter ice cream or raspberry cheesecake.'

She notices Sue and Alison exchanging looks but she isn't sure if the looks are about her choice of desserts or her act of sneaking Tilda into the country. It wasn't difficult to persuade Tilda to lie down in the back seat and be covered by a blanket as they drove onto the ferry. Two white people, one middle aged woman and a young boy, don't fit the profile of people smugglers. Still, it isn't the kind of behaviour Carol normally engages in. She is a law-abiding citizen and can't easily explain to her friends why she would do something so out of the ordinary. In her heart, she knows that Tilda's arrival in her life is somehow linked to the call. But she can't explain that to Sue and Alison.

Instead she sits back down and looks her friends in the eye. 'I know this all sounds kind of weird to you. It does to me as well. The thing is ...' Carol pauses. 'I was going crazy looking after my mum. She's so angry and mean. It's such a relief to have Mum looked after by someone else. You know what's really weird? Mum actually likes being with Tilda. As soon as she got back from her week with John, she took an instant liking to Tilda. They spend hours every day together. She's never been like that with me.'

Carol sniffs wistfully. The dementia hadn't turned her mother angry and mean. Francis had always been angry and mean but only to Carol, not to her brother John and now, not to Tilda. Yes, it is a relief to be free of that anger, but what she really wants is to have a mother who actually likes and appreciates her. *Oh well* she thinks. *Tilda's presence is the next best thing.*

'Anyway,' Carol continues, pushing pointless wishes away. 'It means I can see my friends, have a dinner party, go out to a film, come back to the book group, even read the books. I can't tell you how much I miss our book group. You two still go, don't you? I know Moira does. And the main thing is that I can work without being interrupted. You don't know what that means to me.'

'I'm sorry for being so harsh, Carol,' Sue says, reaching across the table and patting her arm. 'I get it and I'm glad for you. Really.'

'What does Tilda get out of this arrangement?' Alison asks. *She's still got her social worker hat on*, Carol thinks, which is fair enough but Carol doesn't like being interrogated, having to defend herself. Can't Alison see what this means to her?

'Tilda gets free room and board and English lessons,' Carol answers. She isn't sure whether that is really what Tilda wants but it is what she is getting. Francis and Jason are the main teachers. Since both never stop talking, Tilda gets an intensive crash course in conversational English. Unlike Carol, Tilda doesn't get bored or irritated hearing the same stories over and over again. She says it helps her learn English. And learn she does. Carol marvels at the speed with which Tilda learns. Jason also teaches Tilda by including her in his homework and watching TV with her.

'How long is she planning to stay?' Alison says.

'About six months. So it's just for a short while. But so far, it's been great having her. Look, I did something differently than I've ever done before. I listened to my heart, not my head. I went to Ireland on a whim. I met Tilda and invited her home. My life is changing for the better.'

Carol sits up straight and still in the chair. *The way Tilda sits,* she thinks. *I'm on the path to a new me.* She smiles proudly at her friends.

Your sun is but a smoky shadow,
ours the ruddy and eternal glow;
yours is far way, ours is heart and hearth and home;
yours is a light without, ours a fire within,
in rock, in river, in plain, everywhere living,
everywhere dawning, whence also it cometh
that the mountains emit their wondrous rays.

from *The Dream of Angus Oge* by George William Russell, 1897

Chapter 10. Carol

Ever since their return from Ireland five weeks before, Tilda has been making a careful study of each member of her family. Jason and Francis don't seem to mind. In fact, they love Tilda's undiluted attention. Carol has noted the look of adoration on Jason's face whenever he talks to Tilda. She can't figure out what it is about her that attracts him so powerfully. Francis, too, is sweet-tempered around Tilda. But Carol often feels judged and found wanting. Tilda's blue eyes cut through all her defences, leaving her feeling exposed and naked.

One night in early December, Carol is cooking dinner while a barefoot and bra-less Tilda watches her every move from the top of the kitchen table. Tilda is sitting, her back straight and her legs crossed, not wriggling or squirming. Nor does she smile or nod or show any expression. She merely sits and watches. Only her eyes move, following Carol as she bustles about the kitchen.

Sweat drips down Carol's forehead. She drops a spoon on the floor. The rice boils over and spills onto the stove. The broccoli burns. She knows she's overreacting but she is completely unnerved by Tilda's scrutiny of her.

Suddenly she can't stand it any longer. She marches to the table. Speaking slowly and patting the chair as if calling a dog, she says, 'Please stop watching me. I don't want you to sit on the table. Here, sit on the chair.'

Tilda tilts her head and looks quizzically at Carol. Then, without taking her eyes off Carol, she hops off the table and sits cross-legged on the chair.

'Now stop watching me,' Carol says, but Tilda continues to study her closely. No, she doesn't understand. Carol covers Tilda's eyes with her hand. This time, Tilda gets it. She looks away.

'Now call Jason and Francis. Say dinner is served,' Carol instructs. Tilda repeats the command three times without doing what she's been asked. Carol rolls her eyes, walks to the door and shouts,

'Jason, Francis. Dinner is served.' On the third shout, they come into the kitchen and sit at the table. Carol serves the meal. They begin to eat, all except Tilda. She waits silently, her hands in her lap, her eyes on the plate of food in front of her.

Tilda

The kitchen is summertime warm, the cold December evening hidden behind the fogged-over window. Tilda would very much like to continue watching Carol as she whirls around the kitchen doing mysterious deeds with strange and inexplicable objects. It is indeed fascinating. Tilda could watch Carol for hours but clearly Carol does not want to be watched. *How strange*, Tilda thinks. She has always learned by close observation. That is how she became a Wisdom Keeper. How is she going to achieve mastery in the ways of her hosts if she is not allowed to observe them in action? She has already observed what they do when they sit to eat but she cannot do as they do. To eat without first expressing gratitude is like a denial of her very being. Tonight, instead of chanting under her breath in her own language, she says quietly, 'Now for food say fhank you.'

Francis looks up, a spoonful of rice halfway to her mouth. She frowns, then continues eating. Jason stops cutting his fish finger and puts his hands in his lap. Carol tightens her lips and taps her fingers. Tilda chants. She does not translate or try to use any of the English words she's learned. By the time she's finished, Francis has eaten all the rice, all the fish and all the unburnt broccoli on her plate.

'Who are you thanking, Tilda?' Jason asks when she's done. He spears a fish finger and looks at it with interest.

'Who you fhank?' Tilda replies calmly.

Jason considers. 'Nobody but I should thank Mum for cooking the food. I should thank the fishermen for catching the fish and the farmers for growing the rice and the broccoli.'

'And who else?

'Who else? I guess we should thank Tesco and whoever delivers the food to Tesco.'

'And?'

Jason shrugs. 'I can't think of anyone else to thank.'

Tilda is puzzled. She wonders whether she missed something. She didn't catch all of what Jason said but she's sure he didn't mention Mother Earth, the rain, the sun, the plants and animals, let alone Great Mother.

The following morning, Tilda comes into the kitchen to find Carol looking down at her phone, stroking its belly. Phone was one of the first English words Tilda learned in Ireland. Tilda does not yet know what the phone does for Carol when she strokes it. She thinks it may be like stroking a cow's udder before milking, but she is not sure. She doesn't want to annoy Carol by watching her too closely, but she has to learn. She points to a bowl of fruit on the counter and asks, 'Where from orange fruit?'

Without looking up from her phone, Carol sighs and says, 'from Tesco.

Tilda tries again. 'Where orange fruit to Tesco?' She guesses that Tesco is a collection point, not a farm.

'From-Spain,' Carol says in a short sharp voice, without looking up from her phone.

'Where Spain?' Tilda stares steadily at her, willing her to look her in the eye and give her as much attention as she is giving to her phone.

'Where is Spain?' Carol corrects her automatically, still not making eye contact.

'Where is Spain?' Tilda repeats, grateful for the language instruction but aware of a sharp stab of jealousy towards the phone.

'Far away across the ocean,' Carol says, after a pause.

'Farawayacrossvheocean,' Tilda repeats, understanding only the word ocean. 'How orange fruit come here?'

'How did the orange get here?' Carol enunciates the words carefully, looking up from her phone. 'I dunno. By boat or plane or lorry.' She taps the phone firmly and places it on the table.

'What is byboatorplaneorlorry?' Tilda asks eagerly, now that her rival has been silenced.

'Tilda,' Carol says in a rush, running a hand through her hair. 'there is too much to know I cannot pay attention to these unimportant details it does not matter I do not care how the orange gets here I just know that it does my life is too complicated you ask me about things I do not need to think about.' She rises from the table, puts the phone in her pocket and heads to the room where she sits for many hours of each day.

Tilda remains in the kitchen, repeating as much of this speech as she can remember. She recognises several of the words, particularly "I do not care how" which was said with feeling but the meaning of the rest eludes her. She shrugs, wishing Carol was a more patient teacher.

'Charmall, Crogan,' Tilda calls inwardly. 'I am sorely puzzled. Can it be true that Carol cares not from where comes the food that sustains her life? It seems that she believes it should be there for her, as if by magic.'

'I also do not understand,' Crogan says. Charmall murmurs assent. 'It is deeply disturbing. As in our time, Carol is blessed with gifts from all the realms. The Sun, the Moon and the Planets, Earth, Air, Fire and Water, the Animals, the Trees and the Plants, and the Mineral realm provide her with everything she needs to sustain life. Tell us, Oh Wise One, what have you learned about food in this world?'

'The people in this world are well organised.' Tilda chooses her words carefully. 'Carol keeps no cows nor chickens. She does not grow any of the food she eats. She does not help to harvest the food from the farms. Yet she has an abundant supply of food and never goes hungry. She goes to large palaces to collect her food. I have not learned yet where the food comes from.'

'What does your mind say about this?' Crogan asks.

'I am in awe. In this world, the people are as numerous as the ants in an ant nest. To feed them all – yes, it is indeed awesome.' Tilda trails off, not satisfied with her answer. It is not the whole truth.

'What does your heart say?' Charmall asks. 'Your heart speaks the truth.'

'My heart feels their loneliness.
They know not who they are.
They know not their Source.
They are like the waves on the ocean,
enthralled by the rising up and the crashing down,
by their dance with the air,
by the spray and the roar.
Enthralled by their belief in their separateness,
that their lives are due to their own efforts, their own will,
not knowing they are always one with the ocean.
Not knowing they are blessed.
Not knowing they are loved.
My heart feels their pain.'

Crogan wants to know more. 'If Carol does not honour Great Mother and the life-sustaining realms, what does she honour? What does she give her attention to?'

'She honours *m'sheens*,' Tilda replies without hesitation. This she has already observed.

'Now go and learn about *m'sheens*.' Crogan sets the next lesson.

Tilda follows Carol into the room at the back of the kitchen where Carol is paying homage to one of her *m'sheens*. Tilda sits on the floor, her back straight and her legs crossed.

Carol is hunched forward, her shoulders nearly touching her ears. She is peering through a stick with clear round windows that sits on her nose, tapping at little squares with her fingers. Drawings appear on the *m'sheen* as she taps.

'What is *m'sheen*?' Tilda asks, gazing up at her from the floor.

'A-laptop,' Carol says, without turning around or pausing in her tapping.

'What you do wivh alaptop?'

'I am doing my job so I can make money,' Carol explains, with a weary sigh and a heavy droop of her body.

She speaks slowly so Tilda can understand. But Tilda does not understand. There is no word in her language for either *job* or *muh-nee*. Tilda does understand that *muh-nee* is as important in Carol's world as the stones are in hers. She also understands that a *job* and *muh-nee* are burdensome and joyless masters, leaving Carol no time for honouring the life-sustaining realms.

Carol shakes her head, forbidding further questions. Tilda watches in silence for a few minutes more, then leaves the house to visit nearby trees.

Carol

Two hours after asking about her laptop, Tilda sails in the front door followed by a gust of cold, damp air. Carol notices that she's glowing. It seems that she's found a way to recharge her batteries just by being in Nature, hanging out with trees. *Well, that's not my cup of tea,* Carol thinks. *At least not in December.* Yet in Ireland, Tilda had taken them out in Nature every day and Carol had felt that same glow. Carol shivers and turns the kettle on to make herself a cup of tea.

'If you stare at me with those laser eyes again today, I'm going to throttle you,' Carol mutters under her breath. Tilda smiles at her and quickly looks away.

As she loads the dishwasher, Carol says, 'Thanks, Tilda, for not staring at me. I appreciate it.'

The phone rings. The washing machine repair man is on his way. At last; she's been waiting for the repair man for a week. Dirty clothes have been piling up. Her Bad Mother Bubble is nearly full.

Carol catches Tilda glancing at her briefly.

Carol sits down at her laptop and works on the results section of a paper due in less than a week. She reads the same sentence three times. A week is not long enough. A month wouldn't be long enough. Panic sets her stomach churning.

Ten minutes later, she takes a break and listens to the news on the radio. 'No Brexit deal reached. Today was supposed to be when Theresa May came to Parliament to announce that the first stage of Brexit talks was over.' Aargh! Not Brexit mayhem again. Carol tears her hair and switches off the radio.

Tilda shoots her a quick questioning look, her eyes widening in alarm.

The phone rings. The washing machine repair man is stuck in traffic. Damn. How maddening! How absolutely maddening!

Carol returns to the laptop and checks her emails. An overdue bill from the university for Ben's dorm fees for the autumn term. Surely she paid that already. Or did she? She spends half an hour looking through her online bank statements but can't find any record. She's breathing rapidly, wiping the sweat off her forehead.

She glances at Tilda who quickly closes her eyes and looks innocent.

Maybe someone has put a delicious snack in the fridge. She opens the fridge, stares at the meagre contents and closes the door despondently. She makes herself a banana smoothie in the blender and shares a glass with Tilda.

Back to the laptop, she reads the same sentence another three times.

The phone trills. A text has arrived from Jason's school reminding parents to bring in their children's PE kits. She wishes they didn't keep sending these texts. She did send in Jason's PE kit. Or did she? She rummages in the overflowing laundry basket and finds his kit. The Bad Mother Bubble is close to bursting. Her stomach is aching.

There are crumbs on the kitchen floor. Carol gets out the vacuum cleaner and quickly vacuums the kitchen, then carries on to do the living room and stairs. She hates vacuuming but she can't stop. The

Bad Mother Bubble is a bit lighter.

Francis appears in her bathrobe, looking for Tilda. Carol notices a pang of resentment and quickly shoves it away. Wouldn't it be nice if Francis wanted to see her own daughter as much as she craves Tilda's company?

Carol makes her a cup of coffee in her cappuccino machine and settles her in front of the smart TV to watch the next episode of *The Good Place*. Tilda sits with her. Carol stands at the door of the living room. She's still on her way back to work when the episode ends and the next one begins. She catches Tilda's eye. She looks as bewildered and unhappy as Carol feels. That wasn't even mildly amusing. Why does Mum even watch that crap? What a waste of time!

There's nothing in the house for dinner. Her mind's a blank. She hates having to think of meals to make, especially for Jason who's always been a picky eater and for Francis who criticises everything she makes. She jumps in the car and drives to Tesco, after first instructing Tilda to keep an eye on Francis.

Halfway through her shopping, her phone rings. The washing machine repair man is at the house. Carol abandons her shopping and rushes home.

She boils a kettle to make a cup of tea for the repair man and another for Francis, then climbs the stepladder to get a bottle of sherry from the top cabinet. It's the only alcohol in the house. It will have to do. She pours herself a large glass and drinks it all in one long gulp. Clutching her stomach, she barely makes it to the toilet before she vomits it all up.

Tilda stares, eyes wide open, not even pretending to look away.

Tilda

'I observed and I learned about *m'sheens*,' Tilda reports to Crogan. She has spent a week in close but covert observation. She is sitting by her favourite oak tree, basking in the bright sunshine.

'A *m'sheen* has a life and a will of its own, just like a tree-person or a Stone-person, but it also does tasks for people like our stone and bone tools and clay pots do for us.'

'How do *m'sheens* come alive?' Crogan asks.

'From the sun though I cannot explain how,' Tilda says. She is frustrated by her failure to understand how *m'sheens* work. Carol and Jason tried with words and drawings to show her but she still does not grasp the meaning of fossils, fossil fuels and electricity.

Charmall and Crogan disappear to consult. When they return, they say, 'Do not try to understand how the knowledge of this future world is used to make *m'sheens* work. Your task is to observe with the knowledge of your world. What have you observed?'

'What I have observed is this,' Tilda says. 'Carol has *m'sheens* to chop food, to turn solid food to a liquid, to turn liquid food to a solid, to beat eggs, to wash pots and eating tools, to wash clothes, to make food cold, to make food hot and even one that shines light as it sprinkles salt. There are *m'sheens* which flicker and talk, *m'sheens* that play music, and *m'sheens* for talking to people who are far away. And many more in every room, too many to mention.

'*M'sheens* make demands on people and require daily rituals. Every day, Francis sits still and silent before the TV *m'sheen*. She worships it for hours. It tells stories. When I do understand the words, I don't understand the wisdom. They see things in it that I do not. They can't understand why I don't see what they see but I only see flashes of colours and shimmering shapes. When Carol's washing *m'sheen* became ill, she called a special healer to come to restore it to well-being. Her phone is the most demanding of all her *m'sheens*. All day and sometimes at night, it calls for her. She never fails to respond. It is no wonder that Carol has no time to think about where her food comes from. She is devoted to her *m'sheens*. She gives them her full attention. And they make her ill. Very ill.'

'Thank you, Wise One,' Crogan purrs. 'You have learned well. Goodbye.'

Tilda rubs her nose against the tree's rough bark. 'Oak tree, blessed one, beautiful Being of love and oneness. To you I devote myself. How can I serve you today?'

The oak tree stretches luxuriously and waves its bare branches in friendly acknowledgement. 'Grace me with your love, dear one, and I will send love to all Beings through my roots.'

Tilda's heart expands with joy. She stays until she has replenished her spirit.

Chapter 11. Carol

'Mum, is Ben coming home for Christmas?' Jason asks while pretending to wipe the dinner table.

Carol feels a sharp stab of annoyance at Jason for piercing the Ben Bubble, the elastic space at the back of her mind where she banishes thoughts of Ben. She knows she'll have to face facts soon. The autumn term of his university ends in eight days.

'I don't know. I haven't heard from him since before we went to Ireland,' says Carol, thinking what a relief those six weeks have been. Every time he called or texted, she would tense up. Although it's ominous not to have heard from him, she can't deny to herself how glad she is. Ben is not an easy person to deal with.

Now that Jason has precipitously opened the Ben Bubble, memories of her last contact with Ben come flooding out. She stands paralysed by the dishwasher, reluctantly remembering the text he'd sent demanding £50. He'd claimed to be skint. When she apologetically declined to give him the money, he had sent a volley of abusive text messages. Carol tried to get Ben to understand why she refused his request. She explained that she needed every penny she had for her trip to Ireland, that she had limited finances now that she was looking after her mother, and paying for him to go to university. She'd made several helpful suggestions about how he can budget his money better and how maybe he can ask his father. Though she knows that Mike is "between jobs" as usual and has only ever occasionally contributed to Ben's university expenses. Each text Carol sent was matched by a furious rebuttal from Ben.

In the end, she had caved in and sent him the £50. It had seemed easier than fielding his relentless aggression. She could spare £50 if she booked the cheaper dorm room in the lodge in Ireland instead of the en-suite room. He'd accused her of being manipulative and selfish, of caring more for her mother and Jason than she did for him. Is that true? Maybe she does enjoy winding him up, controlling him, playing games with his mind. Maybe she is a Bad Mother.

Carol pictures a Bad Mother Bubble floating near and bumping into the Ben Bubble. She feels laughter bubbling up and imagines blowing the bubbles around the room, maybe even getting a pin and bursting them.

A memory of Ben's so-called thank you text for the £50 makes her stomach hurt. She sits down at the kitchen table, the words of the text seared in her mind: *At last! You need to think about what kind of a mother you are, why you put me through such shit just for a few pounds. Is it worth it to you to feel you have control over me?*

Carol groans as all the wobbly feelings she deposited in her Ben Bubble and her Bad Mother Bubble pour out, submerging her brain in a dense brown fog.

'Hey, forget about Ben,' Carol says. She wonders how she can get Jason off this topic. 'Say, what are we going to do for your birthday? Can you believe you'll be eleven years old in six days? What would you like to have?'

'I'm scared of Ben,' Jason says, ignoring the birthday bait. 'He might just show up any day now. He might, you know. He's done that before. You've got to stop him.'

'I guess we'll have to figure out where he'll sleep,' Carol says through the fog. 'Now that Tilda has got the fold-up cot in the living room. I can put Ben in my bedroom and I can sleep on the sofa.'

'No,' Jason screams. 'No. No. No. Please Mum. Don't let him come here. Why can't he stay with Dad?'

'I don't, um, I don't think that's possible,' Carol says slowly. 'Your dad is not very settled at the moment. I don't even know where he's living.'

'So what?' Jason is still screaming. 'We don't have any room for Ben. He's mean. He's horrible. He beat me up. You can't let him come here. Mum, you don't ever listen to me.'

Carol is stung but she knows he's right. Since their trip, she's been more aware of her youngest son. It's true she hasn't listened to him and she hasn't protected him from Ben. She felt terrible whenever

Ben teased Jason and even more terrible the times when he punched his little brother. But she didn't know what to do.

'I know, Jason. He can be horrible. But he's family. He's my son. He's your brother. He has nowhere else to go and I won't reject him. I would never turn you out on the street and I won't do that to Ben.' Carol's stomachache worsens. An image of handcuffs tying her wrists to Ben's pop into her mind. Yet she sympathises with Ben. Mike left the family when Ben was ten; no wonder Ben feels angry and rejected. It is easier to take it out on her than on someone who isn't on the scene.

'Then I'll leave,' Jason says. 'I'll stay with Sue and Alison.'

'Don't be silly,' Carol says, thinking that isn't such a bad idea. Maybe both of them can move in with Sue and Alison or Moira for the Christmas holidays, leaving Ben with Tilda and Francis. But, as Carol soon finds out, Sue and Alison have a house full of relatives and Moira has another use for her spare room.

When Ben arrives for the Christmas holidays on the 13th of December, Jason is still at home. With his DJ equipment and his many boxes of stuff, it seems that the only sensible thing to do is to move Ben into Carol's bedroom and for Carol to move into the living room on the sofa. It gives Ben privacy from the rest of the family and gives them space away from him.

And so it seems to work for the first few days. Ben stayed in Carol's bedroom, sleeping all day and awake all night. He came downstairs to the kitchen to forage for food when the rest of the family were asleep. Carol kept the fridge stocked with pepperoni pizzas and beer. There was no need to interact. Carol was beginning to think that it might just work out for everyone.

But the peace didn't last. On the third day, Carol is serving dinner when Ben comes into the kitchen. Carol notices his pallid skin and closed expression and instantly feels tense, certain that he is in a mood and might have one of his rages.

'Oh Ben, there you are. Sit down and join us,' Carol says with false brightness. 'We're having grilled salmon, boiled potatoes and steamed broccoli, a healthy meal. I can put another potato on for you, if you'd like. Or of course you can have a pizza. I got the kind you like, pepperoni. But wait, you haven't met Tilda yet, have you? We met Tilda in Newgrange when we went to ...'

She hears herself babbling and knows it's nerves. Ben is not paying any attention to Tilda or to anyone else.

'I need a part for my music system,' he says abruptly, interrupting Carol in mid flow. 'It's on eBay. I need about £40 so can you top up my account now? Make it £85. I need it right away.'

Tilda is watching Ben with curiosity and openness. She has her hands in her lap, her head tilted to one side, ready to be introduced. As she did when first meeting Moira, Sue, and Alison, she is waiting to do the forehead and nose touch greeting. Carol's stomach clenches at the thought of Ben's reaction if Tilda tries that. But she needn't have worried. Ben is not to be deflected.

Jason is busy not looking at Ben and is staring hard at his plate. He barely said hello when Ben arrived and has gone out of his way to ignore his brother on the few occasions they passed each other in the house.

'Mum, did you hear me?' Ben says, scowling at her. 'I need it now.'

'We're eating right now,' Carol says softly, though her stomach is too tense to eat. 'After dinner maybe.'

'I'm. Going. Out. I. Need. It. Now.'

Carol is aware of the threat in Ben's voice and of a sense of shame that Tilda should witness her son bullying her. She realises that it matters to her what Tilda thinks of her. She hopes that Tilda's grasp of English is not yet good enough to follow the conversation. But if there is one thing she has learned about Tilda, it is that she understands emotions and body language. Carol glances at Tilda who is watching her with undisguised interest, her blue eyes taking it all in.

I have no choice. There's nothing I can do to get through to him, Carol thinks. Quickly she goes to her laptop, makes the bank transfer and sits down again at the table. Ben grunts, disappears upstairs and then out of the house. Carol's food is cold, but it doesn't matter. She can't eat anyway, and she can't stop shaking.

'Why did you do that?' Jason whispers, even though Ben is nowhere near. 'Money to fix his music system? Are you crazy? He'll make our lives hell.'

As it turns out, Jason is right. They have two days' grace before the part arrives in the post and the music system is assembled.

Then all hell breaks loose. At two o'clock in the morning, the house is rocked by a barrage of sound, the bass pounding through the walls. Tilda leaps off the cot, looking wide-eyed at Carol who is curled up on the sofa covering her ears with her hands. Jason flies down the stairs, wailing, and hides in the kitchen, though the noise is only marginally less there. Francis emerges from her bedroom and bangs on his door, shouting, 'Stop that noise! Stop it!' Soon a frantic hammering and enraged voices can be heard at the front door as neighbours stream out of their houses to protest. Carol drags herself up the stairs and joins Francis at the door, shouting and banging in a futile attempt to get Ben's attention. Ben does not respond.

Her fist in mid-air, Carol stops banging on the door when she sees Tilda walk calmly up the stairs. There is something about Tilda's manner that strikes Carol as unstoppable, as if she could walk through walls if she wanted to. Tilda looks at Carol with a puzzled expression, as if she is expecting Carol to do something. But the brown fog from the Ben Bubble has descended, rendering her incapable of doing anything. Tilda nods towards the door. Carol is breathing hard and does not move. Then Tilda does something which Carol would never have dreamed of doing. She opens the door and walks into the room. Without paying any attention to Ben, she speaks a few words in her language to the music system and unplugs it.

The sudden silence is shocking. Carol can hear buzzing in her ears, like a shrill silence that ebbs and flows. She hears her heart pounding, her breath ragged as she breathes in and out. She sees her mother, frozen in mid-scream, a purple haze surrounding her in the dark landing, her face taut and agitated. She sees the grain of wood on the door and the striped pattern on the carpet. She feels cold seep into her bare feet.

In the next moment, she senses that a light is switched on and the fog dissipates. A presence fills the space, enveloping her in light. Tilda is walking towards her, carrying the speaker from Ben's music system. She holds it out to Carol and says, 'Vhat's not love. Ben needs love.'

Carol gulps. 'You're right, Tilda. He's really badly behaved, very aggressive. I'm so sorry.' *Having an outsider's perspective is instructive,* Carol thinks. She hasn't wanted to see it before, but Ben's behaviour is over the top. It is totally unacceptable.

Tilda frowns slightly and shakes her head. She thrusts the speaker into Carol's arms and says, 'Karul, love Ben. You must do love.'

Holding the speaker, Carol feels shock waves rock her. Tilda has issued her a clear challenge. For a brief moment, Carol has a sense that a path has been prepared and she is on the way up. Then the fog descends and she loses it again.

Carol is halfway down the stairs with the speaker cradled in her arms when Ben bursts out of the bedroom.

'That's mine,' he shouts. 'Where the fuck do you think you're going with my speaker?'

Carol freezes. Her mind goes blank. Where is she going with the speaker?

'I … um, I … I'm going to, going to, um, throw it in the bin,' she says, her voice wobbling and the words fading away. She is aware of Tilda witnessing this exchange and cannot bring herself to make eye contact.

'Oh no you're not,' Ben sneers at her. He tosses his long greasy hair out of his eyes and puts his hands on his hips.

An image of Ben aged two, flinging himself onto the floor kicking and screaming, flashes into her mind. It is followed by an image of herself standing over him, wringing her hands helplessly, closely followed by a task to put on her ever growing To Do list: make barber appointment for Ben.

'You are so stupid,' Ben shouts. 'I just paid £85 for that speaker. Give it back.'

Carol cringes. He has a point. Throwing away a brand new speaker is a stupid thing to do. It belongs to Ben. It isn't hers to throw away. What is she thinking of? Or is it his? She has paid for it after all.

Out of the corner of her eye, she sees Tilda and has the impression of a tree firmly rooted, its branches swaying in the wind and settling back to their place on the trunk, unbent and unbroken. And then, before she can blink, Ben charges towards her. Terrified that he will hurt Tilda, Carol runs back up the stairs and thrusts the speaker at him.

'Here,' she says quickly. 'Take it. Just don't play your music so loud. Please.'

Ben gives her a look that Carol had seen many times before. It is a look of contempt, as if he is calculating how much he can get away with, mixed with pride that he has got what he wanted. Carol withers under his sneer. She couldn't have done anything else. What if he'd turned round and attacked Tilda?

She glances at Tilda and their eyes lock. For a few seconds, Carol feels strong and clear. She knows what she is meant to do. Then the feeling vanishes as if it had never been.

Ben returns to the bedroom, the speaker under his arm. He turns to face Tilda at the door, narrows his eyes and says, 'You better fuck off out of here, midget! Don't you dare come into my room again.'

He slams the bedroom door shut behind him. Carol can hear the sound of something heavy being moved against the door, probably her oak chest of drawers that she bought when she and Mike first got together.

This could be a scene from a Western, she thinks. There is Ben on one side of the door, barricading himself in her bedroom, preparing for a shoot-out. On the landing are the women waiting for his next move, powerless to prevent another attack. Carol hears Ben humming as he reassembles his music system. She feels humiliated. He is taunting her. Only Tilda is calm and centred, watching Carol with interest, her blue eyes glinting.

Something tugs at the back of Carol's mind. But before she can figure out what it is, Ben fires his opening round, a blast of sound that sends Carol reeling. Tilda sighs. She gives Carol a look that is at once kind and stern, a look that Carol understands as a command to take control of the situation. But Carol has never known what to do when Ben has one of his rages. Nor has she known how to prevent her mother's rages. But neither had her father known or, for that matter, Ben's father. Mike had made it clear that it was up to Carol to manage Ben and then when Ben was ten, he'd cleared off. Carol knows she has failed spectacularly. Her greatest fear is that whatever she does to take control, Ben will retaliate by escalating the level of violence. She also knows from experience that he will blame her for provoking him. It is never his fault.

Tilda mouths the word "electricity". Carol stares blankly at her until Tilda points downstairs to the cupboard by the front door where the fuse box is. A few days before, Carol had shown Tilda the fuse box. Tilda had been fascinated. She had made a systematic study of the box, turning the switches off one by one, then checking to see what happened. For at least an hour, she had dashed around the house, turning lights and appliances on and off. Carol had been uneasy, worried that she might start a fire or break something. She had tried in vain to draw Tilda's lesson to an end.

Even without the brain-paralysing music, it would never have occurred to Carol to turn off the electricity to the upstairs rooms. Yet Tilda's command overpowers her. As if hypnotised, Carol goes downstairs to the fuse box, finds the switch for the upstairs circuit and flips it to off. The silence is such a relief that Carol lets out the breath she hadn't realised she was holding. She allows herself a moment of triumph. She's won a battle but she knows the war is not over.

It takes Ben several minutes to move the chest of drawers out of the way and fling the door open. Tilda is still standing on the landing, in a relaxed but alert pose, facing the door. She gestures to Ben to hand her the speaker. He looks at her as if she is crazy.

'Fuck off, you dwarf,' he snarls. Tilda gestures again, a wordless command. From the bottom of the stairs, Carol can see her six-foot-tall son towering over the child-sized Tilda. She sees him raise a clenched fist, the shadow cast on the wall making him seem even larger. Carol has the sense that he fills the entire landing, that there is no escape. She holds her breath. She can see the scene unfold in her mind: Ben will leap on Tilda from his great height, pound her to the floor and knock her unconscious. An ambulance will arrive and take Tilda off to hospital like the time she was hit by a car in Ireland. The police will come and arrest Ben.

Carol is so engrossed in the scene in her mind that she misses the action. When she focusses, she sees that it isn't Tilda lying on the floor, but Ben. He is collapsed in a heap, crumpled against the bannisters, his face a mask of shock. Tilda is standing in the same spot, one arm extended towards him, calm and composed. Carol is stunned. She hadn't seen what happened even though she'd been watching both of them the entire time. It looks as if Ben tripped and fell into the bannisters and that Tilda had casually sidestepped out of the way. Or could Tilda have thrown Ben across the landing? Carol can't say. Whatever happened had happened in an instant.

Tilda walks the few steps over to Ben and gives him her hand. To Carol's surprise, he lets her help him up. Tilda's manner allows for no other option. She escorts him to the bedroom door where she waits until he emerges with the speaker which he holds out to Tilda.

However, Tilda turns away and calls Carol. Carol creeps cautiously up the stairs. Ben doesn't seem as tall as he'd been before. He looks like a deflated balloon; his black T-shirt is ripped at the collar, a small cut is oozing blood from his forehead and his hair is hanging raggedly over his eyes.

Tilda, by contrast, is as unruffled as one can be in a pair of striped pyjamas. She points with her head from Ben to Carol. Straightaway he hands the speaker to Carol. In a clear and pleasant voice, Tilda says, 'Fhank you Ben. All sleep now. G'night.'

Ben blinks and peers at Tilda as if seeing her for the first time. Carol looks from one to the other. Seeing Ben subdued and compliant, Carol feels a wave of sympathy towards him, the kind of emotion she normally has for the underdog or the victim of injustice. It is the best explanation she can give for what she does next; that and the altered state of mind she is in from lack of sleep.

'Ben, I know you didn't mean to upset everyone,' Carol says, avoiding eye contact with Tilda. 'You're angry and I'm sure you have good reasons for being so angry. Things have been hard for you, what with Mike not being around for you. I'm giving you another chance. Here, take it back.'

She holds the speaker out to him. Ben looks at Carol with what she can only interpret as disappointment. He shakes his head, rolls his eyes and goes back into the bedroom, shutting the door behind him. Tilda doesn't exactly roll her eyes but she does look at Carol with something akin to astonishment, then goes straight downstairs to her cot in the living room. Francis and Jason creep out of the kitchen where they've been hiding, pass Carol on the landing without saying a word, and go to their bedrooms.

Silence fills the house. The bedroom doors are shut, the occupants asleep. All except Carol. She remains standing on the landing, facing her bedroom door. The speaker weighs heavy in her arms. She sees the grain of the wood on the door closed against her, hears loud snoring from her mother's room and is aware of a buzzing in her ears. She is alone, shut out by everyone in her family. She feels the familiar misery of rejection seeping through her. Everyone disapproves of her. She has tried so hard to make things right. She is doing the best she can.

Just as the loop of self-pity is about to spiral out of control, she notices a glimmer of light around the edges of her consciousness. A slight buzz of amazement. She has been shown something she hadn't known was possible. Tilda stood up to Ben and Ben backed down. She has no idea how Tilda did this, but she did. Which means it can be done. There is another way. If Tilda can do it, then maybe, just maybe, she can too.

Chapter 12. Carol

Carol moans and opens one eye. After leaving the speaker on the landing, she had collapsed on the sofa only to be woken a few hours later by Jason wanting breakfast. As soon as the taxi whisked him off to school, red-eyed and yawning, she'd instantly fallen asleep again. Now Moira is shaking her shoulder and firing off a round of questions, staccato style. Carol wonders groggily who let her in. It must have been Tilda, who is hovering behind Moira next to a man with a ginger goatee and moustache. Moira opens the curtains. Bright sunlight streams in. Carol burrows under the duvet, her head throbbing painfully.

'Remember I said I'd bring Pete to meet Tilda. Well, here he is. I'll make some coffee, shall I, seeing as you're still asleep at ten in the morning.'

Moira ushers Pete and Tilda out of the living room and settles them at the kitchen table. Carol reluctantly launches herself off the sofa and staggers in to join them, trying in vain to remember who Pete is and why he is in her home. As she stuffs her arms into her blue terrycloth bathrobe, a glimmer of a clue comes to her. Something about refugees landing on Lesvos. That doesn't help much. She takes over the coffee making from Moira who has abandoned her task and is speaking slowly to Tilda, enunciating each word carefully.

'Tilda, this is Pete. Pete, meet Tilda.' Tilda leaps up, lifts Pete's baseball cap, touches her forehead to his forehead and her nose to his nose. She smiles at him and says, 'Heyyo Pete.'

Pete laughs, his eyes crinkling in amusement. He pulls his cap down over his forehead and strokes his thin line ginger moustache. Then he pulls a piece of paper from his pocket, unfolds it and reads, '*Khoshbakhtam be ashNayee.*' He pauses and peers intently over the paper at Tilda. Tilda peers back just as intently, mirroring the way he thrusts his head forward.

'Uh, excuse me. Pete – hi, I'm Carol. Nice to meet you too. What are you doing here?' Carol ties her bathrobe more tightly around her waist. She is not at her best after the 2 a.m. battle with Ben and cannot keep the irritation out of her voice. Who is this guy with his baseball cap and goatee?

'Hi Carol,' Pete says, without taking his eyes off Tilda. 'I just said "nice to meet you" in Farsi. I'm trying to figure out where she's from. She looks like she could be from Afghanistan.'

Carol bristles. He's talking about Tilda as if she's a specimen being examined.

Moira tuts. 'I told you I'd bring Pete over today. Don't you remember? He volunteered in Lesvos a year ago meeting refugees coming over on boats from Turkey.'

Pete doesn't even glance at Carol. Still looking at Tilda, he says, 'Tilda, *Sobh bekheyr.*'

Carol has forgotten about Moira's plan to identify Tilda's country of origin. It makes her uncomfortable. She detects an undercurrent of jealousy as if Moira is competing with her as to who could be more right-on. *Get your own refugee*, Carol thinks ungraciously. *Tilda's here for me.* She doesn't really think of Tilda as a refugee. Though she had brought her into the country illegally. She does not want to consider the consequences if she is found out.

'How do you know you're saying it correctly?' Carol snaps at Pete. He is altogether too earnest for her liking and he is rude. It feels wrong to be entertaining a man in her bathrobe, especially a stranger who has not even acknowledged her existence. But she offers him a cup of coffee even so.

'White, two sugars,' Pete says, still without taking his eyes off Tilda. '*Esm shoma?*'

'I'll have a coffee too, Carol. Any biscuits or cake?' Moira says, looking around the kitchen hopefully.

Carol scowls and pours out another cup. 'How do you know Pete?'

'We've been friends since uni,' Moira says. 'Sam and I and Pete and Gillian all met in our second year at uni when we moved into a student house share. Last year Pete gave up his job as a firefighter, sold his house and went to Lesvos. You actually donated money to get him there but you clearly don't remember. You're in another world, you are, Carol.'

'*Esm shoma*? It means, what is your name?' Pete says.

There is a pause. Pete is still studying his crib sheet when Tilda suddenly replies, 'Ahmtoshtelay.'

They all look at her in surprise. Carol stares, her mouth open. It was Jason who insisted on calling her Tilda instead of learning to say her real name. Tilda had been good-natured about it. Carol had assumed she didn't mind but here she is giving her real name. That must mean something. Carol bites her lip and can't bring herself to look Tilda in the eye.

'*Az kodam keshvar amadeed*?' Pete asks eagerly. '*USratak min ay WATan*?'

'English,' Tilda says. 'I speak English.'

'She doesn't speak Farsi or Arabic,' Pete says, folding his paper. 'I'll have to try English. What Country Are You From?'

'From Ocean On Boat,' Tilda says, looking at Carol with a twinkle in her eye.

'So she did come over by boat,' Pete says, stroking his goatee thoughtfully. 'Was it one of those inflatable boats or a bigger one? I wonder if she got to Lesvos first and then paid traffickers to smuggle her to Ireland. Or was trafficked ... But why to Ireland?'

'Wivh Poo-Joe on boat,' Tilda says.

'Who Is Poo-Joe? Is Poo-Joe In Your Family?' Pete asks eagerly. 'We're getting somewhere,' he says to Moira. 'Has she mentioned Poo-Joe before?'

'In Karul family,' Tilda says, mimicking Pete's slow talk. She points to Carol and says at normal speed, 'On boat wivh Poo-Joe and Karul and Jason.'

She goes over to the fridge, gets out a pot of yoghurt, carries it to the table and speaks quietly, addressing the yoghurt. Pete tilts his head to one side to hear better, then shakes his head, puzzled. 'I don't recognise that language,' he says. 'Tilda, *keefik?*'

'Don't interrupt her while she's saying grace,' Carol whispers, stopping herself just in time from poking him with her coffee spoon.

Pete is clearly no respecter of the saying of grace. 'She could be from the Sudan or Nigeria or Sierra Leone,' he muses. 'There are Black people with blue eyes from those countries. I didn't meet any in Lesvos though there were people from Africa who got to Lesvos by a roundabout route.'

'Shh,' Carol says, annoyed. Out of the corner of her eye, she sees Tilda grin mischievously.

Moira, who has been uncharacteristically quiet, suddenly bursts out laughing. 'Poo-Joe. I get it. Isn't your car a Peugeot, Carol?'

'She's talking about the trip here from Ireland?' Pete asks Moira. 'No, Tilda. No. Before Ireland. Where Did You Come From?'

Tilda eats the yoghurt slowly with her eyes closed, paying no attention to anyone but the yoghurt. When she finishes, she looks at Pete and says, 'I come from Neeulivikbroomavin.' She raises one hand and points to her fingers. 'Five fhousand years ago. Jason told me. I am very tired. Go back to sleep.' Then she goes into the living room.

Pete blinks at this declaration. Turning to Carol, he asks, 'Do you understand what she means? Who's Jason and what did he tell her?'

'I don't know what to make of it,' Carol says, shrugging. 'Jason's my son. He and Tilda have been talking a lot about Newgrange since we got home. He's been teaching her English by reading books to her about it and showing her documentaries on TV. She made drawings of the symbols on the stones. There's something about that place that fascinates both of them.'

'What happened five thousand years ago?' Pete asks. 'Is that when the Newgrange monument was built?'

'Yes, that's right. In the Neolithic period. Do you want to see my photos of it? It's spectacular.'

'Is there another name for Newgrange, Carol?' Moira asks with a gleam in her eye.

'The Irish name is Brú na Bóinne which means the Palace on the River Bóinne.'

'I get it,' Moira crows. 'Tilda says she came from Neeulivikbroomavin. Neeulivik. That's her way of saying Neolithic. Broomavin is Brú na Bóinne. Tilda. Where did she go? Let's ask her.'

But Carol's had enough. 'Look, you two. We've had quite a night of it. Ben's back from uni and he was playing his music at two in the morning. None of us got much sleep. We're kind of wrecked. Do you think you could do this another time?' Carol yawns. Kind of wrecked, she thinks. More like totally wrecked. She is going to crash out any minute.

'Moira told me you've been going through hell with Ben,' Pete says. 'I've been there too. My son Matthew was a nightmare for about five years. Drugs, rudeness, benders, not going to school, the works. He's twenty-two now and has finally found his feet. I know how it feels.'

Carol's stomach clenches at the thought of drugs, rudeness, benders, not going to school. And what does "the works" include? She takes a closer look at Pete. Maybe there's more to him than she first thought. He seems sympathetic, even genuine.

'I think we should go,' Pete says, smiling sympathetically at her. 'Carol, if you need any help or just want to talk, give me a ring. C'mon Moira. These ladies need to rest.'

Carol nods a vague goodbye and closes the front door behind them. She walks slowly into the living room, yawning, her ears buzzing. Tilda is asleep on the sofa. A shaft of sunlight lights Tilda's black locks and the green cord fabric of the sofa. Dust motes float lazily in the air.

Gazing down at the sleeping Tilda, Carol is struck by how beautiful she is, how perfect. In that moment, she hears the call in her mind, the exact words she's heard so many times before. '*I am the sunlight*

in the heart, the moonlight in the mind. Come with me. Come away.'
It is no figment of her imagination this time. Whatever she is being
called to come away to, she knows it has something to do with Tilda.
Gently, she lays herself down alongside Tilda and tenderly kisses
her forehead and nose. Without opening her eyes, Tilda wraps her
arms around Carol and cuddles her close.

Chapter 13. Carol

All that day, Carol is subdued and thoughtful. She opens her laptop to work but her mind keeps drifting to the traumatic events of the early morning. After a half-hearted attempt to work on her article, she closes the laptop and stares out the window. Instead of stuffing the battle with Ben into the Ben Bubble as she usually does, she tries to makes herself think about it. She replays it in her mind again and again, asking herself what she could have done differently and why she can't say no to Ben. Each time, her mind goes blank. She would like to be able to deal with Ben the way Tilda did but it's easy for Tilda. She isn't Ben's mother and she has no history with him. Carol has been bullied by Ben since he was a toddler. It's understandable that she has trouble standing up to him now that he's a hulking twenty-year-old.

Yet, on some level, Carol knows that Tilda would never allow herself to be a victim to anyone, not to her mother or her husband and certainly not to a toddler. Tilda has a presence and an air of authority that Carol lacks. She wonders if it's possible to acquire an air of authority. The thought occurs to her that she might learn something from someone who's had a similar experience. Maybe Pete could be that someone. She files the thought, not in the Ben Bubble where she might never see it, but near the top of her mind.

Francis emerges from her bedroom, crosser than usual, and pointedly ignores Carol for the rest of the day. Carol is relieved. A sullen silence is easier to bear than an angry tirade. When Jason arrives home from school, he goes straight to his room. No chat about his day. No rummaging in the kitchen for a snack. Carol cringes inwardly but doesn't dare approach him. Ben does not leave his room, except to scurry to the toilet and retreat hastily back. He does not join them for dinner. Dinner is eaten in an uncomfortable silence. Carol feels their disapproval like a thick fog. She finds it hard to breathe.

Only Tilda is cheerful. Every time Carol looks at her, Tilda smiles at her. And every time their eyes meet, Carol feels a jolt pass through her. Tilda doesn't say anything but Carol senses she is pleased. It's as if she can see something in Carol that Carol herself can't see. It gives her hope.

That evening, Sue rings. 'Hi Carol,' Sue chirps. 'I can't talk long now. I just want to tell you about a Singing for the Brain group that's starting up in January. I think your mum would enjoy it. It's for people with dementia. It's every Wednesday. I'm happy to take her.'

'Thank you so much, Sue,' Carol whispers, overcome with gratitude. It seems to her that things are happening without her having to make any effort. She wonders if she can trust it. It's certainly a comfort not to feel so alone. 'I really appreciate it. You're a good friend.'

'My pleasure. And I want to tell Tilda about a winter solstice event at Stanton Drew stone circle the day after tomorrow. I've got a friend who's going and he can take Tilda and anyone else who wants to go.'

When Carol tells Tilda about the invitation, she is surprised to see tears of joy in Tilda's eyes. Carol has never paid any attention to the solstices but clearly it is an important event for Tilda. Carol remembers the demonstration at Newgrange which showed that the monument was designed in such a way that on this one day of the year, the sun would shine into the heart of the chamber.

Jason is drawn in by Tilda's excitement and begs Tilda to let him come with her. Watching Jason and Tilda dance around the living room together, Carol feels as if she's been stabbed in the heart. It's fine for Francis to ignore her, but when Jason does it, she feels devastated. She is about to slink out of the room when Tilda takes Jason's hand and brings him to face Carol. Jason looks down at the floor, his arms crossed over his chest.

Carol takes a breath and says quietly, 'I'm sorry about last night, Jason. I know I've got to change how I deal with Ben. I'm doing my best.' She pauses, then adds, 'And I know it's not good enough. I'll try to do better.'

Jason looks up at her and sighs. 'Can I go with Tilda?'

Carol nods. She hasn't been forgiven but, fair enough, she doesn't deserve it yet.

Tilda

Just before the sun sets on the evening before the winter solstice, Tilda puts her ceremonial garments on over her jeans and fleece. She wraps the necklace of periwinkle shells three times round her forehead and walks to the solitary oak tree by the pond where the grey heron fishes. Throughout that night, the longest night of the year, she chants, drums and dances in preparation for the moment when the sun stands still and is then reborn.

It is strange to be alone for this part of the ritual instead of with the circle of Wise Ones, taking her turn in a continuous cycle of dancing, chanting, drumming and resting. It is even stranger to not be celebrating the most sacred day of the year at the Palace of the Immortals.

But she will be at a stone circle by sunrise and Jason will be with her. She returns to the house at six in the morning, buzzing with the life-force she has summoned during the night. Jason is wide awake, buzzing with excitement and chocolate. He has packed a thermos of hot chocolate, several chocolate bars and a blanket in his backpack. A van arrives to take them to Stanton Drew.

They pass through a gate into a field. It is too dark to see the stone circle but Tilda can hear the stones singing. She breathes a sigh of relief. She had been worried that they might not be awake. In the distance, she can see spots of light from people's torches. Jason shines his torch so they can avoid stepping in cow pats and tripping over tussocks of grass.

Tilda goes to the nearest stone and greets it by touching her forehead to its cold, hard surface. Jason does the same. Taking Jason's hand, Tilda leads him slowly around the stone, chanting softly in tune with the stone's song. With her free hand, she touches the stone. Jason copies her every move.

Working together, Tilda, Jason and the stone draw down the cosmic life-force spiral from above and draw up Mother Earth's spiral from below. The spirals meet, flowing up and down, spiralling around each other, in perfect balance. They are creating a sacred spiralling cradle ready for the sun's return and Mother Earth's renewal.

Tilda and Jason go from one stone to the next. Whether the stones are lying down or upright, each one is singing a song of hope and love. As they circle each of the stones, Tilda feels the life-force growing stronger.

There is a vague hint of light in the eastern sky. People have gathered and formed a large circle in the middle of the stone circle. A tall, grey haired, bearded man wearing a long white robe and carrying a wooden staff lights a fire in the centre. He leads a song, everyone joining in.

The sky lightens. The bearded man points his staff to the north. In a ringing voice, he calls, 'Hail the fertile darkness of the North, life and light is reborn.' Then he steps back into the circle. A red-haired woman steps into the centre. She is wearing a long, purple cape and a purple headband decorated with a gold sun design. She faces east and says, 'Hail the gentle breath of the East, life and light is reborn.'

Fog becomes visible as daylight grows. From across the circle, another white-robed man says, 'Hail the rekindled spark of the South, life and light is reborn.' A green-robed woman faces west, calling in a high-pitched voice, 'Hail the trickling drop of the West, life and light is reborn.'

The sun rises as Tilda and Jason finish the last stone of the circle. The sun, source of life and light, shines weakly through the fog. It kisses the stones who burst into a wild song of joy. Tilda can almost see the life-force flowing out from the stones, revitalising the people and the land around them. Jason is staring at her, wide-eyed and breathless. She smiles and winks at him. She wonders if he is feeling the same sense of joy, of being at one with all Beings, of belonging to Mother Earth, that she is feeling.

She hugs him and ruffles his hair. They insert themselves into the circle of people, all holding hands. The bearded man goes up to each person in the circle and gives them sprigs of mistletoe. When he comes to Tilda, his eyes widen momentarily as he takes in her tunic with the triple spiral design. He bows deeply and Tilda bows back. He moves on until everyone has mistletoe. He takes the hand of the woman in the purple headdress and leads the circle of people in a dance that spirals slowly into the centre. Tilda and Jason are carried with the line, joining in the singing. They walk to the van, still holding hands.

'Light and life are reborn,' Jason says. His eyes are shining as he rummages in his backpack and unwraps a chocolate bar. 'Yes,' he says, munching the chocolate. 'Light and life are reborn.'

Carol

'So, how was it?' Carol asks, yawning. She is in her bathrobe eating a bowl of porridge when Jason and Tilda walk in. There is something about them both that is different, but she can't put her finger on it.

Jason tosses his backpack on the floor. 'It was amazing,' he says. 'You should have been there, Mum. Light and life are reborn. It was even more amazing than at Newgrange. Well, that wasn't the real solstice. This was really the solstice. Wasn't it, Tilda?'

Tilda nods, mirroring his enthusiasm. 'Solstice, yes.'

'Could you see the sun rise?' Carol asks. 'It's so foggy here. I wouldn't have thought you could see anything.'

'Yes, we saw it, sort of,' Jason says. 'It was foggy there too. But the stones were amazing. Did you know that the stones sing? Look, the Druid priest leading the ceremony gave us all some mistletoe.'

'You know what you're supposed to do with mistletoe, don't you Jason?' Carol says, feeling a warm glow of affection towards her son.

'No. What?'

'You kiss under it. Come here, let's do it.' She knows it's a risk to try to kiss an eleven-year-old boy but, to her surprise, Jason holds the mistletoe over their heads and gives her a big kiss on the cheek. That is what is different, Carol realises. He is glowing with happiness.

'Mum,' Jason says, his tone becoming serious. He glances at Tilda as if for support. She nods encouragingly. 'This is important. I want you to listen to me.'

Carol beats back a wave of defensiveness. Tilda's blue eyes are boring into her, making her feel slightly nervous and somewhat exposed. She has the sense that Tilda sees right through her. Where are all her encouraging smiles now? She's taken Jason's side.

Jason shuffles from foot to foot. He takes a breath, stands a bit straighter and pierces Carol with the same look Tilda has. Suddenly Carol feels very nervous and very exposed.

'Mum, I learned something from the stones. It's about Ben. I want you to protect me from him. Promise me that you won't let him stay with us anymore, Mum. Please.' He holds her gaze, his jaw jutting out and tears about to spill over.

'I understand how you feel, Jason, but I … it is, you see … the thing is ..' Carol stutters to a halt. Tears are pouring down Jason's cheeks. Tilda's expression has hardened.

'Last night, Ben came and talked to me,' Carol says. 'He told me he called Mike and asked if he could stay with him for a few days. I was amazed to hear that Mike agreed. He's living in Birmingham with some woman. I'm going to take him to the train station this afternoon. It gives us a breather for a little while.'

It takes a few moments for Jason to digest this information. 'And then what?' he asks.

Carol opens her mouth to speak and closes it. Her head is spinning with questions. Could she make a promise not to let Ben back home? What will Ben do if he can't stay at Mike's or at home with her? How can she throw him out on the street? It is more complicated than Jason knows.

She tries again. 'I don't want him here either the way he behaves, but it's not so simple. I can't just ...' Or can she? She never has in the past but that doesn't mean she never will. Suddenly, she has an idea. She forces herself to look Tilda in the eye. 'I can't do it on my own. Tilda, will you teach me how to say no to Ben? Will you help me?'

Tilda's face softens into a delighted grin. 'Yes, Karul, I teach you.'

Jason gives a surprised yelp and punches the air. 'Thank you, Mum. Thank you, Tilda,' he shouts and runs upstairs, whooping loudly.

Tilda is still smiling at Carol. She picks up the mistletoe that Jason dropped on the floor and holds it high over her head. With her eyes, she beckons Carol to stand under it. Then she gently pulls Carol's head close and kisses her lightly on the lips. Carol feels the kiss move down to her toes, pooling deliciously midway. Her tongue moves of its own accord through Tilda's lips, seeking Tilda's tongue. Her lips press firmly against Tilda's lips. Her arms ache to reach behind Tilda's back and pull her close. The moment seems to last forever.

Then Francis' voice booms from upstairs. 'Carol, is Tilda back yet?'

Carol leaps back, mortified. She doesn't dare look Tilda in the eye. Tilda says softly, 'I go to Francis now. I teach you later.'

Carol closes her eyes and calms her ragged breathing. Oh no. What was that all about? She can't afford to drive Tilda away. Quickly she stuffs her rampaging emotions into a new Did I Really Kiss Tilda Bubble. Then she grabs the Ben Bubble with both hands and marches herself up to her bedroom. It is time to reclaim it from Ben.

Look what has happened with just one kiss.
I never knew that I could be in love like this.
It's crazy but it's true, I only want to be with you.

By Dusty Springfield

Chapter 14. Tilda

Ever since their kiss under the mistletoe, an idea has been growing in Tilda's mind. Like a seedling putting forth its first tentative shoots, Tilda keeps the idea close to her heart. She does not want to risk it being trampled underfoot before it has taken root and can thrive on its own. How best to awaken Carol? Tilda is realising that it won't happen just through talking. Though she is pleased with her command of English and can hold conversations about things that matter, Carol does not seem willing to think too deeply about things that matter.

Krismuss is a good example. 'Why dead tree wivh no roots in house?' Tilda asks when Carol and Jason drag an enormous fir tree into the living room. Its tip reaches the ceiling and its branches cover the TV. The house is filled with the aroma of fir tree. Tilda tries not to show how sad she feels to have a tree corpse in the house.

'Because we're celebrating *Krismuss* and Ben's not here,' Carol says, singing gaily. She opens a box of colourful objects and passes them to Jason and Francis. They hang the objects on the tree corpse, working together without arguing, occasionally breaking into song. Tilda watches, puzzled. Are they so cheerful because Ben is staying away with his father or because of *Krismuss*? But what is *Krismuss*? And what does a dead tree have to do with *Krismuss*?

'Karul,' Tilda says. 'What is *Krismuss*? And why tree wivh no roots in house?'

'*Krismuss* is when we celebrate the birth of Christ,' Carol answers. 'But don't ask me who Christ is because we don't believe in Christ. We just like having a *Krismuss* tree and giving each other presents and having a meal and being together.' She pauses, looking guilty. 'Without Ben.'

Tilda digests this speech, playing it over in her mind several times, before deciding that the words don't convey enough useful information. She listens instead with her body. It's vibrating with excitement and pleasurable anticipation, the way she feels while preparing for the solstice festivals. And there's more; little sparks are shooting between her and Carol every time their eyes lock together. Each time this happens, Carol's face turns red.

Tilda does not doubt her understanding of the signals passing between them. What she does not know is whether her idea of acting on these signals is the best way to awaken Carol. Should she invite Carol to be her lover? While the others are decorating the tree without roots, Tilda leaves the house to walk by the river and ask for guidance.

She asks her body first. Her body says yes, yes and again yes. It sends her little rushes of excitement from deep in her woman's space. When Carol walks into the room, her heart flutters. A spring flows between her legs. When Carol looks her in the eye, her breath comes fast. When she leans against her, when she smiles at her, her knees go weak. Her body says yes.

She asks Crogan and Charmall. Crogan, ever the cautious one, says, 'Be careful with Carol. She is out of balance. She has not had a lover for many years. She may feel abandoned when you leave. Your task is to guide her to love herself and to be open to a lover from her world.'

Tilda feels daunted. She remembers a time when she asked Liedid to be her lover at a full moon festival. He had wanted to partner with her and have children. He believed that she wanted the same. She thought that he knew she had already committed to live with the Wise Ones and forego having children. Only after they made love did they talk and learn the truth. Liedid had been hurt, very hurt. Tilda does not want to hurt Carol but she has no idea what thoughts Carol has in her mind about being lovers.

Charmall is more encouraging. He says, 'Hand over your doubts and fears to Great Mother. We trust you to make the best decision for yourself and for Carol. You are loving and you are lover-wise. But first seek guidance from people in this world. Talk to Sue and Alison. They can tell you about the beliefs these people have.'

Tilda is surprised and nervous, but she finds a way to visit Sue and Alison on her own the day after *Krismuss*.

'No dead tree?' Tilda asks, as she walks into their living room. The room is refreshingly bare of signs of *Krismuss*, except for a few cards on a shelf. Tilda relaxes. She has given up trying to understand Carol's way of celebrating the mysterious festival of *Krismuss* and doesn't want to talk about it with Sue and Alison. She wants lover advice from them.

Refusing their offer of wine or tea, Tilda settles herself on the floor. She launches straight in without wasting her time talking about unimportant issues.

'I come to ask you about lovers. How long for lovers?' She bangs her hand against her forehead in frustration. 'English too hard.'

'Okay,' Sue says slowly, her eyes widening. She puts down her cup of tea. 'You want to ask us about lovers. Why not? It's as good a topic as any on Boxing Day. So are you asking how long we stay with our lovers?'

Tilda nods uncertainly. She's not sure what she needs to know or how to ask.

Alison seems amused. 'That's a good question. How long for lovers? I haven't thought about it that way.'

'What way?' Sue asks. 'We don't plan in advance how long we'll be with a partner. Each relationship takes its course.'

'Well.' Alison's earrings bounce as her head moves from side to side, as if weighing up the arguments on both sides. 'There's this idea in our society that we should be monogamous, we should be heterosexual, we should have sex with one person all our lives until death do us part. And even though we lesbians are not heterosexual, we buy into these shoulds. And we get hurt and devastated when our love affairs end. And yet lovers separate all the time.'

Tilda puts her hand over Alison's mouth. 'Slow please. What is meaning monoga, hetersex, lesbeen?'

'Alison.' Sue rises from her chair and reaches for a bottle of wine.

'Aren't you into monogamy? Please tell me you are. You don't have another lover or two hidden away that you haven't told me about?'

'You thought I was with my dad this morning but really I was popping in to make love to Chantalle,' Alison grins at Sue mischievously. Tilda smiles with them, admiring their ability to tease each other but feeling lost in the banter. 'So Tilda, monogamous means you have only one lover at a time. Sue and I are monogamous. We don't have any other lovers. Just each other.'

Tilda is still confused. 'How long for mongams? You were wivh man before Sue, yes?'

'Yes, but the thing is, I was monogamous each time. I was married for five years to a man and I've been with Sue for twelve. Before I got married, I dated guys and had short relationships, like a month with one guy, six months with another. So yeah, I guess you'd call it serial monogamy.'

Sue looks with interest at Tilda. 'What do people do where you come from, wherever that is? And don't tell me you're from Neolithic Newgrange. I don't buy that story.'

Tilda shrugs and doesn't say anything for a few minutes, while she replays Alison's words in her head. Eventually she says, 'On my home, are many ways to make love because people are different. No shoulds. Some are monogams. I am not. Some women are lovers wivh men only. I am not.'

Both Alison and Sue look intrigued. Alison speaks first. 'Are you saying you have many lovers, some men, some women?'

Tilda nods yes. 'Like you here. But not like you here, not one at a time.'

Sue purses her lips. 'Do you have a lover back home that you're going back to?'

'Yes. Four lovers. I am not monogam,' Tilda holds up four fingers. She is beginning to realise that the gap between her world and theirs is bigger than she had expected. What if Carol is a monogam? What if she expects Tilda to be a lifelong monogam lover? 'I have four lovers: two women, two men. We make love togevher in full moon festivals and wivh one or two at ovher festivals.'

'Whoa, Tilda.' Sue is staring intently at Tilda. She exchanges a look with Alison who has tucked her chin back and has narrowed her eyes. Is she puzzled, shocked, disapproving? Tilda is confused by their reaction.

'Hold on a minute. Say that again. You make love together at festivals? You mean like group sex? Do you live together in the same house?'

'Wivh one of vhe women. I live wivh vhe Wise Ones, in house apart. We have been lovers many years from when we were young.'

Tilda is not sure she is getting the information she needs to know whether to ask Carol to be her lover. Perhaps she needs to be more direct.

'Sue. Alison. I ask you because you know Karul. You are good friends wivh her. I want to make love wivh Karul. She wants to make love wivh me. But I will go home soon. She will be hurt. What is best to do?'

Sue blinks. Alison opens her mouth and closes it. They both start speaking at the same time. Sue stops first. Alison pours herself a glass of wine and takes a long drink.

'Tilda,' Alison says, shaking her head and putting her glass down on the floor. 'We've known Carol for twelve years. Since before Jason was born. Never has she shown any interest in women. Since Mike left, she's only ever wanted another man. She's been on dating sites and met a few men. We've had to hear all about her dates. But women? Never.'

'How do you know she wants to make love to you, Tilda?' Sue asks. She takes a drink of her wine and looks hard at Tilda.

'I know,' Tilda says simply. But the dilemma is the same. Whether Carol makes the first move or she does, she still has to decide whether it is right to be lovers.

'I just can't see it,' Alison says. 'Can you, Sue? Can you see Carol as a lesbian? No, she's definitely heterosexual.'

'Could you be misreading her, Tilda? Maybe you're missing your fivesome group sex thing. Maybe you're just imagining that Carol's coming on to you.'

'Carol wants make love wivh me,' she says, wondering why they would even ask. Of course she knows. 'I go home in six moons. What do you fhink I should do?'

She waits, not sure whether it's fair to ask them or not.

'You first, Sue,' Alison says, screwing her lips to one side. She fiddles with her earrings.

'Right,' Sue says. 'My advice is to leave it for a few weeks. Don't do anything. I think it will become clear what to do over time. I mean, anything's possible. You could be right. Carol may be up for it.'

Alison rolls her eyes. 'That is not helpful advice, Sue. My advice is not to worry. I'm sure Carol is not attracted to you. She is so not a lesbian.'

Sue looks annoyed. 'How is that more helpful than my advice, dearest? You're saying the same exact thing. Let's bet on it. I bet Carol is changing. She went on that mad trip to Ireland and came back with you, Tilda. That's a sign of something shifting.'

Tilda laughs. 'Fhank you Sue. Fhank you Alison. You have been very helpful.'

She's ready to hand it over to Great Mother and leave it in Her hands.

Chapter 15. Carol

Carol checks her diary for the third time. Yes, it is the seventh of January, the date she's arranged to have dinner with Sue and Alison at their home. She pauses at the door of the living room with a bottle of Sauvignon Blanc in one hand and a box of profiteroles in the other. She's changed out of her everyday jeans and sweatshirt into her one and only red dress-up dress. Jason and Tilda are on the floor making a model of the solar system. Francis is snoozing on her chair.

Carol calls out a hasty goodbye and has already turned to leave when she catches Tilda's eye, looking at her quizzically. Her cheeks burn and her stomach lurches. She doesn't dare do a proper goodbye, Tilda-style. What if she can't stop her lips from kissing those bright blue eyes, or her teeth from nibbling Tilda's luscious lips? As Tilda rises up from the floor and starts towards her, Carol stumbles against the door, dropping the box of profiteroles and the bottle of wine. She flees out the front door without them.

Sitting in the car, her head on the steering wheel, Carol gulps deep breaths. Tears drip onto her dress. All over Christmas and into January, the feelings have been growing like mushrooms in the dark. They're so big that she can't think of anything else. How can she carry on living in the same house with Tilda feeling the way she does, knowing that Tilda would be shocked and horrified at her improper intentions? She had to talk with someone and it made sense to ask Sue and Alison for help. She has armed herself with wine, profiteroles and her best dress to give herself courage.

At the door, Alison greets her warmly, switching to alarmed concern when she sees Carol's red swollen eyes.

'Oh my god,' she cries, pulling her inside. 'Whatever is the matter?'

'I brought you wine and profiteroles,' Carol sobs. 'But I dropped them and left them at home.'

Sue rushes out of the kitchen, wiping her hands on her apron and pushing her hair out of her eyes. She looks at Alison, puzzled.

Alison hugs Carol tightly. 'It's all right, sweetheart. I think we'll survive without wine and profiteroles.'

Sue isn't convinced. 'What kind of wine was it?'

'Sauvignon blanc,' Carol says sadly. 'Your favourite.'

'That is a disaster,' Sue says evenly. 'Our favourite, yes. And the profiteroles, what kind were they?'

'Cut it out, Sue,' Alison warns, patting Carol lovingly on the back. 'Come and sit down, Carol. How 'bout a beer? Go get her a beer, Sue, and stop teasing her.'

'I deserve it,' Carol sniffs, stopping herself from wiping her nose on her sleeve. 'Do you have a tissue? I'm such a mess. I'm so confused and, well, ashamed. I can't go on like this. I need your help.'

They usher Carol into the living room and steer her towards the sofa. Sue hands Carol a beer. Alison provides a tissue. They sit down on either side and look at her with concern.

'Is it about your mum?' Sue asks gently. 'You haven't mentioned any more episodes. Has she had any rages since you came back from Ireland?'

Carol blows her nose and shakes her head. No, now that Francis has Tilda at her beck and call, she completely ignores Carol. *Which is great*, Carol thinks wistfully, *though it would be nice to have some of that good will directed to me.*

'It's Ben, isn't it?' Alison continues the interrogation. 'What's he done now?'

Carol sighs. Ben, too, has been ignoring Carol and hasn't been back to the house since the night of the loud music showdown. *Which is great*, Carol thinks, *though again I wouldn't mind a few pleasant interactions with my son.*

'Is it Jason?' It's Alison's turn. 'Has something happened to Jason?'

Carol takes a deep breath and a sip of the beer. 'It's Tilda,' she whispers, looking down at her lap.

Both Sue and Alison look expectantly at Carol. Sue holds her breath. Alison raises her eyebrows.

'So tell us, Carol. What's with Tilda?' Alison says, after a pause. 'I can't stand the suspense.'

'She's so sweet and loving and kind to everyone.' Carol wipes her eyes and blows her nose. 'And I ... well, I, I can't even say it.'

'That is worrying,' Sue tuts. 'I'd be crying too if I had someone living with me who was sweet and loving and kind to everyone. I knew there was something suspicious about her right from the beginning. And this nonsense about her popping over from Neolithic times. I don't think so.'

'Shut up, Sue.' Alison reaches behind Carol and playfully smacks Sue on the back of the head.

'The thing is,' Carol tries again, 'I'm not sweet.'

'Is that the problem? You don't appreciate her?' Alison asks.

'No, I do. Too much. I'm ... I ...' Carol gives up and wipes her nose on the sleeve of her red dress. 'OK, the thing is, I'm in love with her.'

There, she said it. It's out in the open. It's a reality, a fact. Sue and Alison don't say anything. Carol has the sense they are communicating with each other over her head.

'Ha, told you,' Sue murmurs to Alison. 'I won.'

Alison frowns at Sue. 'So, Carol, what are the tears about, love? She hasn't turned you down, has she?'

'No. I haven't let her know how I feel. She doesn't know. I can't show her.'

'Carol, believe me, she knows. Anyway, you're like an open book,' Sue says, laughing affectionately and rolling her eyes. She dodges out of the way of another pretend smack from Alison. 'Of course she knows. You've told us that Tilda understands body language and emotion even though her English isn't great.'

'Oh God,' Carol moans. 'She must think so badly of me. Do you really think she knows? I try to hide it, even from myself. I can't look her in the eye anymore. Yes, she must know. Oh no. This is a disaster.'

But it is also a relief to have said it out loud. Hearing herself say the words makes them seem less outrageous. Not normal by any means, but not monstrous either. She is grateful to Sue and Alison for helping her wrench the admission out of her throat. Yet along with the relief is anxiety.

'What if I'm taking advantage of her, you know, of her dependency on me, using her for my own selfish reasons? Oh God. I'm like those wealthy men who bonk their maids, as if they're entitled to sexual services.'

'Carol, is that how you see Tilda? Like she's your servant?' Alison demands. She withdraws slightly. Carol senses outrage.

'No, no, not at all. But Moira does.' Carol is confused. 'Moira said she's vulnerable. She's not free to do what she wants, that I just scooped her up and brought her over to look after my mum and she can't refuse because she has nowhere else to go, no passport. If I didn't keep her locked up in my house, she would be deported to some ghastly country and tortured. What am I offering her? Nothing, except some English lessons.'

'Leave Moira out of this,' Alison snaps, sounding angry. 'Tilda's not locked up in your house, is she? She's always out and about. Is Tilda here of her own free will?'

'Of course,' Carol says slowly. 'I think she decided to live with us for some reason of her own.'

'OK,' Alison says more calmly. 'So why don't you declare your love to her?'

Carol looks at Alison with surprise. 'Alison, I'm NOT a lesbian.' That sounded rather too emphatic, she thinks, hoping that Alison and Sue won't take it the wrong way. 'I mean, it's not who I am. I'm not against anyone else being a lesbian. It's just not me.'

'I should hope not,' Sue says tartly with a gleam in her eye. 'Not mentioning any names, of course, but is there anyone in this room that you are not against being a lesbian?'

Alison laughs. 'Sue, she's confused enough as it is without you going on at her. Look Carol, we know this is huge for you.'

'All I meant,' Carol says miserably, 'is that I've never had a sexual relationship with a woman.' And the sexual relationships she's had with men have not been worth mentioning.

'So let me get this clear,' Alison says, rolling her eyes. 'You're not a lesbian but you're in love with a woman and you're crying because you shouldn't be in love with a woman because you're not a lesbian. Is that right?!!'

'How do you know you're NOT a lesbian?' Sue says, leaning forward intently. She has a twinkle in her eye, but Carol picks up an edge in her voice. She is challenging in a way that Carol hasn't seen before from Sue.

Carol hesitates, then decides to make a counter move. 'How do you know you ARE a lesbian?' This isn't the sort of conversation she usually has with Alison or Sue.

'I've only had sexual relationships with women,' Sue replies. 'From the time I was a teenager. My first lover was when I was fifteen. I've just never been interested in men, never had desire for men. That's how I know.'

'I was married to a man for five years,' Alison adds. 'I dated boys when I was a teenager. I always thought of myself as normal, you know, heterosexual, but then I met Sue. It was very romantic. We met at work. We were both working at a project for homeless women. I fell in love with Sue after we'd been working together for about five months.'

'I fell in love with you when we interviewed you for the job,' Sue says, leaning over Carol to smile at Alison.

'So much for equal opportunities,' Alison laughs. 'You gave me the job because you fancied me? I thought it was because I met all the essential and desirable requirements for the job. Or was it because you had to up your quota of BMEs?'

'If Alison was not a lesbian when you first met, why did you fall in love with her? I mean, how did you fall in love with her?' Carol turns to Sue.

'Why did you fall in love with Tilda? You're not a lesbian,' Sue retorts. 'Look, Carol, forget about this lesbian thing. People fall in love with each other all the time, whatever they are and however they see themselves. Alison was still married and living with her husband. It's just a natural thing that happens between people. Don't over-complicate it. Let's have dinner. I made spanakopita.'

Alison links arms with Carol and guides her into the kitchen. 'How do you know Tilda doesn't feel the same as you?' she asks as Sue dishes out the food. 'Can't you tell whether she's attracted to you or not?'

'No, I can't tell,' Carol says, feeling stupid. 'She's always kind and sweet to me and to everyone, to my mum, to Jason. How would I know? How did you know, Sue, that Alison felt the same as you?'

'Because Alison is the least subtle person I know. She would blush every time I looked at her a certain way. And when I looked her in the eye, she would go all breathless and wibbly wobbly.'

'No I did not,' Alison says indignantly. 'How would you know I was blushing anyway? You white people can't tell when a Black person blushes.'

'I could tell,' Sue says smugly. 'You're like Carol, an open book, easy to read. So Carol, shall I tell you how to know when a Black person blushes? It will come in handy with Tilda. Or you could skip all that reading of subtle signs and just come out with it. Tell her how you feel and ask her how she feels.'

'Or here's an idea: you could just kiss her and see what happens,' Alison suggests, looking pleased with her idea. 'Look, what's the worst case scenario? She could recoil in horror and say "get off me, you dirty lesbian". Or she could be indifferent and say kindly that she's not interested. If she does, you're in no worse position than you are now. Or she could kiss you back and say, "What's been taking you so long?" Which of those two scenarios are most likely?'

'She wouldn't call me a dirty lesbian. She doesn't know that word, I'm sure.' Carol sits staring blankly at the spanakopita. Both scenarios sound equally terrifying. 'What if she kisses me back and wants to go further? I have no idea what to do next.'

'Leave it to Tilda,' Sue says firmly. 'I'm sure she has enough sexpertise for the two of you.'

'Do you think she does? Why would you think that? We don't know what Neolithic people got up to sexually, do we?' Carol is wringing her hands.

'She's not Neolithic, Carol,' Sue says, putting her hands on her hips.

'She says she is. Whatever, she's here. Anyway, I imagine it's very different from sex with a man,' Carol says shyly. 'Do you have any books I could read?'

'Sue darling, go get the dessert and I'll give Carol a quick sex education lesson,' Alison says, putting her arm around Carol's shoulder. 'You've got to get out of your head, Carol. This isn't something you learn from books.'

'What exactly are you going to teach her?' Sue is drumming her fingers on the table. 'Don't you think Tilda will be the best teacher? Anyway, she left the profiteroles at home. So there's no dessert.'

'Go rustle something up, darling,' Alison says, narrowing her eyes at her beloved. 'Now clear off. Carol and I have important business to discuss. And you're not helping.'

An hour later, Sue and Alison send Carol home with a promise to text them either a thumbs up emoji or a thumbs down.

Chapter 16. Carol

I can do this. It's okay to feel this way. It's okay to feel attracted to another woman. Tilda feels the same towards me. Yes, she does. Sue said so. How does Sue know? Maybe she does. Maybe she doesn't. There's nothing to be frightened of. I'm terrified. What am I going to say when I get home? Tilda will be waiting for me. She'll want to know why I ran out. What if she rejects me? What if she doesn't reject me? Either way, it's okay. Either way is terrifying. Okay, let's do this. Come on, Carol. Get out of the car. Here I go.'

Carol opens the car door. She gets out slowly and deliberately. She closes the car door and locks it. She walks up to her front door and opens it. As she comes in the door, Tilda emerges from the living room and stands in the hallway. There are tears in her eyes. She is rubbing her hands together, obviously distressed. Carol can't bear to see her in pain. Tilda says softly, 'Karul, Karul, I am sorry I upset you. I am so sorry.'

'No, it's not you,' Carol says quickly. Her heart is beating wildly. 'It's me. You haven't done anything to upset me. I upset myself.'

'Why you upset? Please tell me.'

'Oh Tilda, I'm so mixed up. I don't know what I'm doing. I made myself ill.' She pauses, then dives headlong, the words rushing out in a jumble. '...from loving you.' She gulps. That doesn't sound right. After the pep talk from Sue and Alison, is that the best she can do? Faced with Tilda in distress, Carol can't remember what she's been advised to say.

'But loving is good,' Tilda says, the tears spilling down her cheeks. 'Why make yourself ill?'

Carol flounders, opening and shutting her mouth. Why is this so hard? 'I mean I want sex. Sex with you.' Even if Tilda were halfway open to the idea, Carol knows this pathetic seduction line would certainly put her off. She looks helplessly at the floor. If she were to look at Tilda, she'd have to kiss those tears away and she still doesn't have the courage. But she makes herself keep going. 'I'm in love with you, Tilda. But I don't ...'

'No talking,' Tilda says sternly. She has stopped crying and is shaking her head from side to side, frowning. Carol does not notice the twinkle in her eye as she is still looking at the floor. Tilda looks intently at Carol, her mouth pursed and her eyes narrowed. Carol reads her body language and concludes it can only mean rejection. She opens her lips to speak but Tilda's hand covers her mouth.

Tilda leads her into the living room. Sitting down on the sofa, she pats the space next to her. Carol sinks down, her heart heavy. Tilda will be kind and considerate and will let her know in the most tactful way why they cannot be lovers. And Carol can't bear it. She tries to rise but, in that moment, something happens that keeps her glued to the sofa.

It is as if time stops and a force fills the space between them, and they are pulled towards each other as if they are magnets, and their lips touch and their tongues find each other and they kiss for a very long time. And they come up for gulps of air like whales. And they roam wild and free over unexplored territory. And they find caves of precious jewels and hidden lakes with sun-sparkled waterfalls and secret forests with rare and beautiful birds singing unbearably beautiful songs.

And at no time do clouds block the sun and nowhere does danger stop them in their tracks. And they are curious and explore until they reach the highest peak. And they tumble and roll and somersault all the way down. And they land in a sweat-scented tangle of arms and legs and breasts and bellies and tongues and vulvas and skin. And every cell in their bodies is tingling and alive.

And they sleep like love-swaddled babies.

The next morning, Carol sends a text with a thumbs up emoji and twenty smiley faces to Sue and Alison.

Chapter 17. Carol

'Carol, would you stop that infernal singing,' Francis snaps, unaware that Carol has crossed into a parallel universe of lovemaking-induced bliss. Carol is in her bathrobe, her short hair waving in all directions, swaying her hips from side to side as she measures out coffee grounds and throws two pieces of bread into the toaster.

'Oh Mum, I can't stop,' she sings, swooping in for a quick hug before dancing off. 'I'm so happy.' *Five nights of lovemaking will do that to you*, she thinks. Never before in her life has she inhabited her body so fully. It is intoxicating and overwhelming but in a good way, she realises. It makes her incapable of getting stressed and irritated.

'Mum, remember Sue's picking you up in an hour to take you to your singing group.' Carol butters the toast and eats both pieces, standing up. She is ravenous.

'That is my toast,' Francis says, her voice quivering. 'What singing group? You didn't tell me anything about a singing group.'

Without a twinge of impatience, Carol replies, 'It's the same one you've been going to for the last two weeks. You love it. You'll have a great time. I bet you'll be singing more Beatles songs today.'

'I want Tilda to take me, not Sue.'

Oh, that is so not going to happen, Carol thinks.

'I'll help you get dressed Mum. Come on.'

'Wipe that smile off your face,' Francis snarls. 'Where's Tilda? I don't want you helping me, you scruffy slob. Why aren't you even dressed?'

'*All you need is love, love. Love is all you need*,' Carol sings as she leads her mother up the stairs, cheerfully distracted by delicious thoughts of what she and Tilda will be doing while her mother is at her singing group.

Two hours later, a ray of weak January sunlight pierces the thick cloud cover and peers in through Carol's bedroom window. It lights up chestnut brown skin wrapped around pinkish-straw coloured skin. With hearts thudding in sync and limbs entwined, Carol can't tell where her body ends and Tilda's begins. *It's like we're one body,* she thinks. She is so relaxed she feels as if she is melting into the bed.

Tilda opens her eyes and moves her head slowly down Carol's body, kissing gently as she goes. Carol strokes Tilda's never-brushed hair, thinking how it is like a soft woollen blanket. She feels desire bubble up again, amazed at how soon she can be aroused after orgasm. Tilda pushes her hair off her face and looks with interest at the part of Carol's body that nestles between her legs.

Carol feels a wave of self consciousness flow through her. 'Don't look,' she whispers. 'I don't want you to look at me down there.'

She pushes herself up onto her elbows to face Tilda but can't look her in the eye. Looking Tilda in the eye can be unnerving, Carol has discovered. There are times when Tilda's gaze is like a laser, a bit too direct and intense for Carol's comfort. It seems to Carol as if Tilda is looking beyond or through her to someone she could be but isn't yet. Carol is finding it hard to present a good impression of herself when the midday sun shining through her bedroom window is like a spotlight exposing her naked body to view. Although the room is warm, she shivers. She tries to bring her knees together but Tilda stops her and looks up at her.

Two frown lines have appeared on Tilda's forehead and her eyebrows are lowered over narrowed eyes. Carol cringes. Is Tilda offended? Annoyed? Angry? Tilda blinks. She studies Carol's face closely.

Carol feels her face burning. She takes a deep breath and puffs out her cheeks. 'It's the light,' she explains, blowing the air out. 'We've only made love at night. In the dark. So you couldn't see me. I kept my eyes closed.' And she liked it that way. She was able to lose herself in the sensual experience of touch and feel and taste and smell without the distraction of sight and all the judgements she imposed on what she saw.

'Yes. Now we can see,' Tilda says. She doesn't appear to be self-conscious about being seen. Not surprising, Carol thinks. Tilda is small and well-proportioned with none of the flabby bits that mortify Carol about her own body. Carol envies Tilda's ability to be comfortable in her skin and to be at ease touching her own body and Carol's.

'I don't want you to see me, especially that part of me,' Carol says miserably. 'I'm embarrassed. It's ugly. That part of me.'

Tilda gasps, her eyes widening. 'Ugly? What you mean ugly?' The frown is becoming a permanent feature. Carol wishes she didn't have to spell it out. She knows she isn't that unusual. What woman is completely comfortable with her body? Everyone has an issue with some part. Surely Tilda can understand that.

'I mean ugly. It's private. Nobody has wanted to look at it before.' Carol is beginning to feel exasperated. This could be a drawback of lesbian sex, she realises. The few men she slept with had been eager to get inside her and had shown no interest in looking where they were going. But Tilda keeps her eyes open, feasting eagerly on every new sight.

'Let me see if ugly,' Tilda says. Before Carol can object, Tilda has lowered her gaze and is looking carefully at the exposed no-longer private part. Carol sighs in defeat and endures the examination, squirming inwardly.

After what seems an interminably long time, Tilda speaks tenderly. 'I see no ugly. Only beautiful.' She smiles up at Carol, her blue eyes twinkling happily. She spreads her arms out as if there is nothing more to be said. She has settled the matter once and for all. Despite herself, Carol smiles back. That's what she likes about Tilda – her simple though delusional faith that all one's emotional baggage, built up over a lifetime, can just be swept away by making a decision to no longer indulge it.

Carol sighs. 'No one's ever said that to me before. About that part of me.' She pauses. Tears well up and spill over. 'No one's said I'm beautiful.'

Tilda leaps off the bed and lifts a bamboo-framed mirror off the wall. 'You look,' she says, holding the mirror in place so Carol can see herself. Carol squints briefly into the mirror and groans. 'Oh god. I look like a Sumo wrestler.' She peers again out of the side of her eyes, aghast at the unflattering view. There is something weirdly fascinating about seeing herself from this angle. Her belly bulges out and her breasts flop to either side. Pubic hairs stray down her thighs. She can't even focus on her vulva.

'What's a-tsoo-nu-raffler?' Tilda asks, the frown lines reappearing.

'Enormously fat, ugly men from Japan who wrestle semi-naked,' Carol replies, still looking at herself in the mirror. She is intrigued. Only once before has she had a look with a mirror and that was when she was eleven years old. It had been an unpleasant experience and she'd never felt inclined to look again. How come she has never been curious about her own body? Carol realises she has been living most of her life in her head. Five days of sex with Tilda has awakened her body. She feels alive and full of vitality. But not beautiful. That is a step too far.

'Look wivh loving eyes,' Tilda says, holding the mirror in place. 'Your body give you pleasure, give me pleasure. So not ugly. It's beautiful.'

Carol says sadly, 'I wish I could see myself as beautiful, but I don't.'

Tilda is chewing the inside of her mouth and gazing at Carol with a look that Carol can't decipher. That makes her anxious. Gently stroking the inside of Carol's thigh, Tilda says quietly, 'I am sad to hear vat. Great Movher give you beautiful body.' Tilda's fingers travel up to Carol's belly, caressing its wobbly expanse slowly and tenderly. Carol tenses. She sucks in her belly but it doesn't oblige and flatten out. How long has it been since she last had a flattenable tummy? Her mind wanders twenty years into the past to the time when she was pregnant with Ben.

Mike's voice booms out to her from the Mike Bubble at the back of her mind: 'That's disgusting. Cover that ugly thing up,' he had said repeatedly when her belly swelled in pregnancy. After the birth, his sneering had intensified. 'Are you sure there isn't another baby still in there? Go to the gym, for Christ's sake. You've let yourself go. I can't bear to look at you.' And on and on. There was an aggressive side to Mike that he reserved for Carol. No one else saw this side. Carol couldn't blame him. She was convinced of her ugliness and had tried very hard to remedy the situation. But the sit-ups, the diets, a gym membership that lasted two weeks, and a half-hearted attempt to train for a half marathon all ended in failure. The tummy stayed.

Carol surfaced from her reverie to hear Tilda speaking earnestly about Great Mother. 'Great Movher only give beauty, not ugly gifts. You should fhank Great Movher for your beautiful body.'

Does Tilda disapprove of her lack of appreciation of Great Mother's gift? She hasn't encountered this side of Tilda before. She doesn't know what to say. She desperately wants to move on, to recapture the thrilling, exciting mood she'd been in before Tilda had started her forensic examination of her genitals.

Tilda points to the window. 'Look at tree. Is ugly?' she demands. Carol cringes inwardly. She knows when she is being told off. Outside the window, a bare-branched sycamore tree is waving in the January noon sun. 'Tree is beautiful because is gift from Great Movher. Beautiful every day, every season. Beautiful roots. Beautiful leaves. Beautiful what you call tall middle part?'

'Trunk,' Carol mutters, glancing nervously at Tilda. She can't bear Tilda to be angry at her.

'Chung? Chruck? How you say it?'

Carol rolls her eyes and nods vaguely. She is not in the mood to give Tilda an English pronunciation lesson.

'Beautiful chruck. All of tree beautiful. All parts needed.' *Tilda is like a dog with a bone*, Carol thinks. *An attractive dog but annoyingly stubborn.*

'Yes. Yes. I get it,' Carol says quickly. 'I don't mean any disrespect to your Great Mother. Please don't be angry at me.'

Tilda throws up her hands. 'Yours too. Not my Great Movher. She is for all living beings. She loves you. She is love.'

This reaction does not reassure Carol. Tilda is definitely cross with her. *Everything I say comes out wrong,* she moans to herself. The lovemaking session is not going how she wants.

'I'm sorry, Tilda,' she grovels. 'I don't believe in Great Mother. I can't see her anywhere. I'd never heard of her before I met you.'

'I not angry at you,' Tilda says in between kisses. 'I admire your beautiful body. I love you.' She smiles, her blue eyes lighting up. Carol can't help smiling back until she hears Mike's voice in her head again. 'No one can admire your fat body. No one can love you.' Carol closes her eyes in pain. Of course Tilda is angry with her. She has just disrespected her God or Goddess or whatever she believes in.

Tilda is chewing the inside of her cheek again, her eyes flitting from side to side, as if looking for the best words to say. 'You not see Her because your eyes are closed, Karul. Great Movher is here in every breafh you take, in every part of your body. She created you.'

'Oh Tilda. I don't know what you're talking about,' Carol says wearily, revelling in the warmth of Tilda's body against hers. She doesn't want to think and argue and understand with her mind. She just wants to cuddle, to feel, to sense with her body. But arguing is a compelling hook for her. Sighing, she says, 'I grew up with a God that judges and punishes. He doesn't give gifts. He isn't love. I stopped believing in him when I was a child. I don't believe in a God who created the world in six days. I'm a scientist. I believe in evolution.'

Tilda is silent, the frown lines deepening. 'Who made your body?' she asks eventually with a serious expression on her face. Carol groans and wishes she hadn't succumbed to arguing. Why couldn't she just let it go? What does it matter what Tilda believes?

'No one. It just happened,' she says and kisses Tilda on the nose. Delicious sensations arise from between her legs and travel up through her belly. She doesn't care in the slightest who made her body or how it came to be. She just knows for the first time in her life that her body is an exquisite instrument of delight, capable of far more than she had ever dreamed.

Tilda draws back slightly, still frowning. 'No one made your body?'

Carol closes her eyes in frustration. How can she put an end to this ridiculous conversation? 'It's like this,' she says quickly. 'All life evolved by random chance occurrences. A few molecules got together and started reproducing themselves. It's like a machine. There's no design, no purpose. Just a blind indifferent universe.' Carol trails off, realising she is spouting someone else's ideas. She is finding it hard to remain indifferent to the feelings pulsing blindly within.

'Karul, you talk too fast. If like a *m'sheen*, vhere has to be a *m'sheen*-maker.'

Carol starts giggling. She puts her finger over Tilda's mouth. 'Okay. Okay. Fair point. You're a good arguer. I am not a machine. Great Mother made me and gave me a beautiful body.'

'You mean it?' Tilda asks, looking uncertain but hopeful.

'I'm sure I will mean it if I hang with you long enough. Now can we stop wasting our few minutes alone together and get back to the important business of making love?' She pauses and looks Tilda in the eye. 'Thank you for telling me I'm beautiful.'

Chapter 18. Carol

D on't stop, please,' Carol moans. Tilda has been languidly and sensuously stroking Carol's G-spot when she suddenly stops and lifts her head to listen. Carol is lost in the sensation, all of her attention focussed on that one tiny spot of her anatomy. The feeling has been expanding and radiating out to every nerve ending of her body.

'Carol! Let me in. Where are you?' Francis calls through the door.

'Damn her,' Carol mutters. 'She shouldn't be home for another hour.' The delicious liquid desire that has been building up deep inside evaporates. Could her mother's timing be any worse?

'Carol?' Sue's voice joins Francis'. 'I texted you. We had to leave early. Are you there?'

'Carol!' Francis calls again, her tone demanding an immediate response. 'Open this door right now.'

'No. Go away,' Carol mutters. 'Please Great Mother, make her go away.'

Tilda slowly withdraws her fingers and puts them over Carol's mouth. 'Hush,' she whispers. 'It's okay. I will let her in and come back to you.' Her voice is tender and soothing.

Tilda rummages around on the floor for her jeans and green fleece. Carol shakes her head in exasperation as Tilda dresses without putting on underwear. As well as child size jeans and two green fleeces, Carol bought Tilda several pairs of knickers, socks and a bra when they arrived back from Ireland. Tilda examined the knickers and bra without comment, then hid them under the sofa.

'She hates me. And I hate her,' Carol explains to the room when Tilda leaves. 'I don't want her here anymore. I've had it.' Hearing the words spoken out loud shocks her. She senses a charge in the atmosphere, as if the empty room is a witness to her rebellion. Something is listening to her. What's more, it is hearing her. A door has opened to an idea that had been unthinkable before.

From the corridor, Carol hears their voices, Sue's apologetic,

Tilda's soothing and melodic, Francis' grating and querulous.

'Heyyo Sue. Goodbye. Heyyo Francis. How was singing?'

'Where were you, Tilda? I wanted you to take me, not Sue.'

'I was here wivh Karul.' Their voices are getting louder as they walk up the stairs.

'You be careful, Tilda. Carol will take advantage of you. I'm tired. I need a back rub.'

'Okay. I give you back run.'

Furious, Carol mutters under her breath, 'Don't you dare, Tilda. Get back here now.'

Francis directs her voice at Carol's bedroom door. 'Tilda's giving me a back rub. Carol doesn't deserve one.'

Tilda chuckles quietly, 'Oh I fhink she does. Come, Francis.'

'You haven't finished mine,' Carol shouts. Under her breath, she mutters through gritted teeth, 'and it's not my back I want rubbing.'

Lying alone on the rumpled bedclothes, in the highly charged atmosphere of the bedroom, a dangerous fiery feeling builds in Carol's belly and radiates out through every cell of her body. Each minute that Tilda is with Francis feels like a lifetime. After what seems like an hour of waiting but is probably less than ten minutes, Carol sits bolt upright with an energy born of rage. She flings on her bathrobe and marches across the corridor to Francis' room. She bursts in to a cosy scene: Francis, her mottled skin sagging, nightie buttoned up to her neck, tucked up in bed with her eyes closed, and Tilda, straight back, sitting cross-legged on the floor, singing. At her arrival, Francis opens her eyes and screams, 'Get out. Go away. She's with me.'

Carol's fury boils over. 'No. Tilda's with me. Not you. You get out. Tilda, come back to my room.' Then she crashes out of the room followed by Tilda's intense gaze. How embarrassing! She doesn't know what to do with her wild angry energy. She can hear Francis shouting and Tilda soothing her. She considers throwing things around but can't bear the thought of tidying up afterwards. She contents herself with slamming the bedroom door several times.

Tilda comes in quietly and sits cross-legged on the floor watching her. She is not smiling and her blue eyes are not twinkling. Her mouth is set in a straight line. Carol realises she's gone too far. Tilda must be disgusted by her behaviour. Maybe she'll leave and go home early.

'I, um, I don't know what came over me,' Carol whispers, glancing up quickly and then down at the floor again. 'I just got insanely jealous. I want you to myself.'

Tilda shakes her head from side to side. 'Why jealous? I was short time wivh Francis. She was almost asleep. I was coming to you.'

'I want you to be mine,' Carol says, not looking at Tilda. 'You left me to be with my mother.'

'Kårul, I make love to you. I make sex to you.' Tilda runs her fingers over her hair, pushing the matted black locks off her face. 'I make loving kindness to your Movher. I not make sex to her.'

Carol fumes. Why should Tilda show her mother loving kindness after the way Francis has treated her own daughter? She feels a flash of anger at Tilda for betraying her. Tilda should stand up for her, tell Francis off, not be kind to her. Francis would be horrified if she knew that she and Tilda were lovers. Would she turn against Tilda if she knew?

What does she know about Tilda's sex life? Tentatively she asks, 'Have you had many lovers in your life, like me? Women lovers?'

'Nobody like you but ovher women lovers, yes.'

Carol both does and doesn't want to know more. Questions pop into her mind but don't come out her mouth. How many? For how long? What kind of sex? Were they better lovers than she is? Were they prettier with flat tummies? How old were they? Is she the oldest?

She pulls the bathrobe tighter around her waist. She is out of her depth. She is fifty years old and has never had a woman lover. She hadn't even known what she was missing. But now that she knows, she can't imagine how she has gone without for an entire lifetime. There just have never been any opportunities that she could remember to have had other lovers, women or men.

'Have you ever been jealous?' she asks.

'Not of my Movher,' Tilda says, looking amused.

Carol covers her face with her hands. Her stomach is twisting with anxiety. She whispers, 'Now I know what I've been missing and now I'm terrified of losing it. I need you, Tilda. You make me feel complete, whole.'

Tilda reaches over and pulls Carol's hands away from her face. 'You are perfect already and beautiful. You are complete. Don't need me for make you complete.' Her eyes are soft and loving.

'I want you to be mine,' Carol says in a low voice. 'I want you to need me.'

'I don't understand,' Tilda says, frowning. She holds Carol's hands in hers and looks deep into Carol's eyes. 'You want own me like your *m'sheen*s and car and house?'

'No. Of course not,' Carol huffs, shocked that Tilda would even see it that way. 'I want us to make a commitment to each other. I want you to promise to only make love to me.'

'I promise make love only to you right now.' Tilda's face relaxes and her eyes twinkle. She leans closer to kiss but Carol stops her.

'Do you promise to only make love to me for the rest of our lives?' Carol says. Did she really say that? They only became lovers five days ago and she only met Tilda two months before. What has got into her? Surely this is rash, premature. Tilda has had many lovers. She is obviously an experienced lover. She has never said she would give up other lovers.

'Did you promise only make love to Mike for rest of your lives?' Tilda counters.

'Yes,' Carol admits. She wonders why. She never felt towards Mike what she feels for Tilda. 'We got married. We said our vows. But we shouldn't have. I should have left him about six months after

I married him. Make that six months before.'

'Karul. Karul. Why make promises can't keep?' Tilda playfully pushes Carol over until they are lying side by side on the floor. 'Great Movher gave us beautiful bodies so can make beautiful sex. She wants joy for us, not us be jealous.'

Carol feels confused. There is something not right about what Tilda is saying. Or something unsaid. 'I want to make beautiful sex with you too, Tilda. But why can't we make promises to each other and keep them?'

'Vhat's not love, Karul.' She abruptly sits up and looks down at her lap. Carol too sits up. She senses a shift in the atmosphere. Tilda seems hesitant, less confident somehow, more serious.

'What do you mean? You make me feel so alive, so real,' Carol says. 'Being with you, a woman, feels so natural. I love you. I need you. I want to be with you forever. I can't bear the thought of being without you. I didn't feel this way about Mike, ever.'

'Karul,' Tilda speaks, still not making eye contact. She falls silent. Carol feels her gut twist with anxiety.

'Look at me, Tilda. Be honest with me. If you don't love me, you must say.' Brave words but could she bear the truth if the truth is not what she wants to hear?

Tilda hangs her head, then looks Carol in the eye. 'I love you. You are perfect and beautiful.' Carol has no doubt that Tilda is genuine but senses a big "but" coming.

Tilda wraps her arms around her knees. She lowers her head so that her hair covers her face. Carol feels the air drain out of the room. *She's going to leave me*, she thinks, *and I will not survive*.

Without looking up, Tilda says, 'Love is now in vhis moment. Love is here always. Now you feel alive, awake, you see love everywhere. I didn't make you feel love. I told you when we first met I stay six moons. I don't belong here. You know, yes?'

'I know, but it's different now we're lovers,' Carol whispers, hearing her heart break.

'I understand,' Tilda closes her eyes. 'But now you are awake, so you find ovher lovers when I go home. You will find love everywhere, not just in sex. Sex just one way. Are many ways. But Karul, we can stop. I understand. You want stop?'

No. we shouldn't stop, Carol thinks in panic. They shouldn't stop and she can't stop, even if that were the sensible thing to do. But to hell with the sensible thing to do.

'Do you want to stop?' Carol asks, holding her breath. Tilda shakes her head.

A Tilda Bubble is growing at the back of her mind, filling up with desperate schemes and despairing thoughts, all swirling around in a stomach-churning mess. *How can I make Tilda stay? What an idiot I was, clinging and whining. I shouldn't show her all my insecurities. She doesn't need me. She's got better lovers at home. She'll see through me soon, get tired of me. I can't give her anything she needs. She doesn't like it if I'm too needy. I must be more self-contained. She'll stay if I'm a better lover.*

Carol pushes the Tilda Bubble as far to the back of her mind as she can manage. Discarding her bathrobe, she wraps herself around Tilda and murmurs, 'As you said before, Tilda, and you do know Her better than I do, Great Mother wants our joy. We've got these beautiful bodies so let's make beautiful sex while we've got the chance.'

Does she imagine it or does Tilda look worried? However, Tilda very sweetly and gently puts their beautiful bodies to good use.

Chapter 19. Tilda

Carol and Francis are snarling at each other in the kitchen, like a couple of angry bears. *They are fighting over me,* Tilda realises, and her heart feels heavy. Is it best to stay and help them or leave them to it? Her heart says go. Without further deliberation, she calls goodbye and slips out the front door before either of them notice.

She skips down through the woods to the lake, grateful to be outside. As she skirts the lake, avoiding the hard, unmoving strip along its edge, a squat brown dog stops for a pat, his tail wagging cheerfully. An older man, wrapped warmly against the cold, follows the dog. He nods a brief greeting without slowing his pace. A loud buzzing sound approaches from behind. Startled, Tilda turns and sees a swan flying across the water. It crash-lands, running along the surface, its great webbed feet smacking the water. A heron preens itself amongst the reeds. A pair of coots quarrel and peck each other. More dogs, walkers, cyclists, birds. Tilda's heart lightens with each fleeting encounter.

She stops by a chestnut tree and closes her eyes. She is ready to focus inwardly.

'Great Mother, I am grateful to You for showing Your face to me,' she chants out loud. 'Great Mother, take my doubts and fears from me. I hand over to You my arrogance that I can make Carol and Francis feel or be something they are not ready to be. I hand You my impatience and my pride, my irritation. I will make no decisions on my own. Thank You for Your loving guidance.'

Charmall joins her. 'Speak to me of your holy union with Carol.'

'Oh Charmall, I am on a fast-moving river but still afloat.

Amongst the thicket of thorny vines that surround Carol,

white flowers have bloomed,

purple berries have ripened, plump and juicy.

The vines have withered, uncovering the entrance to a cave.

Deep within the cave, there slept a bear.

But the bear slumbers no more.

She heard my call, the call to love.
And she awoke and came to me.
I called her to dance and she dances
as if her feet have never been still.
I called her to sing and she sings
as if her voice has never been silent.
I called her to laugh and she laughs
as if her laughter has never dried up.
Not forgotten, the ancient wisdom of the body.
A magnificent animal she is.
I worship her beautiful body, her wild aliveness,
her abandonment to pleasure.
We join together in the sacred dance of love.
We become as one body, one animal.
We make love and there is just us,
two soft animals, exulting in our bodies,
at one with the stars and the moon,
the trees and the earth,
as Great Mother flows through us.
Though thousands of solstices have passed between us,
the body wisdom remains.
In that time, different paths have been followed,
Other ways to live together.
A new mind-wisdom has come into being,
one that knows not Great Mother
or who we are in the sacred web of life.
Great Mother is here amongst them
but their eyes are closed.
I am Great Mother's voice, Her eyes, Her lips
the body She uses to be love.
But Charmall, the bear fears the world outside her cave.
In the bright sunshine outside the entrance,
she sees her own shadow cast upon the ground.

Frightened, she crawls back into her cave
and pulls the vines over the entrance.
I grab the vines to tear them off but the thorns pierce my hands.
My hands are bleeding. My heart is sore.
I call Great Mother again and again.
I await her guidance.
What do you say to me?'

'Dear one, Great Mother sent you on this journey with your body. You are here for Her. She sent you into the dream world to heal and awaken Carol and Francis. Be at peace. It is not for you to know what to say or do. Great Mother will guide you. She is here with you always. You will be healed as you let Her teach you how to heal.'

Opening her eyes, Tilda glimpses a flash of sky blue and setting-sun orange as a tiny bird streaks by. She heads back to the house, her step lighter and her heart at peace.

Chapter 20. Carol

Where are you taking me? I want Tilda. Who are you anyway?' Carol stands at the front door until Sue has manoeuvred Francis into her car and is driving off down the road. After last week's premature homecoming from the singing group, Carol is determined not to be interrupted again.

'C'mon Tilda,' she says, pulling Tilda off the kitchen floor and into the living room. 'We have no time to waste.' Within seconds, they are on the living room floor, kissing fervently among a rapidly growing pile of discarded clothes. Just as they achieve total nudity, the doorbell rings.

'Ignore it,' she mutters to herself. 'They'll go away.' But they don't. After the fourth ring, Carol angrily pulls on a T-shirt and jeans and yanks open the door. Moira marches in, talking non-stop.

'Carol, I know I said I would come every Wednesday but things have been hectic. I am sorry I haven't been around lately. Aren't you cold? You're just wearing a T-shirt ... I've been busy painting some seascapes.'

Carol zones out. She follows Moira into the kitchen, quickly closing the living room door so Moira won't see a naked Tilda and their clothes scattered all over the floor.

'... popped into Lidl to buy you this lemon drizzle cake ...'

The cake emerges from Moira's handbag and lands on the kitchen table just as Tilda appears at the kitchen door, dressed to go outside in her Doc Martin boots and green fleece. She greets Moira who smiles warmly at her without pausing the flow of words. Tilda looks expectantly at Carol, who is standing mute by the kettle, sending desperate pleas with her eyes.

'I go walk,' Tilda announces abruptly, narrowing her eyes at Carol. The image of a pack of wild dogs barking ferociously and pinning her into a corner comes into Carol's mind. Tilda shakes her head unsympathetically and leaves.

'... Dunster Beach. I hired a little chalet and went by myself for a few days. Have you ever been there? It's really undeveloped and peaceful, especially this time of year.'

'Look Moira,' Carol begins.

'I meant to come over and help you out but I wonder if you need me anymore since you've got Tilda with you,' Moira says, cutting into her second piece of cake.

'Well, yes. Thank the Goddess. I'm not so stressed anymore.' *And I'm having passionate sex with a woman*, she adds to herself, trying to hide the smile that creeps out. *Or I would be if you hadn't come by.*

'Thank the Goddess?' Moira opens her eyes wide. 'Since when do you thank the Goddess? Is this Tilda's influence?'

Carol grins but doesn't answer. She is tempted to ask Moira about her sex life. She has no idea what Moira and her husband Sam get up to in bed. Is their sex life as exciting as hers and Tilda's? Or is it more like the boring sex she used to have with Mike? Is lesbian sex intrinsically better than heterosex, as Sue claims? Or does it not matter what gender your sexual partner is, as Alison and Tilda claim?

'What are you thinking about?' Moira asks and, unusually for her, waits for a reply.

'Nothing. Nothing,' Carol says, walking restlessly around the kitchen.

'Yes, you are. I can tell. What is it?'

Carol stops pacing, surprised by Moira's interest in her. 'I was thinking about ...' Carol makes a face and tries desperately to think of something safe to say to Moira. 'Um, about work.'

'Oh yeah? What about work?' Moira is clearly not convinced.

'Well, I haven't been able to do it. I've missed deadlines. I've had a warning. I just can't get into the right headspace.' As soon as the words are out, Carol realises the enormity of what she's just said. This is a problem she is going to have to face soon. But not yet.

Moira gasps and raises her eyebrows. 'Carol, this is mega-serious.

Are you about to lose your job?'

Carol takes a deep breath. 'Actually, yes. It's a real possibility. I just can't make myself think about it or do anything about it.'

Moira stares at Carol, speechless. She gulps. 'You don't seem appropriately concerned. Are you on something?'

Carol laughs. *Why would I need drugs*, she thinks, *when I've got sex-induced endorphins pulsing through my body for free?*

'Don't throw in the job yet, at least not until you've found something else. Carol, are you listening to me?'

Carol isn't. She is dancing around the kitchen, singing, '*Cause you started something, can't you see that ever since we met you've had a hold on me. No matter what you do, I only want to be with you.*'

'Carol, would you stop jiggling around for a minute? The reason I dropped by was to invite you for dinner. I thought that you could come, now that you have Tilda to babysit.'

'Oh.' Carol skids to a halt, surprised. She hasn't been to dinner at Moira's for years. She isn't sure she does want to go and leave Tilda to babysit. What she really wants is for Moira to babysit while she has dinner with Tilda. But how nice of Moira to invite her. She feels a stab of guilt for not appreciating her friend more.

'Thank you, Moira. That's really nice of you. When would you like me to come?'

'Why not tomorrow night? Come about seven.' Moira packs up the remains of the lemon drizzle cake, wraps herself in her coat and scarf and heads for the door. As she goes out, she calls back casually, 'Oh, Pete will be there too. See you.'

Carol is interested. She'd been meaning to talk to Pete about his experience with his wayward son but hadn't got round to it. She knows it is still an issue for her. Although Ben did stay with Mike over Christmas, he's likely to come back. It would be useful to hear how Pete managed his son. Moira has just given her an opportunity.

But Moira may have another reason for getting them together, one that is no longer relevant. Carol has complained about her unwelcome single status to Moira many times. Moira, to her credit, has given plenty of advice but so far hasn't come up with a suitable match in her self-appointed role as matchmaker. No wonder, Carol thinks, having a sudden light-bulb moment. Moira had been looking at the wrong gender. As she had been as well, before Tilda.

The next evening when Pete arrives at Moira's with a bottle of wine, he looks as if he's put some effort into his appearance. Carol has deliberately dressed down and is wearing her slob-around-the-house jeans and a rumpled jumper. Moira leaves the two of them in the living room while she disappears into the kitchen. Carol remembers that Moira is a gourmet cook who tends to spend several hours in preparation. She fiddles with a hole in her jumper and resists the urge to break the awkward silence.

Pete clears his throat. 'Um, has Tilda said any more to you about where she's from?'

Carol shrugs dismissively. 'She says she's from Neolithic Brú na Bóinne so I guess that's where she's from.'

'Yeah, that makes sense,' Pete says. He grins at her.

'I don't think about it much. We're too busy with other things to talk about where she's come from. Anyway what does it matter? She's here now.' Carol stretches the hole in her jumper a bit more. She's feeling awkward and finding it hard to say outright what she means. She wonders why it's so hard but decides it's not his business to know about her sex life. 'Actually, Pete, I would like to find out more about how you dealt with your son's bad behaviour, if you don't mind.'

Pete is very willing to tell her about his experiences with Matthew and to hear Carol's stories about Ben. They are still on the subject when Moira calls them to the dining room. As she serves dinner, Moira contributes her views on the topic. Carol groans inwardly. Given that Moira has never had anything to do with teenage boys, she finds Moira's opinions irritating. She is pleased when Pete steers the conversation onto his trip to Lesvos.

When Moira leaves them alone together to get the dessert, Carol remembers that Moira had once said something about Pete's wife, but can't remember the details. 'What happened to Gillian?'

A look of pain crosses Pete's face. 'She died five years ago. She left in the most terrible way imaginable.'

'I am sorry,' Carol squeaks, alarmed. 'You don't have to talk about it if you don't want to. I'm just being nosy.'

'I don't want to talk about it. But I think I should. And I don't mind you being curious. I like that about you.'

Carol waits, but Pete can't bring himself to say more. Just as she is about to change the subject, Pete speaks abruptly. 'She took an overdose. I found her body.'

Horrified, Carol flounders, trying to find words that don't sound trite or insincere. 'That's terrible.' She pauses. 'For you and for Matthew.'

'He was seventeen. Not a good age to lose your mother to suicide.'

Tears spring to Carol's eyes. 'I … well, I don't know what to say. That is so terrible. I am so sorry I put you on the spot like that just being nosy.'

Pete reaches over and pats her hand. 'Hey, don't apologise, Carol. Really. Thank you for being nosy and … and for being so lovely. I feel safe to talk about it with you. My counsellor says I should talk about it more, make it a more normal part of the story of my life.'

Carol offers him more wine and pours another glass for herself. The house seems too quiet. What is Moira doing in the kitchen? It can't take that long to make dessert. The image of Pete finding his wife dead looms large in her mind. She wonders what he did when he found her, how he had felt.

Pete wipes his eyes and says softly, 'You always think what you could have done to prevent it. But I still don't know. I didn't see it coming.'

He takes a sip of his wine and looks at Carol, a sad look that pierces her heart. She wants to take him in her arms and comfort him. Maybe there is something in her eyes that frightens him because he suddenly draws back and says, 'That's enough for now. Let's change the subject. Moira told me that you've been working for a pharmaceutical company and you're fed up with it. I'd like to hear more about that.'

Carol is relieved. She doesn't want to get drawn in to Pete's issues. She has enough of her own and suicide is way out of her repertoire of life experiences. The fact that Pete is interested in her work surprises and excites her. She's never had anybody to talk to about her work. For something that has taken up so much of her time, it has been a lonely and isolating part of her life.

Eagerly, she begins, 'I've been writing up drug studies for years. I could do it in my sleep. But since Tilda came into my life, I've started seeing it in a new way. You see, there's an unwritten requirement to produce papers that show positive results. My job was to go on a fishing expedition through the data until I found the positive results the company wanted.'

'A fishing expedition? That sounds almost sinister.' Pete is giving her his undivided attention.

'It was. I had to manipulate the data with various statistical tests and draw ambitious generalisations about the drug's usefulness with different populations. And you certainly don't publish papers showing a new drug to be worse than an existing one. You keep repeating the trials until one of them gives the results you want. But I can't and won't do it any longer.'

Pete is nodding energetically. 'Wow, you really have an insight into this field. I never knew about this. So, you're burned out, I guess.'

'Maybe I am burned out,' Carol says, rubbing her forehead. 'But it's more than that. I'm sick and tired of manipulating data for a pharmaceutical company that's just out to make a profit. I want to do something with integrity. I want to find a new way to make a difference in the world. I want to use my creativity, to express myself. I want to shine my light into the world.'

Pete keeps nodding. 'Sounds exciting, Carol. I really hope you find a way.' He leans forward. 'Let me tell you about my new passion ...'

'Dessert's ready,' Moira calls, carrying an enormous platter of pavlova into the room. Fruit and cream have been artistically arranged on top of the meringue. No wonder it took her so long. Pete whistles appreciatively and Carol shakes her head in admiration, saying, 'That is gorgeous but how can we possibly destroy your beautiful artwork?'

Moira takes a photo and serves generous portions to each. She's looking pleased with herself. Carol suspects it's not just about the pavlova. She clearly thinks her matchmaking has been successful.

Chapter 21. Tilda

'Jason, I have story for tell you,' Tilda says as they are walking by the River Frome. It is a dry day in early February. Jason is by her side, tossing a stick from hand to hand.

'Once upon a time.' She pauses. She is using the starting phrase that he taught her. It's their signal. He stops tossing the stick and gives her his full attention. 'Before breasts grew on my chest, I began my training to be Wisdom Keeper. I moved into House of Wise Ones.'

'Wow. That's young, isn't it?' Jason shifts the backpack from one shoulder to the other. Tilda can't believe the amount of stuff Carol packed into his backpack for a walk of but a few hours.

'How young are you when begin your training?' Tilda asks. The cold damp air is biting her neck. She regrets not accepting Carol's offer of her soft sun-coloured woollen scarf.

'Do you mean school? We start when we're five, in reception. So your training is like our school?' He nods, satisfied. He has another question. He asks it casually as if he's just a bit curious, as if it's not that important. 'Did you leave your parents when you moved into the House of the Wise Ones?'

'My Movher was a Wisdom Keeper. I came back to her when I moved into House of Wise Ones. She left when she had no more milk for me. I stayed wivh my favher and ovhers, aunts, uncles, one brovher, cousins, not all from vhe same family, friends too.'

Jason is taking this in. He frowns, holding the straps of the backpack with both hands. He is looking at the ground, biting his lower lip. 'Did you see your dad and your, um, your clan after you moved?'

Tilda laughs. She is thinking how strange it would have been not to have seen them. 'Yes, nearly every day. Did not you see your favher after he moved?'

Jason shakes his head and shrugs as if he wants her to think he doesn't care. But his shoulders sag and his wellies tap loudly on the concrete path beside the lake while Tilda's moccasins leave no sound.

'You miss your favher,' Tilda says. It's a statement, not a question. Jason shrugs again. He unwinds his scarf and stuffs it roughly in his coat pocket. It doesn't fit and he tries again, his movements jerky and fierce. Tilda feels a stab of pain in her heart and knows it is his pain. They walk on in silence. When Jason says no more, Tilda continues with her story.

'One day, we hear somefhing bad happen to sacred web of life. A man, his name Marfeen, would not give his portion of milk, cheese and meat to vhe full moon feast.'

'What's a full moon feast?' Jason asks.

'At full moon, people come togevher for feast. Everyone brings food. We all share: goats and cows for milk, animals to kill and cook for meat, dried meat and cheese. We have feasts many times for many reasons. Feasts are for share, for even spread of food. Feasts are so no one has not enough and no one has more than vhey need. We fhank Great Movher for all she give us.'

'So what do you mean? Are there no poor people and no rich people in your town?' Jason asks. He takes off his hat and runs his fingers through his curls. They walk past three ducks who look at them hopefully and then paddle away. A heron stands on one leg on a branch hanging over the lake. It is studying the water intensely.

'No one has more vhan anyone else. All need food. All should have enough food. How do you say it?'

Jason frowns. 'Do you mean that everyone deserves food? Maybe that's the word you want.'

'Yes, de-serves. De-serves. De-serves. If Great Movher gives life, vhen deserve to eat.'

Jason opens and closes his mouth several times. No words come out.

'Vhe feast-collectors came to Marfeen. Marfeen's demons attacked vhem wivh words vhat were strange to us. He said, "I own vhis meat. Vhis milk is mine. I made vhis cheese. It belongs to me. I will not share." Vhe feast-collectors ran away. Vhey were frightened and confused. Vhey ran to House of vhe Wise Ones.' Tilda stops, seeing the puzzled look in Jason's eyes.

'What's wrong with having things?' Jason asks. He pats a small dog that has come to greet them. 'If Marfeen did all the work, why couldn't he keep all the things he made, the meat, the milk, the cheese? I don't get what's wrong with that. Why should he share? That's not fair.' The dog wags its tail and prepares to jump on Jason when a man walking past orders it down.

Tilda chews the inside of her cheek. 'It is not our way. We are all equal, all part of vhe whole. Vhe task of Wise Ones is to keep all in balance. So we have feasts.'

They pause at the weir and watch the water splash and leap and roar over the stone wall. A duck swims to the top but isn't swept over. Tilda marvels at the power of the river and the skill of the duck to stay in balance.

'Two Wise Ones – Crogan, smiling fearless woman and Charmall, blue eyed wise man – took me wivh vhem to speak wivh Marfeen, to help him wivh his demons. How do you say vhis, Jason?'

'Help him fight his demons? Help him overcome his demons? I don't know,' Jason says.

'Like when goat kicks and you make her calm, not kick. What is word?'

'Oh. Tame. You tame the goat. You went to help Marfeen tame his demons?'

'Tame, tame, tame.' Tilda commits the word to memory. 'Crogan and Charmall later passed into Ovherworld and still guide me today. But vhen, I was under vheir care day and night. As vhey were brave and calm, so was I. As vhey showed no fear, nievher did I.'

'Tilda,' Jason says, looking at her with a cross between a smile and a frown on his face. 'You were a little girl. Were you really not scared? I would have been.' They are crossing a narrow bridge.

Jason drops a twig into the river and dashes to the other side to see it float by.

Tilda's eyes crinkle up. 'OK, was small fear in my heart. But I tried not to show it.

'Before sun rise, we prepared for journey. Crogan and Charmall dressed in vheir sacred long robes wivh vhe triple spiral design. Vhe same as mine. You seen it. Vhey covered vheir hair wivh necklaces of periwinkle shells.'

They cross a stone bridge and walk down four concrete steps to the riverbank. They stare at the brown swirling water. It has been raining for several days and the river is high.

'As I was a child, I did not have my sacred necklace. I wore short robe. We entered vhe Palace of vhe Immortals. Crogan, first, she held a burning torch and chanted as she walked to vhe chamber. Vhe chamber where you went. Remember?' Jason nods. 'Charmall followed, he beat a drum. Vhen me. It was my first time in chamber. My heart beat like drum and my legs wobbled so vhat I feared I could not stand in vhe presence of vhe stones and vhe ancestors. Great Movher blessed our mission and we left chamber, still chanting.'

Jason skips from one foot to the other, the backpack banging heavily against his back. The path leads to an opening with tall sycamore and chestnut trees on the riverside and a thick bank of brambles on the other.

'Tilda, can you see Great Mother with your actual eyes?'

'No. She has no body.'

Jason takes the bottle of water and the thermos of hot chocolate out of the backpack and empties them onto the ground. 'That's better.'

'We left vhe Palace of vhe Immortals and came to river. We walked for many hours, sometimes chanting, sometimes in holy silence. Blessings flowed to us from vhe salmon of knowledge who swam beside us, from vhe birds and butterflies, from vhe trees who bowed to us as we passed. Vhe sun shone encouragement.'

Jason's eyes light up. 'I wish there was salmon in this river. I saw an otter once. Not here. Further along. Look. See that streak of blue flashing by? That's a kingfisher. King-fish-er.'

'King-fish-er. King-fish-er.' Tilda repeats the word three more times and it's added to her stock of English words. She loves Jason's enthusiasm for nature and his patience in teaching her English. He is like a younger version of Charmall, Tilda thinks, remembering the love she felt for both Charmall and Crogan, but particularly Charmall. She shakes her head to bring herself back to the present.

'It was warm and vhe journey long and slow. We carried only small pouches wivh dried meat and kefir. Crogan and Charmall stopped many times to let me drink, pick berries and rest. I was not strong enough to walk long distances. Vhis mission was part of my training and vhey were patient and kind.

'Vhe sun was setting as we arrived at vhe long house where Marfeen and his people lived. When Marfeen saw us, his eyes grew wide wivh awe and fear. Never before had Wise Ones come to his home. Marfeen bowed low and kissed vhe hems of our robes. He brought us water. As is our custom, Marfeen honoured us with a bowl of kefir, fhanking Great Movher before passing vhe bowl around. After eating, we sat around his firepit. In silence. Watching vhe flames dance and leap and crackle, I soon fell into a deep sleep, leaning against Charmall.'

Tilda halts at the side of the road. She waits nervously until a car drives past, then holds Jason's hand to cross the road. They go through a gate to a dirt path in the woods. The path climbs steeply uphill. Jason sits on a fallen tree trunk. He opens the backpack, offers a peanut butter sandwich and an apple to Tilda. She takes the apple. They sit and eat in companionable silence. Tilda resumes her story.

'Next morning, I wake. I am lying on floor of vhe long house where Charmall had carried me vhe night before. He and Crogan had already dressed, eaten and asked Great Movher to bless our journey. Marfeen had a goat on a rope. Vhe goat was loaded wivh pouches of dried meat and hard cheese. It was my task to lead vhe goat back.'

'I bet that was hard,' Jason says. He stops to catch his breath. The hill is very steep and rises high above the river.

'Yes, vhe goat wanted to stop and eat every step of way. I had to pull her and push her and smack her on vhe bottom to get her to move. I did not like vhat goat. I cried all vhe way home.'

'Didn't Crogan and Charmall help you?' Jason asks. 'You were just a little child.'

'No. Vhey trusted me to work it out myself. Vhat's how I learned.'

'But you cried. Leading the goat was too hard for you. That's cruel to treat a child that way. I don't like Crogan and Charmall.'

'But Jason, I was so proud of myself. I told vhe story over and over. A little girl walked all day with vhe most stubborn, lazy, bad-tempered goat in vhe land. A goat vhat hit me wivh her head when I pulled her rope. A goat vhat kicked me when I pushed her. Everyone praised me. It was wonderful feeling.'

Tilda is smiling at the memory and amused that Jason has taken a dislike to Crogan and Charmall. She is looking forward to telling them later about Jason's strong reaction. She catches herself in mid thought. She isn't being truthful. There were times when she did resent both Crogan and Charmall for giving her tasks that were too hard for her. No wonder Jason thinks it was cruel to make her responsible for the goat.

Jason is thoughtful. The path has reached the top of the ravine. Down below is the river. Holding on to tree trunks and exposed roots, they slide down the path as it descends sharply back to the river. Jason stuffs his hat and scarf in the backpack. He ties his coat around his waist and looks expectantly at Tilda.

'On vhe way back, we chanted. Vhe sun was high in vhe sky when we took our first rest. A sycamore tree gifted us with shade. Vhe river gifted us with cooling water. I tied vhe goat to vhe tree. She ate vhe rope and escaped. I found her drinking by vhe river side. I chased her. She pretended not to see me and waited for me to get close. Vhen she ran. Vhe sun was not as high in vhe sky when I finally caught her. I shouted at her. I was very angry. Crogan put her hands on my head and helped me calm down. Vhen I made peace wivh vhe goat.'

'But Tilda, what did Crogan and Charmall say to Marfeen? How did they make him give his share to the full moon feast?'

'Not a fhing. Great Movher said it all.'

'So they didn't arrest him or tell him what a selfish, bad man he was or threaten him or give him a fine or beat him up?'

'No. Vhat is not our way.'

'That wouldn't work here.' Jason scuffs his wellies against the path. He is swinging a stick from side to side, hitting the stone wall of the bridge they are crossing. 'So is that the end of the story?'

Tilda nods.

'Then you have to say The End.'

'Vhe End,' Tilda says.

Jason hits the stick against the stone wall so hard that it breaks in two. He walks quickly, his head down, frowning. Tilda trots to keep up. He stops suddenly and faces Tilda.

'Tilda, would you go talk to my dad? He lives in Birmingham. You'd have to go on the train. Would you?'

'What you want me to say to him?'

'I don't know. Maybe, just remind him that I'm his son too. Not just Ben. He could send me a Christmas present or a letter or call me every now and then. Or even come to visit. Or let me visit him.' He pauses, waves the broken stick some more and tosses it aside. 'Actually, I don't care. Don't bother. You'd have to arrest him to get him to do anything. Mum has tried yelling at him and it didn't work. So never mind.'

Tilda pulls him into a hug. He doesn't resist but leans into her. 'Jason. You and Karul must talk and decide togevher what to do. Okay? You will talk wivh Karul, yes?'

She looks at him out of the corner of her eye. He looks back out of the corner of his eye. They grin at each other.

'Race you to the water mill,' Jason shouts, and runs out of her embrace, his wellies clacking against the concrete.

Chapter 22. Tilda

It is a bitterly cold February night. Tilda feels like she is suffocating under the too-warm duvet in Carol's hot, airless bedroom. She wants to reach out to the stars and receive their blessing, but the windows are locked shut and heavy curtains hide the midnight sky. Lying awake in bed, she's engaged in a marathon battle with an army of demons. The demons exaggerate the sounds of Carol's breathing, of a clock ticking, of the fridge humming in the kitchen downstairs, of her own rapid heartbeat. They whizz random thoughts and impressions through her mind. A feeling of dread overwhelms her. Lying awake another minute becomes intolerable.

She decides to visit Darren. She smiles, remembering meeting him on one of her night walks. He is currently living under the motorway in a tent he was given when his last tent was set on fire. He is often awake in the night and grateful for anything she brings him. She heats up the rest of the chicken soup Carol made for dinner and fills a thermos. As she tightens the lid, she admires the thermos and thanks it for its service. How much better it is for carrying hot liquids than the pig bladders used at home. She has no doubt that Darren will need some more warm clothing. She wraps Carol's yellow woollen scarf around her neck and shoves a woollen hat on her head.

Standing before the front door, she closes her eyes and runs through the steps Carol insisted she do in order to leave the house. Open hall closet door, open alarm box door, check green light is flashing, press four squares, which ones? Wait for steady green light. No, first take keys off the hook in the kitchen, then open hall closet door. She is sweating with the effort of remembering. If she makes a mistake, a sound as loud as Ben's music attack will blast everyone out of their beds and make her ears ring for hours, as she has found out on several occasions. There have been nights when she gave up and stayed inside, feeling like a trapped boar and just as angry. But tonight, her mind is clouded by an overwhelming urge to get outside. She has to get out. She puts the thermos on the floor, sits beside it and chants until her mind is calm enough to remember the sequence of steps to turn off and reset the alarm system. Success at last! She stands outside on the front stoop, relishing the cold air cleansing her lungs and face.

'Crogan, I need you,' she calls as she starts walking to meet Darren. 'I have a sense of foreboding. I am afraid of what I know not.'

'Great Mother is with you,' Crogan replies, but Tilda does not feel reassured. The dread is like a thick mist around her.

In half an hour of quick walking, she reaches Darren's abode – an outdoor space of concrete surrounded on all sides and above with car-frenzied road. Not even a blade of grass or a solitary dandelion softens the merciless concrete. A drawing of a kingfisher on a pillar only serves to highlight the chasm between Nature and this lifeless place. Tilda feels her energy drain out of her body.

Darren is sitting outside his tent smoking a roll-up, wrapped in a thin blanket. He is shivering and his lips are blue with cold. Scattered around the tent and in one of the shopping trolleys Tilda has seen at Tesco, are his possessions and his rubbish. He greets Tilda with a delighted smile and pats a square of cardboard beside him. She sits down cross-legged on the cardboard and rubs her nose on his.

'Hey Tilda,' he says, laughing. 'You are the only one who visits me after midnight.' Tilda guesses that she is his only visitor.

'I'm sorry I have nothing to offer you,' he says regretfully. Over the weeks that Tilda has been visiting him, she has graciously, but firmly, refused his offers of cigarettes, alcohol and pre-packaged food.

'Your friendship is all I want.' She takes off the woollen hat and scarf and puts them on Darren's head.

'Some day, you'll tell me your story, friend Tilda. When you're ready. Did I tell you about the time I was in care? That was a bad time. I'll tell you one day. Hey, I wish I knew when you were going to visit. I'd tidy up my patch first.' He looks around at the mess and shrugs. Tilda makes a mental note to ask Carol what "in care" means. She doesn't want to interrupt Darren's flow by asking too many questions.

'My asthma is bad again. I'm going to give up smoking one day. And look at this leg ulcer.' He rolls up his trouser leg to show a dirty bandage. 'They said at the hospital it's because of my diabetes.'

Tilda notices that Darren is looking paler and his body odour is more pungent than the last time she visited. She doesn't show it but she is shocked and outraged at the state he's in.

'You are good man. You deserve better,' she tells him. He smiles sadly at her and she sees that he's lost hope or interest in getting out of his predicament. And though he's cold and sick, she knows he'd rather be free than confined in a sterile, soulless hostel. Tilda admits to herself that she feels the same. She just wishes there was another option for him.

She glances at a car stopped at the traffic light less than three metres away. Loud music is blasting through the closed windows. The occupants are warmly dressed, sitting on cushioned seats, laughing and chatting. Tilda shakes her head in disbelief, her matted locks flying about her head. 'Cars are powerful Beings,' she says. 'Vhey rule vhis world.' Darren nods in resigned agreement.

She opens the thermos, about to pour steaming hot chicken soup into Darren's tin mug, when three men emerge from the night. They stand in a row, legs akimbo, sneering down at her and Darren. Even before they utter a word, they radiate a gleeful anticipation of violence. It flows out on their sour breath, from the ugly sneers on their faces and from their veiled, unseeing eyes. Darren whimpers. The smell of urine wafts up from his trousers.

'Great Mother,' Tilda calls inwardly. 'Are these demons or human beings? What do you ask of me?' She is sweating despite the cold and her heart is racing like the cars speeding along on the motorway above.

Great Mother responds instantly. Tilda takes a deep breath. She's not sure if this is good news or not. They are human beings but ruled by powerful demons. Her task is to touch their hearts and to bring them back to their humanity.

Her training has taught her ways to touch hearts, but she has never encountered a situation like this, nor had to deal with it on her own. At home, there is a wealth of experience to draw on to weaken the grip of demons and to reach the person under their spell. Normally, she would consult Crogan and Charmall. She can sense their presence at the edge of her mind. She knows they are calling to her but she is distracted and her mind divided. A part of her is telling her to grab Darren and run. Another part is paralysed with fear and indecision. Still a third part is saying she must do what she has been trained to do.

Tilda heeds the third part. While the men walk around, kicking out at random, Tilda sits very still and chants under her breath. The men shout and whoop, a constant stream of incomprehensible abuse spewing from their mouths. Tilda listens to the feelings beneath their words. Anger, rage; hatred, certainly. Excitement, thrill – definitely. And underneath: fear.

One of the men has a painting on his neck and cheek that looks like a spider. He digs a lighter out of his pocket. The other two hoot with excitement. They kick and throw Darren's stuff onto the tent, shrieking and shouting. They are winding each other up into a frenzy. Painted Man lights the lighter and gleefully waves the flame in Darren's face. Darren stumbles onto his feet and runs. Tilda watches, her stomach twisting in horror, as he is chased and knocked down, kicked and punched. He runs into the road, screaming and pleading, and then his voice becomes fainter as he gets further away.

Tilda directs her attention to Painted Man just as he flicks the lit lighter onto the tent. The stuff bursts into flames. The fire roars loudly behind her. His face glows eerily in the light of the flames. Tilda wonders if she misunderstood and he really is a demon. There would be no point trying to touch his heart if that were the case. Briefly, their eyes meet. Too brief to make meaningful contact but long enough to convince her that there is a human being somewhere within. She seizes the opportunity.

'I am Tilda,' she says clearly and confidently, pointing to herself. 'Tell me your name.' She thinks there is a slight shift in his energy.

'Fuck off, you Paki,' he says. His voice is slurred and his eyes are unfocussed, but he has responded. Encouraged, Tilda tries again. 'Come. Sit down and talk to me.'

'Shut the fuck up,' he shouts, then spits in her face and curses her in words she doesn't recognise. She focusses on sending a beam of light directly from her heart to his. It is the hardest act of concentration she has ever done. She imagines the beam is burning through the demons and travelling to his heart. She visualises the light carrying a message of pure love. She breathes into the light. Great Mother is filling the space between them. She enters a dimension without sounds, without smells, without images, without thoughts. Time itself stops.

And starts again. She sees a look of confusion cross Painted Man's face. He leaps to his feet and runs off into the night, his two mates close behind.

Tilda is on her own, a scene of devastation around her. Her teeth are chattering. She is shaking from the cold and the shock. She waits for Darren for what seems like hours until Charmall advises her to go home. When she creeps in the front door, Carol is awake, sitting on the sofa wrapped in a duvet.

'Tilda, where have you been? I've been so anxious. Are you all right?'

Tilda crawls into the duvet and cuddles Carol tightly. If she weren't so worried about Darren, she would enjoy the feeling of safety and warmth, of being held in Carol's arms. When she stops shivering, she says, 'I went to see my friend Darren, but angry men came. Vhey made fire. I don't understand why. Explain to me, please.'

Carol asks a lot of questions, becoming more agitated with each answer. Tilda is surprised by her reaction. Instead of sympathy,

Carol seems angry, not at the men who attacked her and Darren, but at Tilda. She speaks in a low, fierce voice, throwing words as if they were rocks. 'What were you doing after midnight sitting in the motorway underpass with a homeless man? That's asking for trouble. You should have stayed home. It's not safe to be out on the street like that.'

Tilda disentangles herself from the duvet and moves away so that she can see Carol's face better. She understands that Carol is frightened for her. She wishes, not for the first time, that Carol were more direct and able to admit her fear, rather than hiding it under anger and blame.

'But Carol, why not safe to go out in night?'

Carol expels her breath noisily and throws more rock-words. 'Because there are men like that roaming the streets, full of hate. They were probably out of their heads on drugs or alcohol. Looking for someone, anyone, to beat up. A homeless man is an easy target. Women are and Black people are. They could have killed you or raped you.'

'Who are vhese men? Why are vhey full of hate?' Tilda asks. She is beginning to understand why Carol believes she must lock the doors and put an alarm on every night.

'It's just human nature,' Carol says. She sounds impatient. 'Throughout history, from prehistoric times, people fight and hate anyone who's different. Don't tell me there's no violence where you come from.'

'Of course not. No. Vhere's no violence. Not like vhis,' Tilda says abruptly. 'We argue, we disagree and vhen we come togevher. We talk and listen and chant. We do ceremonies to bring us back into harmony. We have Great Movher to help us.' Her voice has grown louder.

'Well, I've never heard of such a place,' Carol says flatly. 'This is real life, the way it is in this world.' She turns away, scowling.

Tilda isn't ready to drop the subject. She takes Carol's face in her hands and looks into her eyes. 'Carol, I want to know. Tell me, please, what is vhe way it is in your world? Who are your Wise Ones? Where are vhey? What do vhey do to bring harmony, to take hate away from men's hearts? And why so much hate in vhere hearts?'

Carol shakes her head. 'Tilda, I can't answer those questions. It's four in the morning. Could we talk about it another time?'

Tilda sighs. She wonders whether Carol will ever answer her questions, whatever the time of day. Over the next few days, whenever Tilda brings the subject up, Carol has an excuse for not talking about it. On the third day, while Francis is with Sue at her Singing Group, Carol and Tilda meet Alison in a cafe. While Carol is at the counter ordering drinks and food, Tilda seizes her chance.

'Alison, tell me who are Wise Ones here. Why men have hate in hearts and attack me and Darren?'

'Whoa, Tilda,' Alison cries. 'Right in the deep end yet again. You sure don't go in for small talk, do you? Who attacked you? What happened?'

While Tilda tells the story, Carol appears with a tray of drinks, chatting about the food. Tilda pays no attention. She senses this is another one of those times when Carol doesn't want to talk about the attack. She is grateful that Alison does. When Tilda describes the spider painting on one of the men's necks, Alison asks her to draw it. She gasps when Tilda shows her the drawing.

'That's a swastika,' Alison says, taking her hand off her mouth. 'It's the symbol of white supremacists, racists, white people who hate Black people, Jews, immigrants, homeless people, everyone really who's not white. That's why they attacked you. It's because you're Black and Darren is homeless.'

Tilda closes her eyes and thanks Great Mother for the turmeric tea Carol has given her. 'I don't understand. What means white people, Black people, Jews, immigrants?'

'You're Black, like me. Carol and Sue are white. Look at our skin colour, our hair colour, our eyes.' Alison seems surprised at Tilda's ignorance. Tilda stares at her, suddenly aware that her knowledge of words for colour is inadequate. She thinks that her own skin colour is brown, like the colour of Mother Earth's rich soil. Carol's skin is definitely not white, like a white cloud against a blue sky. Tilda looks round the crowded cafe.

'Is she white?' Tilda asks, pointing to a woman with jet black hair and brown eyes sitting at a nearby table.

'No. She's Chinese,' Alison replies, in a low voice. Tilda guesses she doesn't want the woman to hear her.

'But her skin colour and eyes are same as Carol's,' Tilda says.

Carol mutters under her breath. 'It's not just skin colour, Tilda. Anyway, my eyes are hazel, not brown.'

Tilda stares at the Chinese woman, aware that she is studying her as if she were an object rather than a human being. The woman glances at her, frowns and quickly looks away. Tilda knows she has hurt her and feels a stab of guilt.

'Alison, my eyes are not brown. Vhey're blue but you said I am Black.'

Alison sighs. 'Yes, you are Black because your skin is dark brown and your hair is kinky and black. It's mainly skin colour.' She pauses. 'Except when it's not.'

'What if I want to be white or Chinese? Can I choose?'

Alison shakes her head and frowns. 'Sorry, mate. You can't choose. It's chosen for you by other people. It's just who you are. And you should be proud to be Black.'

'Why should I be proud of colour of my skin? Should I be proud of my blue eyes? Are you proud to be white, Carol?' Tilda says, staring intently at Alison. Clearly, she doesn't understand the word "proud". She thought it meant to be glad of one's achievements. She's proud of learning English, of healing her body after the car hit her, and of getting out of Carol's house without setting off the alarm.

Maybe "proud" means appreciating one's beautiful body. Carol certainly struggles with that. So she isn't surprised when Carol says she isn't proud to be white.

Carol shoots an anxious glance at Alison. 'But that's different. I don't really think about being white. I'm not racist. It's just not something that comes up in my life, I guess.'

Alison sniffs. 'It's something I'm aware of every moment of my life.'

Tilda tilts her head to one side and looks from one to the other. There's an atmosphere between them, like a disturbance in the air. Something is not being spoken. Tilda waits but neither woman speaks. They're both not looking at each other.

Finally, Alison says, 'Where you come from Tilda, is everyone brown skinned like you? And what about the leaders, the people on top. What colour are they?'

Tilda thinks for some time. Eventually, she says, 'I am one of ten Wise Ones. Yes, we are leaders but we are not on top. Some of us have light coloured skin, ovhers darker like me. Some have brown eyes, some blue. We all have beautiful bodies. We don't fhink we're ugly. We train for many, many years to be Wisdom Keepers. We're proud we bring harmony and healing to our people. We're proud we have no violence. But here, so much violence and hate. Where are your Wise Ones?'

Alison snorts. 'They're not our politicians, that's for sure. They want people to be divided so they can rule over us. They create the conditions that lead to violence and hatred.'

'I know. Vhe trees tell me,' Tilda says. She has heard the same story every time she talks to trees – the story of disconnection. 'In your world, people see trees as separate fhings, as different, as not part of web of life. And not just trees, but animals, birds, the earth and even people.'

Alison is listening intently, nodding her head. She seems to understand. Tilda feels encouraged. Perhaps she is expressing herself clearly. It's hard to tell what Carol is thinking as she's looking at her soup.

'Before we cut down a tree in my world,' Tilda continues, 'we talk to tree, ask tree to forgive us, ask Great Movher for blessing. Vhat is how it should be. But sometimes, people forget. Sometimes, vhey cut down trees wivhout asking for Great Movher's blessing. It is happening more and more in my time. I see now where it leads.'

Alison nods. 'It leads to the slave trade, to wars, to a collective psychosis, the illusion that people with dark skin are not fully human.' She sighs. 'Tilda, you ask questions that sound like you don't know about racism or about the modern world. I know you said you came here from Neolithic times but that doesn't make sense. I don't believe it. Where are you from really?'

Carol looks up, suddenly interested.

Tilda takes a deep breath. 'It is true. I come from five fhousand years ago. It is first time I did travel to different time. Great Movher told me to come. I go home in two moons.'

She can see that Alison is not convinced. Her eyes are narrowed and her lips pursed. She searches Tilda's face, then shrugs. 'OK, whatever. Look, I'm sorry you were attacked. That's a horrible experience. What about your friend? How is he now?'

'I can't find him. I look every day. I worry for him.' A tight knot has formed in Tilda's stomach at the mention of Darren.

'Maybe I can help,' Alison says kindly. 'I know where all the shelters are for homeless people in Bristol.'

Tilda nods. She is grateful but doubts that Darren would go to a shelter. She makes a silent promise to Darren to keep looking until she finds him.

Chapter 23. Carol

*D*amn, *her aim is good,* Carol thinks, dodging a barrage of clothes her mother has thrown at her. Cautiously, she creeps up the stairs. She doesn't know how she will calm her mother down, but she is determined to try. Sue and Alison are coming over for dinner in an hour and she will not let Francis spoil her evening.

'You drove Tilda away,' Francis shrieks as she lobs a white cardigan on a wooden coat hanger at Carol. 'Where is she? She's been gone for days. You made her go.'

Carol grits her teeth. It's true; Tilda has been gone for days. Two days and five hours, to be precise. During each minute of those two days and five hours, Carol's stomach has been twisting and churning and aching. She knows that Tilda is looking for Darren, that she's been looking for him ever since the attack. It's been four weeks and she hasn't yet found him. Why can't Tilda give up her search and accept that Darren has left Bristol? Or better still, why can't she just leave Great Mother to sort Darren out? Carol would like to tell Great Mother a thing or two.

This is the longest Tilda has stayed out. Before she left, she assured Carol that she would be back for the dinner with Sue and Alison. But Carol hasn't slept. She hasn't eaten, done any work, cooked any meals or done any housework. And now Francis is having one of her rages.

With each step she takes, Carol's grip on her self-control slips. She feels like a volcano on the verge of erupting. As she reaches the landing, she starts screaming, 'Shut up. Shut up,' over and over. Francis backs away, shocked. To Carol's surprise, she sinks to the floor, covers her face with her hands and sobs. Carol feels no sympathy.

'I can't take it anymore, Mum. I can't do it. You can't do this to me. You have to stop it. Put the clothes away and come downstairs when you're calm.' Carol speaks in a clipped, merciless tone and marches back downstairs just as Sue breezes in the front door.

'Hi Carol. I can't see a thing. My glasses are all steamed up. Here, hold this.' Sue hands Carol a damp cardboard box and a bottle of wine. She hangs her dripping rain gear over the radiator. 'Could I have a towel, please? My raincoat is not as waterproof as I thought.'

Carol takes a few breaths to calm herself and gives her a kiss. 'Did you swim over? Where's Alison?'

'She's with her dad. She'll be here in half an hour. This rain is incredible. Here, I brought you profiteroles for dessert and some wine. So, how are you?'

'Sue, thank god you're here. Everything's falling apart. Mum's just had one of her rages. She's been throwing her clothes at me. Ben is threatening to leave uni and come here, like, tomorrow. Tilda's gone walkabout and I haven't slept in days. I don't know if I can go on.' She ends on a sob and stands in the hallway with her arms hanging helplessly by her side.

Sue pulls Carol into a hug and pats her on the back.

'And I almost forgot,' Carol mumbles into Sue's shoulder. 'I got a final notice from my job. They're going to fire me.' She ought to be wailing by now, but she's run out of energy.

'I'll pour you a glass of wine,' Sue says. 'Now you go sit in the living room and I'll make dinner. Go on. Don't worry about a thing.'

From the living room, Carol hears Sue bustling in the kitchen and Francis singing loudly off-key: *'Do you need anybody? I need somebody to love.'* She seems calmer. Maybe she should yell at her mother more often.

Soon Sue is singing along: *'Oh I get by with a little help from my friends. Mm I get high with a little help from my friends.'*

Alison arrives with another bottle, wearing dangling earrings and a large crystal around her neck. She joins Carol in the living room and talks at length about her father's prostate cancer treatment.

Tilda is not back. She said she would be back tonight.

Sue's bottle is drunk by all except Jason, who grumbles his discontent not to be allowed a taste.

Carol is convinced that Tilda is living on the street, that she has abandoned Carol, preferring Darren.

A simple dinner of baked potatoes and fish fingers is served. Carol eats nothing.

Tilda's profiterole is fought over and shared between Francis and Jason.

Dishes are washed.

A vivid image of Tilda lying in a ditch by the side of the road, dead, flashes into Carol's mind.

The World's Greatest Dancer is put on BBC iPlayer and watched by Jason and Francis in the living room.

Alison's bottle is opened.

The front door opens. Tilda strides through the front door, looking as if she's been in the shower with her clothes on. She is not wearing the raincoat she'd gone out in. Her head is bare, water streaking her coarse black hair. She is shivering, her T-shirt, jeans and moccasins soaked.

Carol gasps and is about to rush to her, but stops. A man is hovering in the doorway behind Tilda. Tilda's raincoat is draped over his shoulders and her fleece is wrapped round his head like a scarf. He is as wet as Tilda and shivering even more violently. His teeth are chattering and his skin is a jaundiced yellow with bright red spots on his cheeks.

'Vis is Darren. He's very ill,' Tilda announces. She guides him into the living room. Jason and Francis are on the sofa, their eyes glued to the TV. Tilda has to call them several times before they notice her and the sick man. Reluctantly, they relinquish the sofa and back away. Tilda helps Darren lie down. She covers him with a blanket without removing the raincoat or his shoes, then sits on the floor where she begins chanting.

No one speaks. Carol has silently moved out of the kitchen followed by Sue and Alison and is standing with Jason and Francis in front of the TV, watching Tilda stroke Darren's head.

'He's getting the sofa wet,' Francis complains. 'Who is he?'

'He's Darren. He is very ill,' Tilda interrupts her chanting to answer. 'Make tea please.'

Carol is rooted to the spot. She barely notices that Jason leaves the living room and returns with a cup of tea. He offers it to Tilda who tries to get Darren to sit up and drink. Darren is too weak. Tilda resumes chanting.

Alison strokes the crystal around her neck and says to the room, 'We need to call an ambulance and get him to hospital.'

Tilda shakes her head. 'He needs herbs. Needs to be dry and warm. Needs to sleep. Come help.'

Still chanting, she unwraps her fleece from Darren's head and pulls the raincoat off him. Just as she is about to remove his shoes, Alison shrieks, 'No, don't!' It is too late. The shoe comes off and it is like a stink bomb has exploded. Tilda recoils. Darren groans, his teeth chattering. Francis and Jason flee upstairs. Jason comes down soon after, holding his nose with one hand and a box of paracetamol in the other. He hands them to Tilda, then retreats to the other side of the room. Carol has not moved. She is in shock. It's one thing for Tilda to befriend a homeless man and visit him on the street. It's something else entirely to bring him into her home.

Alison has already dialled 999. Carol can hear her say in her authoritative, social worker voice, 'His name is Darren Smith. I think he's having a heart attack.'

'He's not having a heart attack,' Francis snarls when Alison hangs up.

Alison shrugs. 'I've worked with homeless people. I don't know if he has a heart condition or not. He probably does. But if I didn't tell them that he does, then he would have to wait for several hours for an ambulance. I'm sorry, Tilda, there are many people in Darren's situation. You cannot save them all.'

'He's my friend,' Tilda says, stroking Darren's forehead.

'I know,' Alison says. 'He's clearly very ill. He needs medical care. They'll look after him in the hospital.'

Tilda looks at each of them in turn, then shrugs and nods. In half an hour, the ambulance arrives and whisks Darren away. Once Darren is gone, Tilda disappears upstairs. Carol hovers at the bottom of the stairs, wondering whether Tilda is upset or angry. But Tilda is smiling when she comes back down, dry and comfortable in the plaid nightie Carol bought for her a few weeks before.

'Why did you bring that man here?' Carol demands, her anger overtaking her anxiety. Before Tilda can answer, the volcano erupts. Carol starts shouting. 'All of you. Leave me alone. Go away. I've had it.' Even as she utters the words, she knows she doesn't mean them but before she can take them back, they all melt away. Sue and Alison slip out the front door and go home. Tilda ushers Francis upstairs. Jason goes to his room.

Carol is left on her own in the kitchen. She finishes the half-full bottle of wine left on the table and drifts into a stupor, her head on the kitchen table. Some time later, she lifts her head and sees Tilda watching her from the doorway. Carol struggles to her feet and collapses on the kitchen floor where she lies, looking up at the ceiling.

She's vaguely aware that her head is in Tilda's lap and that Tilda is stroking her forehead and chanting quietly. Times passes, whether hours or minutes she can't say. Eventually, there is a shift. The tears flow down her cheeks, then sobs rack her body. Then wailing. She feels she will never stop crying. The backlog of tears is a bottomless pit. Tilda props her up and hands her paper towels.

More hours go by and still she weeps and still Tilda strokes her forehead and chants. Finally she sleeps. It is dark when she wakes. She is lying on the kitchen floor, covered by a blanket. Tilda is asleep next to her, holding her tight.

This time, she wakes to rage. She begins muttering and soon graduates to shrieking and flailing her arms. She kicks her feet on the floor, then gets to her feet driven by the impulse to find something to throw. Grabbing a chair, she throws it across the room. Before she can throw anything else, Tilda wraps her in the blanket and holds her tightly on her lap. Carol thrashes and yells but the blanket is an effective straitjacket. Eventually she lies still and lets Tilda rock her back and forth.

At first light, Jason appears in his school uniform, humming '*I get by with a little help from my friends.*' He is on his way to the fridge when he nearly trips over Carol. Startled, he yelps and jumps into the air.

'Mum, what's wrong? What happened?' He kneels down beside Carol who stares through him. She can't make her eyes focus. She dimly registers his look of panic and Tilda's urgent instructions to call Sue, Alison and Moira.

As Jason leaves to make the phone calls, Francis wanders into the kitchen. She takes one look at Carol lying on the floor and starts screaming abuse at her. Carol leaps to her feet, flinging the blanket away. If Tilda hadn't stopped her, she would have strangled her mother. Carol starts ranting loudly and pacing frenetically. Francis flees back upstairs. Jason is sobbing with his hands over his ears. Tilda is standing nearby, keeping a close eye on Carol and efficiently moving knives and throwable objects out of sight.

'I've had enough. I hate everyone. Fuck you, Mum. Fuck you, Ben. Fuck you, Tilda and Great Mother. Fuck you, Mike. It's not fair. You have no right to treat me this way. I'm not doing it anymore. You can all fuck off.'

Carol continues screaming as Sue and Alison walk in. She sees Alison's mouth moving and Tilda collapsed on a chair looking exhausted. She hears Alison speaking comforting words in a soft, soothing voice. She watches Alison gradually move closer and closer. When Alison reaches her, Carol falls into her arms weeping.

'I can't go on. I can't go on.'

Alison takes charge and convenes an emergency case conference. She orders everyone into the kitchen. For once, Carol is not irritated by Alison in her social worker role. Still crying but subdued, she allows herself to be settled on a chair. Moira arrives and is bundled straight into the meeting. Jason has not gone to school and stands next to Carol, patting her on the shoulder. Francis is brought down by Tilda who parks her as far away from Carol as she can get. Sue makes cups of tea.

'We need to work out what you need and what we can do to help you, Carol,' Alison says. 'Can you stop crying so we can talk?'

Carol takes a shaky breath. The tears keep flowing.

Alison studies her, making a rapid assessment. 'We better call your GP, get an emergency appointment. I can take you.'

'No,' Carol moans. 'No bloody drugs. No. No. No GP.'

She starts hyperventilating, her breathing getting more and more shallow and rapid. Tilda steps quickly in behind Carol's chair and puts one hand over her forehead, the other around her front. She hums a wordless tune, softly and lovingly, holding Carol firmly.

Jason holds Carol's hand. 'Let's sing her a lullaby. She used to sing this one to me. Do any of you know Hush Little Baby?'

It turns out that everyone but Tilda knows the lullaby and she picks it up by the second round. They surround Carol with a choir of sweet voices. Even Francis joins in, having no trouble remembering the words. Carol closes her eyes and relaxes, letting herself be soothed. Her crying eases gradually, her sobs weaving in and out of the singing. She doesn't want the lullaby ever to end. Why can't she have this every day?

A memory comes to her. Years ago, before Francis moved in to live with her, she took five-year-old Jason and fifteen-year-old Ben to Thailand. They spent a day at an elephant sanctuary near Chiangmai where abused elephants were rescued and rehabilitated. A thin, wiry man, called a mahout, guided a group of visitors to sit among the herds of elephants. While they watched, an elephant standing slightly apart from the others suddenly let out a loud trumpet call. Jason had grabbed Carol's hand in fear. Even Ben had run to her side, but the mahout had remained calm.

'Don't worry. She just wants to be admired,' he'd said, smiling fondly at his charges. 'She had a hard childhood. Here in this sanctuary, the elephants heal each other.'

As they watched, four other adults ran over to the trumpeting elephant and stroked her with their trunks. They kissed her and caressed her for half an hour. Carol had been touched by the sight. There was something very tender, gentle and loving about their caresses. It occurred to her that people could learn a lot about healing from elephants.

Carol pats Jason's hand. 'Do you remember the elephants we met in Thailand, Jason, how they caressed each other with their trunks?'

Jason nods eagerly and rubs his nose against his mother's cheek.

'I feel a bit better now,' Carol says. 'Especially with you kissing me with your trunk.'

Tilda faces the group and makes an announcement. 'Friends, listen. In my home, to help each ovher, we talk. Use talking stick.' She picks up a wooden spoon. 'You talk when you hold vhe talking stick. You start, Karul.'

Carol takes a deep shaky breath and reaches for the spoon. 'I need to get away for at least a week. No responsibility. No work. No Mum. No Ben.' Her words begin tumbling out faster and louder. 'No house. I'm sorry Jason, but I can't even cope looking after you. I need a break, a rest, just for a while. I'll come back.' The tears start again.

Alison takes the spoon and faces Jason. 'You can stay with us while Carol's getting better. Is that okay with you?' He nods, wide-eyed.

She passes the spoon to Francis who holds it angrily. 'I don't know what's the matter with you Carol. You go off, do what you want. You always do. Think about nobody but yourself. I'll stay here with Tilda.'

Several voices rise up in protest. Carol feels the rage bubbling up and before she can stop it, she leaps to her feet and screams wordlessly at Francis. Francis raises the spoon as if to hit Carol. Only Jason's terrified face brings Carol to her senses. She sits back down, breathing heavily and fuming. Alison wrestles the spoon off Francis and hands it to Tilda.

'I stay wivh Karul,' Tilda says carefully but without hesitation, and passes the spoon to Moira. Carol blows her breath out, feeling weak with relief. Tilda has seen her at her worst and is still willing to be with her.

'I have an idea. It may just work,' Moira says excitedly, waving the spoon in front of her. 'There are lots of chalets available at Dunster Beach this time of year. I often go there to paint. We could book two of them near each other. I could stay in one and Carol, you and Tilda could stay in another. It's by the sea. There's lots of fresh air. What do you think, Carol?'

Carol nods. She looks shyly at Tilda who smiles back.

'Two weeks,' Carol says. 'Minimum.'

Moira still has the talking stick. 'Francis, how about spending some time with your son? You stayed with him when Carol went to Ireland, didn't you? It could be a really nice holiday for you.'

Francis agrees on one condition. 'I want Tilda to come with me.'

Moira hands the spoon to Tilda who looks Francis in the eye and says, 'I stay to look after Karul.'

'Carol's not ill,' Francis spits out. 'She's weak and useless. She wants attention. I knew this wouldn't work. I want you, Tilda, to look after me.'

Tilda simply shakes her head and gives the spoon back to Moira. Carol glares at her mother.

'Well then, you have no choice,' Moira speaks sharply. 'If Carol's unable to look after you for whatever reason, you'll have to go somewhere else. Could you talk to John, Alison? You've got that professional manner. He'll take a social worker more seriously than an artist.'

She hands Alison the spoon. 'Is that okay, Carol?' Alison asks. 'Shall I call John and tell him that I'm your social worker and he has to take care of Francis?'

Carol nods. 'He did take her last November but said he couldn't do it again. But maybe he'll listen to a social worker.'

'He'll put me in a home,' Francis bursts out, sounding distressed and panicky. Her face crumples and she covers her mouth with her hand. Carol feels a twinge of sympathy which quickly fades as she remembers what Francis has just said about her.

Alison turns to Francis and says in her professional, no nonsense voice, 'Let's see what happens when I've talked to John. Until then, we have to accept that there are no alternatives. We have to focus on getting Carol back to functioning. Are there any other issues to discuss?'

Sue waves her hand and asks for the spoon. 'I'll call your work and tell them you're sick. You will have to go to your GP for a sick note. They can prescribe something for you.' Before Carol can object, Sue quickly adds, 'You don't have to take it.'

'What about Ben?' Carol asks.

'What about him?' Alison says. 'Is there any point calling Mike? Or shall I ask John to keep an eye out for him? What does he need anyway?'

'Money for his uni fees and stuff,' Carol says. 'Me to rant at.'

'That's not top priority at this moment,' Alison says, ignoring the second need. 'We'll deal with that later. This is a crisis meeting. You could send him a text saying you're ill and will be out of contact for a few weeks, but you don't have to even think about him right now. OK?'

The meeting ends. Carol is tucked up in bed with a hot water bottle. While she sleeps, phone calls are made and arrangements finalised. Three days later, Carol has been to the GP, Jason has moved in with Sue and Alison, Francis has been collected by John's wife Sheila for her London holiday and Moira has booked two chalets at Dunster

Beach. Carol knows just how the elephant felt when her mates caressed her with their trunks.

Chapter 24. Carol

On the day of departure when Moira arrives, Carol is in her bedroom staring vacantly at her wardrobe. An empty backpack is on the bed.

'Should I take two long-sleeved tops or three?' she asks Moira, paralysed by the enormity of the decision. Without further discussion, Moira scoops out the contents of Carol's chest of drawers and dumps everything in the backpack. She clears out the wardrobe and carries as much as she can to the car. Carol follows her, carrying a pair of flip flops. Tilda is walking around Moira's car, talking to it gently.

'What are you doing, Tilda?' Moira asks as she stuffs Carol's clothes in the boot. Carol hovers nearby, staring blankly at Moira. How does she move so quickly? It's exhausting watching her.

'I am making friend wivh car,' Tilda is saying, patting the car's metallic blue bottom. 'What is its name?'

Moira rolls her eyes. 'It's a car. It doesn't have a name. OK, yes it does. It's a Nissan Qashqai. Right, get Carol in the front seat, would you Tilda? She seems to be in some kind of dream world.'

More like a nightmare, Carol thinks. Or like wading through treacle. She woke at three in the morning, her mind racing, and hadn't been able to sleep for several hours.

'I call it Nissan,' Tilda says.

'Whatever!' Moira jumps into the driver's seat and starts the car. Carol wonders why she's so impatient to get on the road. Perhaps she regrets agreeing to look after her for two weeks. But the thoughts drift away as soon as they begin.

'I'm stopping at the next service station,' Moira announces, shortly after getting on the motorway. 'I want to talk to you, Carol, on your own. Tilda, would you mind leaving us for a while?'

Carol watches nervously as Tilda climbs out of the car and trots across the car park, her head swivelling rapidly from side to side. She heads towards a small patch of green grass with a solitary rowan tree. Carol holds her breath, praying that she won't get hit by one of the cars driving in and out and around the car park.

'Carol,' Moira says, taking a deep breath. 'Alison took me aside yesterday and briefed me on your care plan, as she calls it. Now, as a crucial member of your support team, she thought I needed to know a few salient details about what's going on for you. She was rather surprised that you hadn't seen fit to tell me that something rather, let's say, momentous has been going on between you and Tilda and that it's been going on for more than two months.'

Carol is sliding down in her seat, feeling distinctly uncomfortable.

'And I'd like to get this out in the open because I've signed up to be part of your so-called care plan and I really need to be in the loop, if you don't mind. So is there anything you'd like to share with me, Carol, or do I have to get all my information second-hand?'

Carol winces. She opens her mouth to speak but no words come out. This is what I want from my life, to act from love, she reminds herself. She hasn't acted lovingly towards Moira in the past, but she can remedy that now. Moira is giving her a chance. On the other hand, she is in the middle of a major nervous breakdown and can't be expected to be rational and courageous. Why can't Moira give her a break? What if this confrontation triggers another fit of rage or sends her spiralling into an unstoppable outbreak of weeping? Carol feels resentment towards Moira building up. This isn't fair.

She can see Tilda sitting on the grass across the car park leaning against the tree. Is she sending a message with her eyes? Carol doesn't exactly hear any words but she senses Tilda's voice commanding her to drop the resentment. Easier said than done, she pouts. Nevertheless, she sits further up and rubs her sweaty hands on her jeans.

'You're right,' she mutters. 'I'm sorry. I should have said something before.' Moira doesn't seem satisfied. The resentment surges up again. 'But you're so judgemental. I couldn't face it.'

'Oh I see. It's my fault, is it?' Moira cries, smacking her forehead. 'You're blaming me for something you should have done. You didn't even give me a chance to be judgemental. You just assumed I would judge you.'

Carol clams up. She looks out the window at the cars moving restlessly around the car park, like the thoughts roaming through her mind.

'I'm sorry, Moira.' It seems like the right thing to say but the words stick in her throat. Still, it is the best she can do at the moment.

'Don't say you're sorry, Carol. That doesn't mean anything. What are you sorry about? Are you sorry that I'm challenging you or what?'

'I don't know. I'm ... well, I find it hard to, you know, stand up to you. Or to anyone. That's why I'm in this mess. I'm pathetic, useless, like my mother says.'

'No Carol, you're going to have to do better than that. Don't hide behind your self-pity.' Moira grips the steering wheel and bangs her head against it.

Carol grimaces, wishing Moira would stop being so dramatic. 'I can't help it. That's why I've got to get away. That's why you set up the care plan. I want to do better but I can't get there yet. Please give me some time.'

Carol feels a murmur pushing into her mind. *Shut up, Tilda*, she thinks. *That's the best I can do right now. Give me a break. Don't pretend you're talking to that tree.*

'I hate it when people make assumptions about me,' Moira is nearly shouting. 'It's true I have strong opinions and not everybody can deal with that. But I don't judge you for having a relationship with Tilda. Why would you think that? Do you really think I'm homophobic? Really? Me?! That hurts that you think that about me.'

Carol looks over at Moira's stricken face and feels even more dreadful.

'It's the things you said about Tilda being a refugee, about me using her to look after my mother. I thought you were accusing me of exploiting her. Of being like a man screwing the maid.'

Moira gasps. 'I never said anything like that or even thought it.'

There is silence. Carol can't remember clearly if Moira has said something explicit or whether she's made it up. Glancing at Moira's red face, her hands gripping the steering wheel, Carol feels a longing to be real with her friend, to see her for who she is. Slowly and carefully, she chooses her words. 'I made assumptions. I didn't check out those assumptions with you.'

She pauses. There is more she wants to say but she isn't used to having this kind of conversation with Moira. *Speak the truth, the whole truth,* she thinks she hears Tilda say in her mind. *It's so hard to do,* she thinks back. Moira is still waiting, still gripping the steering wheel, staring straight ahead through the windscreen.

'Moira, I don't mean to hurt you. I didn't think how you might be feeling. Your friendship means a lot to me. I appreciate what you're doing so much.' Screwing up her face, she reaches for Moira's hand. Moira unclenches her hands from the steering wheel and grasps Carol's hand. Carol breathes a sigh of relief.

Moira nods slowly. 'I can kind of see how it happened that you thought I was judging you for bringing Tilda over. I have been thrown by what you've done, smuggling her into the country. Nobody knowing anything about her, where she's from, other than this fantastical story about time travel from the Neolithic time. It is rather, um, unusual. And so not like you. I am sorry if I came across as judgemental.'

The air sizzles, like an electric current has been switched on and is flowing between them. She smiles at Moira and closes her eyes.

Moira smiles back. 'Let's promise to be more honest with each other in future. Check things out more. I'll try to be more mindful of what I say. I'm really sorry if I gave you the impression that you were exploiting Tilda.'

'Thanks, Moira. I've got to crash out now, sleep for a bit.'

As soon as the words are out of her mouth, she falls asleep. Tilda appears at that moment and settles herself in the back seat, chanting quietly. Moira puts the radio on to Classic FM and drives the rest of the way without talking.

Carol doesn't wake up until they drive into the Dunster Beach site and up to their chalet, at which point she is overcome by panic. The chalets are smaller than she'd expected and the sea is closer and bigger. The word chalet evoked an image of a cute Swiss cabin with overhanging eaves nestled in the snow in the mountains, but these are square wooden boxes, not much more than a large caravan. A row of the tiny chalets lies along a flat, bleak beach which stretches interminably in both directions. Lying in wait, biding its time, is the channel, choosing its moment to rise up in a tidal wave and obliterate the beach and the chalets.

Moira clearly loves the place and is eager to show it off, but Carol barely notices how cosy the chalet is. Her chalet is decorated in a nautical style which she would take delight in if she hadn't been feeling so agitated. The double glass doors opening on to an outdoor patio and then to the sea make her feel exposed. There is no escape from the sight or the sound of the sea and the wind.

As soon as Moira parks, Tilda bolts out of the car and runs to the water's edge where she stays for some time looking out to sea and skipping around. Carol guesses she is thanking Great Mother for their safe arrival. Carol does not feel thankful. She wraps herself in a blanket and sinks into the sofa, her back to the sea. Moira hums happily while she unpacks, stocks the kitchen cupboards in both chalets and set up her easel in the next door chalet.

Tilda bounces back to the chalet. 'Come see animals,' she cries, trying to pull the blanket off Carol. 'What are animals?'

She's just like Tigger in Winnie the Pooh, Carol thinks ungraciously. She won't come and see anything, let alone animals. Moira appears from the next door chalet and says, 'Let me show you where the shower blocks are and the little shop. And there's a cafe in the shop.'

'What you call vhe little animals in holes in ground? Vhere.' Tilda points.

'Those are rabbits,' Moira says dismissively. 'They're everywhere. They're a big nuisance.'

'You eat vhem?' Tilda asks. 'I catch one for dinner.'

Moira looks at Tilda in horror. 'No. Are you crazy? I'll make dinner tonight. Come over to my chalet to eat in about an hour. Carol, are you going to have a nap?'

Carol nods, burrowing deeper under the blanket.

'I go explore,' Tilda says, heading for the door.

'No,' Carol cries. She hadn't meant to scream but the thought of being left on her own terrifies her.

'Come nap in my chalet, Carol,' Moira offers.

Tilda waves and disappears out the door to explore. Carol's panic spreads through her body until she feels certain she will never see Tilda again. Sobbing, she calls out to Tilda. 'Come back. Moira, get Tilda. She's gone. She won't come back, ever.'

'Don't be silly Carol. She'll be back. Come and have a cup of tea. You don't need to get so panicky.'

Moira bustles about, making tea and preparing a cosy nest for Carol to cuddle up on the sofa in her chalet next door. But Carol is hyperventilating. When she doesn't calm herself down, Moira volunteers to go out and find Tilda.

'Don't leave me on my own,' Carol pleads. 'The sea is coming. I know it's coming.'

'No, honestly, Carol. There's nothing to worry about. I've been here many times before and the highest tide is down at the bottom of those wooden posts.'

Tilda isn't out for long, much to Carol's relief. Over dinner, a plan is agreed that Moira will be around for Carol during the day and Tilda at night. Moira takes over meal planning and cooking.

Carol feels reassured for the first night and the next day, knowing there is a plan. But late in the evening of the second night, waves of rage begin coursing through her body. Quietly at first, she starts muttering a constant stream of angry invective against everybody.

The muttering escalates into loud ranting and cursing and pacing around the tiny chalet. The urge to throw something grows within her. As she picks up a chair, Tilda runs out and brings Moira from next door. Carol is vaguely aware of the two of them trying to soothe her and of Moira on her phone.

'I just phoned Alison,' Moira says. 'She thinks we should give you the tablets the GP prescribed.'

Carol refuses. She finally crashes out and falls asleep when Tilda swaddles her in a blanket. Moira goes back to her chalet, fully expecting to be called again in the night.

Carol wakes suddenly. Where is she? Nothing looks familiar. She tries to sit up but she can't. The darkness is suffocating. She cries out in panic, waking Tilda who's been lying beside her on the fold-out sofa bed.

'Untie me. Let me go. I need to pee.'

'It's okay, Karul,' Tilda speaks soothingly and helps her out of the restraining blanket. Carol feels the fury rising up. Her mind is racing. A tsunami of grievances threaten to overwhelm her. The only way she can get relief is to move but there is no space in the tiny chalet. Carol flails about bumping into furniture, knocking over the fold-up table, kicking the sofa bed. When Tilda tries to embrace her, Carol pushes her away with such force that she falls on the floor and knocks her head.

Tilda manages to get up and wrestle Carol through the patio doors, grabbing a blanket as they emerge into the wild windy night. Barefoot and without coats, Tilda drags Carol onto the grassy area just beyond the patio.

'Stand on Movher Earfh,' Tilda shouts above the roar of the wind and the waves. 'Movher Earfh takes your anger. She happy to take your anger. Vhen you get balance.'

She wraps the blanket around Carol who is shivering in the cold night air, her teeth chattering.

'Shake your arms. Shake your legs. Stamp feet. Give to Movher

Earfh.'

Carol surprises herself by doing as she is told. After half an hour of downloading her anger into the ground through her bare feet, the grip of the rage eases. She feels drained of energy, but calmer. Her mind clears and she looks at Tilda, suddenly aware of what she's done.

'Oh god, Tilda, I am so sorry I hurt you,' she wails, wringing her hands. 'I don't know what came over me. I've never done that before. Please look at me. I love you. I didn't mean to hurt you.'

Tilda points to her head and grimaces. 'You hurt me, Karul. Vhat is not love. You are out of balance. Like Ben. Like Francis. You do not know how to find balance. Come wivh me. We walk.'

Chastened, Carol hangs her head and walks along the beach with Tilda, the sea on their right, a persistent menacing companion. Carol wants to hold hands, like a small child. She needs reassurance that the sea won't rise up and drown her. She needs to know that Tilda still loves her, but she doesn't dare reach over. How can Tilda forgive her? Yet Tilda did invite her to walk. That must mean something.

'Talk to me,' Tilda suddenly says, as if she knows that Carol is carrying on a conversation in her head without her. 'What do you want?'

I need somebody to love. Could it be anybody? I want somebody to love. The Beatles song comes into her head.

'Love,' she says. 'I want somebody to love. Not anybody but somebody who loves me. Not like my mother or Ben who treat me like shit. I'm sick of their rages. That's not love.'

'Love is here wivh us now,' Tilda says quietly.

'Yes. You love me but you want to leave me.' Carol glances at Tilda to see if she will be angry. Tilda merely nods as if there is no glaring contradiction between these two statements.

'I love you so much that I ...' Carol chokes up. Can she admit how devastated she feels to the lover that has no qualms about leaving? It makes her feel needy and humiliated. If she says what she really feels, would Tilda be more likely to stay or more likely to leave with a sigh of relief to be rid of her?

A gust of wind tears the blanket from her shoulders. As Tilda bends to retrieve it, Carol murmurs under her breath, half hoping that Tilda won't hear, 'I love you with all my heart. I can't live without you, Tilda. I'll fall apart if you go. How can you say you love me and plan to leave me? That's not love.'

'You hurt me,' Tilda says again, pointing to her head. 'Vhat's not love.'

'I know. I did exactly what my mum has done to me. I learned about love from her. I am sorry. I don't know how to do love.'

'Time to learn about love. Learn from Great Movher.'

They walk on in silence. The sea is like a barking dog on a leash, about to charge at her at any moment. Carol does not want to learn about love from Great Mother. Great Mother is nowhere to be seen. She wants Tilda to rescue her. She grabs Tilda's hand, but Tilda's loving squeeze does not reassure her. *Kiss me,* she pleads inwardly. *Please Tilda, save me.*

'We have satnav,' Tilda said. 'Like in Nissan.'

Carol feels confused and angry. What a random comment. She remembers that Tilda had been fascinated by Moira's satnav on the drive to Dunster Beach. The satnav had a lot to say once they left the motorway, especially when Moira took a wrong turn. Many curt commands were needed to get on the right road.

'Satnav is in here.' Tilda puts her hand over Carol's heart and kisses her on the lips.

'I don't think my satnav is switched on,' Carol says ruefully.

Tilda laughs. 'Satnav always on. You need to listen. Your satnav tells you what to do. Satnav says fhirsty. You drink. Satnav says hungry. You eat. Satnav says tired. You rest. Satnav says pee. You pee. Satnav says angry. You listen, welcome anger, hold it wivh love. Always, whatever Satnav says, you listen and get back in balance, on right road, right direction.'

Carol grunts. 'Easier said than done. What if my satnav tells me I'm scared of a tidal wave that I know won't happen? Do I run and hide? That's stupid. The fear is irrational.'

Tilda shakes her head. 'Accept fear. Fear comes to protect you. No wonder you are scared. You are off balance. You don't know Great Movher. Hold fear wivh love like you holded baby Jason close to your heart. Like Great Movher holds you now wivh love.'

Tears prick Carol's eyes. She feels something shift inside, as if a door has opened, not far, just a crack. Through the door is light, a welcome, a glimpse of what she wants. She wants to be held with love. Tilda makes it sound possible, even for her.

'Karul, my precious one,' Tilda says, kissing her neck and nose and mouth. 'My satnav says cold and need to make love wivh you. We go back now.'

Carol doesn't object. Her satnav is saying the same thing.

Chapter 25. Carol

She wakes, her face wet with tears, her heart thumping. The rage is hovering just out of sight, waiting to send her flying out of bed on a path of wanton destruction. The urge to wreck everything she can get her hands on is growing stronger. Her fingers itch to grab whatever is nearby and throw it as hard as she can.

But they have a contingency plan. She and Tilda talked it over before they went to bed. They decided what she will do first, what she will do next, what Tilda will do and what Tilda won't do. If only she could remember what the first step is.

What an idiot! They only made the plan a few hours ago and already she's forgotten. There is only one thing she does remember and that is the reason for the plan. She does not want to hurt Tilda. She really, really does not want to hurt Tilda. This thought has a calming effect.

She sits up and takes a deep breath. And another. The rage recedes slightly but she can feel it waiting to pounce. It's not far enough away. *Stop focussing on the rage*, she tells herself. What else can she focus on? She looks through the patio doors at the beach. Clouds are galloping across the sky like a herd of wild horses running free. In the spaces between the clouds, the moon bursts out and illuminates the beach. As the clouds pass the moon, the landscape is plunged in darkness. The sea lurks, threatening to swarm onto the beach and rise up over the sand to cover the chalet.

The rage slinks behind the chalet and panic takes its place. She pulls the duvet over her head and hugs her knees. Can she wake Tilda? Is that part of the plan? She can't remember. Maybe she's supposed to face her fears on her own. Tilda will be gone in a few months. She's got to learn to be strong and independent.

OK, she'll face them. Slowly, carefully, so as not to wake Tilda, she creeps out of bed and walks to the door. She leans her head against the glass and looks out at the wild, windy night, at the moon and the clouds, at the sea crashing against the sand.

Is the moon dancing with the clouds? Or playing a game of hide and seek? Each time the moon peeks out from behind a cloud, it's laughing, it's happy. It seems to be inviting her to join them. Yes, she's coming. She's on her way, expanding out to the sky, to a space of utter peacefulness. When the clouds pull back and the moon shines forth, the light is not of this world. It is a gentle light, revealing every ripple and wave in stark detail, almost like a photograph or a painting. Yet the light is not coming from the moon. It's shining from within the sea, as if the sea itself is not real but a mask for something else, something she can only describe as holy.

She turns her back on the night sky and shifts her gaze indoors. Amazingly, the holiness is in the chalet as well, in everything she gives her attention to. She can feel it in her thudding heart, in the cold of the floor on the soles of her feet. She feels the holiness in the cloth of her pyjama trousers as it strokes the skin of her leg when she takes a step. She takes another step and doesn't fall over. Tears of gratitude come to her eyes at this miracle of balance. She notices the holy shape of the sink, its perfection. She turns on the tap, acutely aware of the hardness and smoothness of the metal. The water dances and sparkles and flows, as if alive. She hears it singing joyfully. She puts her hands in the water and watches as it pools in her palms. She splashes the water onto her face and savours the wetness. Everything is amazing, everything is holy: the vibrant song of the kettle, the tea bag's potential for flavour, the solidity of the mug holding the water, the vivid whiteness of the milk. She laughs out loud.

Tilda is sitting up on the sofa bed when Carol turns round, holding her cup of tea.

'From the Great Mother through my hands to you, my precious friend,' Carol declares, bowing low. She holds out the mug as if it is the most holy drink in the world and Tilda her most honoured guest. Tilda accepts it graciously, bowing her head in return. She looks appraisingly at Carol and seems satisfied that Carol is not about to burst into tears or explode with rage.

'Great Mother is here,' Carol says dreamily. 'She's been here all along.'

Tilda nods and puts the mug down, undrunk. 'Of course, here. Always here.' She yawns. 'Coming back to bed? It's middle of night. Come and sleep.'

Carol sleeps her first deep sleep in weeks. She is woken by Moira pounding on the door, shouting, 'They're here. Are you two decent?'

She opens her eyes to bright sunshine, a glorious blue sky and a view of the Welsh coast across the channel. A freight ship is parked just offshore. Everything is crystal clear. The water is calm and peaceful, no longer threatening to engulf her.

'Why can't I go in?' she hears Jason ask.

'Because I don't know what state she's in. She and Tilda might not be dressed.' Moira sounds flustered. She barged in the day before and barged straight back out again when she discovered both of them asleep naked on the floor.

'I've seen Mum in her pyjamas before.' Jason sounds puzzled.

'Just a minute,' Carol calls and quickly puts her jeans and fleece on. She throws open the chalet door and hugs Jason.

'I am so glad to see you,' she cries, kissing and cuddling him. It has only been a week but she feels like she's been away for a year. He is so precious, she feels she will burst.

'Mum! Let go.' Jason wriggles out of her embrace and runs into the chalet. 'Wow, what a mess.' He runs to the patio doors. 'Hey, look at the sea. This is so great. Is that Tilda by the water?'

Jason flings open the patio doors and gallops down the beach to Tilda. He throws his arms around her. Carol watches, smiling as they skip about the water's edge together. She turns to greet Sue and Alison.

'Thank you. Thank you. I'm so glad you came,' Carol says. She can't stop smiling. 'Was it okay getting time off work, Alison?'

'Not really but I managed it. Sue cancelled her clients for a week.

It's fine. It was more difficult persuading Jason's school to let him take a week off. The head was itching to call in the education welfare officer but I said I was Jason's social worker and am looking after him while you're having a nervous breakdown. Which is true. I didn't say it, but I gave her the impression the local authority is considering care proceedings. She bought it. Anyway, we're here.'

Carol gulps and wrings her hands. Does Alison really mean what she said about care proceedings? She can't tell with Alison. She says things with such a straight face.

'Alison,' she says hesitantly. 'Is the council going to take Jason into care?'

Alison rolls her eyes and purses her lips. 'It depends on what happens this week, how you respond to treatment.' Carol gasps and Alison laughs. 'Of course not, Carol. Don't be silly. We're going to settle in to our chalet. There's a bunk bed for Jason in ours. Then let's meet up in Moira's chalet for lunch and a meeting to discuss what we're going to do with you.'

With Alison in charge, Carol begins to relax and let herself be cared for. She can take the pressure off Tilda. After lunch with the dishes washed and the table folded up, Alison convenes a meeting. She has a pad of paper and a pen and sits, tapping the pen against the pad until everyone has settled with their cups of tea and hot chocolate.

'Right,' she says in a brisk tone of voice. 'The agenda for today's meeting is to set up an intensive healing programme for Carol for the week. I will chair the meeting. Jason, I'd like you to write down what we agree. Each one of us has their own form of expertise. Start with Sue.'

Carol has not seen Alison in her professional role and isn't sure she is completely comfortable with her business-like manner. Sue quickly puts her tea down, sits up straight and offers two sessions a day of one-to-one counselling. Moira offers art therapy sessions for Carol as well as for anyone else who wants to join in, which ends up being everybody. Jason offers Exploring Therapy which he explains means exploring the area and organising sightseeing outings to Dunster Castle and Minehead. Tilda's gift is Nature Therapy. She offers to take Carol on long walks outdoors whatever the weather and at any time of the day or night. Alison focusses on practical matters. She wants to sit down with Carol to talk about her work, long-term care of Francis and her relationship with Ben. She also organises a cooking and cleaning rota for the week.

By the time the programme has been written up by Jason and time slots allocated, Carol's head is spinning.

'When do I have time to just sit and do nothing?' she complains. 'I think it's too much.'

'We have ways of ensuring compliance,' Alison growls, looking severely at Carol. 'Moira, where are those tablets the GP gave Carol?'

'OK. OK. I'll do whatever you say,' Carol mutters. 'Everyone always bullies me, even my so-called friends.'

'It's hard to resist bullying you, Carol,' Alison says, getting up from the table. 'Maybe one sign of the success of our programme is that you start standing up for yourself and stop playing the victim. In the meantime, WE know what's best for you, so you have to do as we say. The programme starts in an hour with a session of Exploring Therapy led by Jason.'

'Don't be ridiculous, Alison,' Carol huffs, outraged. 'Could you step out of your social worker role please? A little bit of power and it goes to your head. I'm in crisis here. I need your support. I don't need to be bossed around.'

Tilda leans over and strokes Carol's hand. 'Yes, you do. Alison is good leader. Do what she say.'

Jason is brandishing a leaflet. He holds it aloft and shouts, 'Assemble by the cafe, everybody. We're going to the castle.'

'In an hour, Jason,' Carol moans. 'Give me a break.' But she's in her hiking boots with her backpack, waiting by the cafe an hour later. Though it isn't quite as intense as in the night, she can still see the holy light shining through and she can still feel Great Mother's presence wherever she looks.

Chapter 26. Carol

I did the same thing to Tilda that my mother did to me,' Carol confesses to Sue. 'I went into a mindless rage. I had no control. I was swearing and muttering just like Mum. And then I hit out and pushed Tilda and knocked her over and she hit her head.'

They are sitting in Carol and Tilda's chalet with cups of tea, Carol curled up on the sofa and Sue sitting on one of the fold-up chairs. Carol has been awake since four but she made herself lie still and doesn't feel as bad as she thought she would. When Sue arrives at nine sharp as per the schedule, Carol is ready for her. Jason has taken Tilda off for an expedition in the rain, both bouncing with excitement, happy to be out exploring. None of the others joined them.

'She was just trying to calm me down. She didn't say or do anything to provoke me. The thing is, I love her. The last thing I want to do is hurt her.' Carol is staring into the abyss, horrified at what she's shown herself to be capable of. She's never lashed out at her children or at Mike or even her mother though all of them have triggered her at one time or another. Maybe not Jason but certainly Ben and Francis have pushed her buttons. Why didn't she ever attack them? Why Tilda? Carol puts her head in her hands and groans.

'Carol,' Sue interrupts gently. 'Um, I just want to explain that it's not my usual practice to counsel friends. So this is ...'

'I know. I know,' Carol interrupts. 'I just want to talk and you to listen. And not tease me or judge me or give me advice. Alison is going to give me all the advice I need. You can do that, can't you?'

Sue nods and is about to say more when Carol continues speaking, this time with anger. 'I don't want to turn into my mother. I don't want to try to understand her or put any energy into figuring out why she's the way she is. And you can't make me.'

Sue puts her hands up in a gesture of surrender and keeps a poker face. Carol glares. 'I don't care why she has her rages. Do you know how many years I've spent trying to figure out what I did to set her off? It probably started when I was a baby. Ever since I can remember, since before I can remember, I was on guard, monitoring her mood, watching what I said and did. Constantly blaming myself. Constantly being blamed by her. She was always yelling at me, telling me how stupid I was, how clumsy, how ugly, how fat. Blaming me for Mike's desertion, for Ben's behaviour. Comparing me to John. He's so successful, so rich, has such a lovely family. What a failure you are. Blah blah blah.'

Carol is breathing heavily. She has opened the Francis Bubble and is rummaging inside, bringing everything out for inspection. To her surprise, there's nothing of value. Without regret, she discards every single thought and memory she's kept stored in it. Why did she keep all this crap?

Carol burrows into the sofa. Suddenly, she leaps to her feet and flings open the patio doors. Running out, she shouts into the rain, 'Here, Great Mother, take all this shit. You can have my entire Francis Bubble. Do whatever you like with it. Just take it off me. And don't give it back, any of it.'

She stands in the rain until she's soaked through. Sue takes her arm and gently guides her back inside. She wraps her in a towel. Carol crawls back onto the sofa.

'You know what?' she whispers to Sue. 'The thing is, if I could lash out at Tilda who I love, then maybe ...'

The thought is so crazy and unexpected that she stops speaking and stares, appalled, at the floor. No, it can't be true.

Sue opens her mouth and closes it.

'Sue, what if Mum really does love me but can't control herself or doesn't know how to show her love? What if it's not me and never has been me? Maybe something's wrong with her. When I went to university, I went through a phase of researching possible diagnoses. I was convinced she was bipolar. Then I read about borderline personality disorder. She certainly ticked all the boxes. But then along came adult ADHD and I was sure that fit her. Or character disorder. That made sense. I eventually gave up and decided she's just mean and that I can't understand her and never will.'

Outside, the rain is less intense, the clouds less heavy, the wind a bit calmer. Inside the chalet, the room feels cosy and comforting.

'All these years, Mum has been criticising me and saying hateful things to me and it's made me unbalanced, like Tilda says, instead of pure and beautiful and loving and deserving of love. Maybe that happened to Mum. I always wondered why we never saw our grandparents.'

They sit watching the raindrops drip down the glass doors. Carol closes her eyes. It is nice to have a witness, especially someone who has no expectations of her, unlike Tilda who clearly expects her to learn how to do the love thing properly. She opens one eye to check that Sue is still there and is not bored or disapproving. Sue is there, looking interested and fully present. Carol snuggles deeper into the sofa and falls asleep.

Tilda

'Mum, wake up. It's time for your nature walk with Tilda. C'mon. It's on the schedule.' Jason is kneeling by the sofa trying in vain to wake Carol. He's nearly crying with frustration. Tilda is standing beside him, gazing out to sea. The rain has become heavier and she is content to wait. She is unused to schedules, except those set by the sun and the moon, the tides and the seasons.

'Jason, leave Carol. Sleep is best healer. Come walk wivh me.'

'I want to help Mum,' Jason says. 'I want her to get better. We set up the schedule to help her. We had a meeting and we all agreed. She's supposed to come on a nature walk with you now.'

Still, he puts on his raincoat and follows Tilda out of the chalet, looking back over his shoulder several times. They walk in silence, the wind in their faces, the rain pelting into them. The sea is restless. Tilda struggles to keep her balance on the soft sand.

'Great Mother,' Tilda calls inwardly. 'I know you will place in my mind the words I need. I will worry no more. You sent me here to awaken and to heal. I will be healed as I accept You as my teacher.'

The first words that Great Mother places in her mind are not what she expects but she says them anyway. 'Let's turn around and walk wivh our backs to vhe wind.'

'Can we go back and see if Mum is awake now?' Jason pleads. 'Maybe we can do an indoor nature walk. Mum won't want to be out in this storm even if she is awake.'

'Yes, okay.' Tilda is relieved to go back. She listens and hears more words behind the wind and the roar of the sea.

'Jason, listen, schedule not important. We six are healing circle. We all help your movher get better. Vhat is our purpose. We do it togevher, we are one, so healing very powerful. Great Movher is in our circle. She heals all of us wivh Her love.'

'Do you think Mum will get better, Tilda?' Jason's face is wet with tears.

'Yes. In time. Be patient. Great Movher give Carol all she needs and all you need too. Trust Her and call Her. Ask Her take away all your fears and worries.'

Jason looks at her with his big shining eyes. She senses his gratitude. As they near the chalet, Tilda sees Carol holding a mug in one hand and waving to them from the patio with the other. Jason runs ahead and Tilda watches as they embrace and disappear inside.

'Here's a cup of tea for you.' Carol offers Tilda a steaming mug of the tasteless brew that is served at their gatherings. Tilda has learned to accept the strange drink when offered but has never drunk a cup after the first unpleasant sip. She has often wondered what the purpose is. Now, she sees that the cup of tea is glowing and she understands. It is the healing balm of Carol's world. And judging by Carol's radiant smile, it appears to be working well.

Chapter 27. Carol

Y ou don't believe Tilda, do you Mum?' Jason asks. His tone is grumpy. Carol is cradling a cup of tea, feeling warm and cosy inside the chalet. She has got over her fear of a tsunami and is facing the sea, looking out at the night sky and at Tilda dancing ecstatically by the shore. The rain has ceased and the sea is settled. Without the lights of the city, the stars are clearly visible.

'You don't believe that she time travelled from Neolithic Brú na Bóinne. Do you Mum?'

'Well, Jason, I don't know what to make of it. You have to admit it's kind of unbelievable. It doesn't make a lot of sense. So I just don't think about it. I've put it in a bubble at the back of my mind. Anyway I've got other things on my mind.'

'Tilda tells me lots of stuff about herself that she doesn't tell you. Mum, you haven't like, really been curious about Tilda, have you?'

Carol feels as if she's been hit with a hammer. Tilda has evidently shared more about herself with her eleven-year-old son than she has with her lover. The sense of grievance rises instantly to stun her.

Jason huffs, tapping his foot impatiently. 'It's because I'm a child, Mum. I'm open to things that you adults think are impossible. 'Cause I don't know what's possible or impossible in this life. I didn't, like, sneer or dismiss what Tilda told me.'

Carol realises that Tilda may have been more present for Jason in the last five months than she has been. Her heart is beating fast, her face flashes hot. She has been shown up as self-centred and uninterested in anyone but herself. She thinks she's been sensitive by not interrogating Tilda, having assumed that Tilda would share what she felt comfortable with sharing as her English improved.

'Of course I'm interested in Tilda,' she mutters. 'But she took on the role of being my teacher. She even said it wasn't appropriate for her to talk about her personal issues. I thought she only shared what she chose to share with me.'

Jason jiggles his feet. 'But Mum, Tilda was my teacher too. Haven't you wondered what Tilda and I have been doing together? You even took us on trips to Avebury and Stonehenge and Stanton Drew and other places. You've been right there while Tilda was teaching me. I wanted to talk to you but you wouldn't listen. You just look bored when I start talking. You always tell me to stop.'

Carol gasps. Surely that isn't true. But her mind is set on the grievance with Tilda and she can't switch tracks. She feels hot and uncomfortable and wants to be doing anything other than being confronted by her son. She looks out the patio doors but she can't see Tilda.

'I assumed that since we became lovers, she would share more with me.'

It was Jason's turn to gasp. 'Are you and Tilda lovers, Mum?' he asks, his eyes wide. 'You mean, like Sue and Alison? But you didn't tell me.'

'No, it's private,' Carol says, crossing her arms. 'It's not your business.' Seeing Jason's stricken face, Carol regrets her abruptness.

'Mum! That's not fair. You don't listen to me. You don't tell me important things.'

'I'm sorry, sweetheart,' Carol says, forcing herself to give her attention to Jason. She's always found it hard to listen to him. He gives so much detail that she can't concentrate. Her mind wanders when he explains something he is interested in and she isn't.

But what has she missed? Surely she would have heard him say something about Tilda. Yet the only topic he's talked about since Tilda came to them five months before is the Neolithic time period. He's been obsessed with everything Neolithic, talked of nothing else, read every book he could get hold of, begged her to take him to Neolithic sites, watched every documentary he could find on anything Neolithic.

Carol is bored by the subject. Her original interest in Newgrange was triggered by the mysterious call she'd received but she hasn't sustained an interest beyond their trip. She realises that Tilda and the call are somehow connected, that Tilda has a connection to Newgrange and that Newgrange is a Neolithic stone monument. But beyond that, Carol can't get these random facts to connect. So she created another bubble in her mind where she parks inexplicable data. The Where-Is-Tilda-From Bubble floats somewhere behind the Ben Bubble and the Bad Mother Bubble and a newly emerged and about to burst Work Bubble.

'Are you saying you've been telling me where Tilda's from and I haven't been listening?' Carol asks, searching her mind for clues.

'Yes,' Jason nearly screams with frustration. 'Like, every day.'

'Jason, I have listened to you and to Tilda. She has said she's from the Neolithic time and you have talked a lot about the Neolithic period. Which is quite interesting. But all right, it's true. I am not as interested in it as you are. And I can't take it on board that Tilda is from that time.'

Jason jiggles about on his chair. Eventually the words come tumbling out in a rush. 'Mum, listen to me. This is what Tilda told me. She was sent to us by Great Mother. She was sent on a mission. She's here to prepare us for what's to come. It's coming soon. Maybe in a year or a few years, everything in our world is going to change. We have to get ready.'

'Ok, I know that's her view,' Carol says. 'That fits with everything she's been saying, but what has that got to do with where she's from?'

Jason takes a shaky breath. 'We know where Tilda's from. We met her in Newgrange. She's from Newgrange. It's about when. She did time travel from five thousand years ago. She's from the time just after Newgrange was built.'

'Jason, I know that's what Tilda says. I'm sorry but I find that hard to believe.'

'She's part of an elite group of people who are sort of in charge. Not really in charge like bosses or politicians or army people. The job of this elite group is to keep everybody in balance with Great

Mother, with the ancestors and with Nature and with the planets and the Sun and the Moon; like, with everything.'

He takes a breath and exhales slowly. 'It's all about harmony and love. They're the wisdom keepers. Tilda is one of the wisdom keepers. She's like a healer but more than that. They don't have writing, you know. She has all the information in her head. She knows astrology, how planets' and stars' movements affect us and about herbs for healing and about chanting and about farming and hunting; about everything really. And she knows how to travel to other dimensions; like when someone dies, she can go with them to the otherworld and she can come back again.'

Jason grinds to a halt and looks intently at Carol. She blinks rapidly, trying to keep up with the flow of words.

'OK Jason. Go back to this time travel business. How does that work exactly?'

'I don't know exactly. Tilda said it's the first time they were asked to do it. They are guided by Great Mother. She tells them what to do, like, about every little thing and, like, every big thing. Like what to eat and where to go, stuff like that. They ask the stones in the Palace of the Immortals. That's what they call Newgrange, you know. Great Mother speaks through the stones. She told them to choose one of the wisdom keepers to do the travelling, that was Tilda, and the rest of her group of ten made it happen by chanting and then something about the triple spiral. You know, Mum, the triple spiral?'

Carol nods vaguely. She is feeling confused and lost in the excited babble of words Jason is spilling out into the room.

'Tilda was in the egg-shaped bowl while her mates chanted and drummed and focussed on sending her to the future. You see, the Neolithic wisdom keepers have special powers. So when they got the order from Great Mother to time travel, they just did it. They believe that Great Mother does everything for the best, so they wouldn't question her command.'

'Special powers? You mean, like Superman?' Carol is wondering whether Jason got these ideas from one of the Netflix series he's always watching.

Jason jumps up. He is so excited he can hardly contain himself. 'Like lifting six tonne stones,' he shouts, miming a lifting of something heavy. 'Tilda told me how they built the Palace of the Immortals. Her grandmother or great grandmother or somebody in her family was part of the group of people who went and got the stones from the Wicklow Mountains, they're in Ireland, like, seventy kilometres away. I found them on the map. They carried them by boat and made the monuments. Everybody who's written about Neolithic stone monuments today is, like, amazed that Stone Age people with no metal and no technology like what we have today could make these incredible things. But they did.'

A thought is hovering at the edge of her mind. Carol is frowning with the effort of catching it. At first she doesn't notice that Tilda has come into the chalet.

'It's something to do with the call, isn't it?' Carol says suddenly.

'Mum?' Jason asks. 'What call? What do you mean?'

Carol peers closely at Tilda, taking in her matted black locks, her blue eyes and something she's never noticed before: green waves radiating outward from the outline of her body.

'I can't describe it.' Carol feels like she is floating, ungrounded. 'It's something I sense, or something I experience, every now and then. It's very nice, very peaceful. It's like a presence filling up everything. I don't know what to say about it. It's kind of nebulous. Sometimes I hear words, like before I went to Ireland, I heard "come with me. Come away." I just had to go with it. But most of the time, it doesn't say anything. It just makes me feel safe and peaceful, like everything's all right.'

Tilda's eyes are wet, glistening with tears. She whispers reverentially, 'It's Great Movher. She blesses you.'

Carol takes Tilda's hands in hers. 'You healed yourself, didn't you, when you were hit by the car in Ireland? You were chanting and drumming and then your broken arm was completely mended in just one day, wasn't it?'

Tilda nods, as if there is nothing remarkable about it.

'Look, I think of myself as a rational person,' Carol continues. 'I have a scientific background. I'm not into vibes or God or spiritual stuff or other dimensions. Never have been. But I couldn't explain what happened then. So, clearly you do have special powers, but that doesn't mean you brought them here from five thousand years ago. That's not proof of time travel.'

Carol puts her hands on her head to keep her crazy thoughts from bursting out. 'So I wondered if with the call and all that mysterious stuff happening to me that maybe I had lost my mind and was in some kind of fantasy dream world. And that I'd made you up.'

Tilda smiles at her, the green waves radiating out further from her body, moving closer to Carol. Jason shakes his head and rolls his eyes. They wait in silence. Finally, Carol puts her hands down and looks first at Tilda and then at Jason.

'How do we know what's true and what's real? I mean, maybe our lives are really some kind of fantasy dream world and we go back to the real world when we die. Sometimes I think that. When my father died, you were about three, Jason. I went into the hospital at five in the morning to be with him in his last moments. He had been in a coma for a week and was lying there with his mouth open and his eyes closed. He couldn't speak or move any part of his body. All of a sudden he opened his eyes, took a gulp of air and closed them again. That was it. He was gone. Yet he was still there, not in his body, but his presence. It was peaceful.'

'You never told me that before,' Jason says, staring at Carol as if mesmerised.

'No, I thought you were too young to talk about death and dying. I did what I thought was best.'

'Were you freaked out?' Jason asks.

'No, like I said, there was a sense of peace in the room, a spirit of love, that was coming from him. Almost right away I could see that his life spark had gone from his body. It was a shell, no longer him. But where had he gone?'

'I wonder about that too.' Jason comes over and puts his arms around Carol. Tilda joins them and kisses each in turn.

'It does not matter if you believe me where I come from or if I'm real. It does matter if you believe vhat vhere is great love here for you, vhat love is real. More real vhan anyfhing in vhis world. Do you know vhat?'

Both Carol and Jason nod. In that moment, Carol knows with all her being that the great love Tilda speaks of is the only true reality. She lets herself be held by the two of them and gives up trying to make sense with her mind.

Jason breaks the spell. He jumps free of their hug and says excitedly, 'Tilda, tell Mum about the trees. Like, every day you used to take Nan for walks, rain or shine to listen to trees. And you took me when I wasn't in school. You knew that, didn't you Mum?'

Carol nods, dazed by the sudden shift in mood and topic. She knows that her mother did things with Tilda that she'd never done before. Walking in Nature, talking to trees, was one of the things that she would not have believed her mother capable of or willing to do. The effect had been almost miraculous. Francis had regained some of her memory and much of her vitality. Now that she thought about it, maybe that was another one of Tilda's special powers.

Jason leaps about the chalet. 'Do you remember the Tortworth Chestnut Tree, Tilda? One day you asked me to find the nearest, really, really old tree. That's in Gloucestershire. It's one thousand two hundred years old! It took you ages to walk there. You even slept on the tree.'

'Slow down, Jason,' Carol says, sighing. 'I don't get it. Why are you going on about trees? You talk so fast that I get lost.'

Tilda puts her hand on Jason's arm and says quietly, 'I talk now.' She turns to Carol and looks her in the eye. 'Most trees are asleep or lonely, cut off from each ovher and from Movher Earfh. Vhey're not in forests, like vhey used to be. Like vhey are in my time. We cut down forests in Neolivhic times too, for farming. Vhat was start of it and it's just got worse and worse until now, vhere is hardly any true forests left.'

'Did you say the trees are asleep or lonely?' Carol asks, resisting the urge to roll her eyes.

'Yes. I wake sleeping trees. Great Movher speaks wivh trees like she does wivh stones. When I got here, I had to wake up vhe trees before vhey could speak Great Movher's words. Vhe Tortworfh Chestnut was already awake. It made its own little forest rooting branches into vhe ground. It sent up chrucks so what looks like many separate trees are really one.

'Vhe Tortworfh Chestnut and vhe trees vhat could be wakened all told me vhat vhe people now in vhis time are out of balance. You're not connected to Movher Earf. You aren't living in harmony wivh Nature. You do fhings out of fear and you're into money and some people have power over ovher people. And people are suffering and you're hurting Movher Earfh. And She's going to teach you to get back in balance.'

'How is Mother Earth going to teach us to get back in balance?' Carol asks. 'Is she angry at us and going to punish us?'

'No, not punish. She teach by making you pay attention. Because people don't change unless vhey have to. She sending warnings for a long time: wildfires, hurricanes, storms, droughts, very hot wheavher, flood and diseases. Vhere will be more and more warnings until people get it.'

'You mean like the plague in the Middle Ages, worldwide pandemics?' Carol asks. She usually avoids these discussions and listening to the news or reading about them. It is too painful and leaves her feeling paralysed and overwhelmed. She wonders what Tilda expects of her. She doubts she could live up to any of it.

'We know all this but what are we supposed to do?' she asks, wringing her hands. 'How can we get in balance and live in harmony with Nature? We know about climate change and environmental destruction and mass extinction but what can we do?'

'It's okay,' Tilda says. 'Don't be afraid. You're lucky to be born at vhis time because you have a chance to leave vhis old way of being and make a better way of being. You are safe. You are protected and you can do it. Children will lead vhe way. Vhat's what Great Movher told vhe trees to tell me to tell you.'

Jason is following every word Tilda says with shining eyes. 'Yes. We can do it. Now do you see why Tilda came to us, Mum? We're going to find new ways of being. We're going to make a difference.'

Through the patio doors, the night sky is alive with stars. The sea is dancing with movement and light and sound. In the chalet, everything Carol looks at glows and shimmers: Jason's eager face, the blue blanket on the sofa, the framed photo of the beach on the wall, Tilda's sparkling blue eyes, a cup of half-drunk tea on the table, her own hand with its pink splotches and brown freckles. They seem to her to be joined together in a coherent, organised network of connected parts. And somehow that adds up to a vast sense of peace that encompasses them all.

We but mirror the world. All the tendencies present in the outer world are to be found in the world of our body. If we could change ourselves, the tendencies in the world would also change... A wonderful thing it is and the source of our happiness.

By Mahatma Gandhi

Chapter 28. Carol

'Tilda, do you think in one of my past lives I was a trainee Wisdom Keeper in the Palace of the Immortals and you were my teacher?' Carol is examining Tilda's necklace of periwinkle shells, admiring the craftsmanship. She looks up to see Tilda's perplexed expression.

'Look at me, Tilda. See how straight my back is. I've been practising sitting the way you do, so still and centred. Do you think you could train me to be a Wisdom Keeper?'

Tilda grunts. 'You lost wivhout your *m'sheens*. In my world, no phone, no TV, no washing *m'sheen,* no car, no electricity, no toilets ...'

'All right, all right, you've made your point. But do I have the qualities you need to be a Wisdom Keeper?'

'No,' Tilda says.

It wouldn't hurt Tilda to humour me occasionally, Carol thinks, *but that is not Tilda's way*. Tilda looks at her without smiling and says, 'You have everyfhing you need to be who you are.'

Carol sighs. She wishes Tilda could give her a little pat on the back. It's been a week since they got back from Dunster Beach. Carol can see she's made tremendous progress. She has a new sense of purpose, a lot more self-confidence. She has crossed a threshold and can leave the old ways behind.

Or she could, until she encounters the first challenge - which is Ben.

His text is curt: 'I'm coming home. Fed up with uni. Heard from Uncle John that Nan is staying with him. You didn't bother telling me. So I can have my room back. Get it ready.'

Carol doesn't start hyperventilating immediately. She waits until Jason has gone to school and Tilda has returned from a dawn walk. As Tilda walks in the front door, Carol ambushes her.

'Ben texted. He's coming home. I can't have him here anymore. I can't. What am I going to do?'

Tilda rolls her eyes. 'It's a gift from Great Movher,' she says and wanders into the kitchen where she rummages in the fridge for yoghurt and milk.

'I'm really grateful for the gift,' Carol murmurs, trailing after her like a puppy. 'Really grateful. I was just about to thank her myself but I can do without this gift. Can I give it back? I'm not ready. Not strong enough yet.'

'Yes you are,' Tilda says, drinking the milk straight out of the bottle. Carol has given up training her in 21st century ways.

'Great Mother really needs to do better in the gift-giving department,' Carol mutters.

Seeing that neither Tilda nor Great Mother are any help with this situation, Carol phones her support team. But Alison is at work, Sue is with a client and Moira isn't free until the evening.

'What will you do?' Tilda asks placidly when Carol has exhausted all possibilities. She takes another swig of milk from the bottle.

'I don't know,' Carol wails. 'Ben cannot be here. I cannot have him in this house, not while he's in this arrogant, disrespectful, aggressive adolescent mode. He's twenty. Why can't he act like an adult, get a job, get a flat, go travelling, whatever? Why does he want to hang out with his mother and eleven-year-old brother?'

'Say no. He can't come. At my home, vhere's no violence. Adult man loves and respects his movher. They live togevher in harmony.'

'How is it loving for me to say he can't come home? Shouldn't I be the mature one until he grows out of this phase?'

Tilda shrugs. 'You're very confused, Karul. Talk to Great Movher. She knows best. I go now to tree in field. Come wivh me.'

But Carol has not got the hang of communicating with Great Mother at will and she feels silly talking to trees. So far, none of the trees Tilda has introduced her to has told her anything at all, let alone anything of value. Tilda shrugs again and goes without her.

Journal writing! That's something Sue recommended in their counselling sessions. Why not? Carol finds a pad of paper and a pen and sits looking hopefully at the blank page for some time. She writes the date, 9th April, and sits for some more time. Then her pen starts moving:

What is the role you've been playing with Ben?

Carol studies the question, surprised at what she wrote. She answers:

I am the proverbial door mat. I am intimidated by Ben. He's a bully. I'm always appeasing him. I am scared of him. I can't stand up to him. I get wobbled when I'm around him. I can't meet his needs and I can't meet mine.

Now she really feels terrible about herself. Maybe this isn't such a good idea. Her pen writes again, *The old way must be left behind. It is dangerous for you.*

She sighs. *Easier said than done,* she mutters to herself. She writes:

I know, but Ben's my son. I should be there for him. I don't know what to do.

Say goodbye to the old role you used to play.

Goodbye, old role, she writes and waits for the next piece of advice. It soon arrives:

See through the masks.

That's it. Nothing more. *A bit cryptic,* she thinks, feeling disappointed. Still, the journalling exercise has given her a little boost of confidence. She writes a text to Ben, saying: *Stay at uni. You can't come here unless you can behave. You're not respectful.*

She deletes the text before sending it. That is giving him a chance, not setting a boundary. He could say he's going to behave and then act just as aggressively as he'd done in his December visit.

She tries again: *Stay at uni. The consequence of your behaviour last time is that you can no longer come home. I hope you learn how to respect us.*

She isn't sure that gets her point across. Ben has an amazing ability to turn anything around so that he is never to blame, and she always is. Carol decides to rewrite:

Stay at uni. No room for you here. Don't come home.

Even that short text contains superfluous words. It is unnecessary to tell him to stay at uni. Where else would he go? And there is room for him at home. All she needs to say is, no, don't come home.

She stares at her phone in an agony of indecision. Such an abrupt text goes against her natural tendency to explain, defend and justify. Alison has warned her many times of the danger of long, reasonable explanations and wordy justifications. Still, the beauty of a text message is that she can't indulge that tendency. Her finger hovers over the send command and before she can think about it anymore, her finger falls and the text is sent.

Ben doesn't bother to reply. He arrives the next day while Carol and Tilda are out with trees. Moira is babysitting.

'Ben alert! Ben alert!' Moira hisses dramatically into the phone when Carol answers. 'He gained entry at sixteen oh ten. Jason answered the door. Ben marched straight up the stairs to his old bedroom. He is taking possession at this very moment. I'm ready and willing to deal with this right now but Jason insisted I get Tilda to apply her Neolithic superwoman powers. I await your orders.'

'Oh, shit,' Carol gulps. 'We've got to get home now, Tilda.'

Tilda, however, is in the midst of an intimate conversation with a stand of trees by the River Frome. Carol is desperate. 'Please Tilda. Please help us. The trees will still be here tomorrow. Moira, what's he doing now?'

'He's carrying his stuff upstairs. Are you guys coming home or not?'

'Mum, can I talk to Tilda?' Jason takes the phone from Moira.

'Tilda, it's Jason,' Carol says, waving her phone at Tilda. Tilda frowns and shakes her head. Jason starts sobbing. Moira comes back on the phone. 'This boy is freaking out, Carol. You better come home with or without Tilda. How soon can you get here? What are you doing anyway? It's pissing down.'

'It'll take me at least half an hour to walk back. Tilda's talking to some trees and is not willing to be drawn into another Ben psychodrama.'

'Oh for God's sake,' Moira expostulates. 'What have you been doing while Tilda's communing with the trees?'

'Getting drenched and miserable,' Carol admits. 'I haven't got the knack yet.'

'Carol, just get yourself home and deal with your sons please. Both of them. In the meantime, I've got the rolling pin in my hand and I'll whack Ben with it if he comes within striking distance.'

'Thanks Moira. I really appreciate it but please try to avoid violence.' Carol's voice is wobbling. She's let Jason down again. Before Christmas, he'd begged her not to let Ben come to the house and she promised she would. As she hurries home, her mind clears. For Jason's sake she has to stop being a doormat to Ben's bullying.

Moira does not rely only on the rolling pin. By the time Carol squelches back in the front door, Moira's ginger-haired friend Pete has come over and is upstairs talking to Ben.

'Leave them for now,' Moira urges Carol. 'Go get yourself dry. Dinner will be ready in twenty minutes. I've put this rolling pin to good use and made a quiche from scratch. One of my specialities. Go on Carol. Drip somewhere else. Jason, wash your hands and set the table for six. I won't ask where Tilda is.'

'Mum, why won't Tilda help us?' Jason asks, as Carol removes her dripping rain gear.

'She's busy talking to some trees. Anyway, this is our business, not hers. She trusts me to sort this mess out myself, I guess.'

Carol grimaces. *See through the masks. Say goodbye to the old role. This is a gift.* She repeats the phrases as if they are a mantra. She has no idea what it means to see through the masks but it boosts her confidence to say it to herself. She keeps repeating the phrases while she changes into dry clothes. By the time Moira calls them for dinner, Carol feels slightly more ready to take Ben on. But first she needs to deal with Pete.

Carol intercepts Pete as he is about to walk down the stairs. She feels a pang of irritation. *What does he think he's doing, butting in like this?* She knows he's had a similar situation with his son Matthew but that doesn't give him the right to come over and sort out her situation.

'Pete,' she says, putting her hand on his arm. 'Thanks for coming over but I'll take it from here. I think Moira over-reacted by calling you. I don't need a man to fix things in my life. I can manage just fine by myself.'

Carol is surprised at how defiant she sounds. Can she manage just fine? She doesn't need Pete, that's for sure, but she could do with Tilda's help. And Tilda has made it clear she isn't going to help.

Pete steps back and covers his mouth with his hand. 'Oh Carol, I'm so sorry. I didn't mean... I mean I didn't think. I mean Moira stepped in and helped me with Matthew and I thought ... well, sometimes, someone outside the family can calm everything down. Look, I'll go now. I'm really sorry.'

Pete flees down the stairs and out the front door before Carol can change her mind. She marches into the kitchen. Ben comes soon after and sits at the table next to Moira. Jason is sitting as far away as possible from Ben. What would Tilda do if she were here? An image flashes into her mind of Tilda sitting still and upright, making eye contact with Ben and speaking the truth.

Carol smiles to herself and gives herself a quick pep talk. *I can do this. Yes, I can.* She looks Ben in the eye and says, 'I sent you a text telling you not to come home. You ignored me. After the way you behaved last December, I can't believe you would have the nerve to come back. You can't treat us like that. You have no respect. You intimidate us. You're violent. You wear the mask of being my son, a member of our family, but you're not a loving son, grateful for the support your mother provides for you. Who do you think pays for you to go to university? I do. Mike has never paid for anything. Well, I see through the mask and I've had enough. You have to go.'

Ben looks down at the table. *He appears to be uncomfortable which is unusual and a good sign,* Carol thinks. 'I'm going to give uni another chance,' he says. 'Put more effort in. Pete suggested I change my major, because music technology isn't really my thing anymore. I don't know what else I could do. Pete said he'd help me look around.'

Carol bristles hearing of Pete's intervention. 'Did he say anything else?' she demands. *Like, how you're going to change your behaviour,* she thinks.

'Oh yeah, he says I should apologise to you.'

Carol waits. *This will be a first.*

'I said I apologised,' Ben says irritably. Carol glares at him. 'OK, OK, I'm sorry,' he mutters in a low voice.

'Sorry for what? Letting the chickens out!?' Moira snaps.

Ben grunts. 'Sorry for barging in after you told me not to come home, though what right do you have to cut me off like that? It's my home too.'

Carol narrows her eyes.

'I'm sorry for disrespecting you,' Ben says. 'Though you disrespected me first. Why don't you apologise to me?'

'The only thing I'll apologise for is not setting clear boundaries. And the apology is to myself and to Jason.'

'Hear! Hear!' Moira mutters under her breath.

'I'm considering whether to stop paying for you to go to university,' Carol says. 'There's a contract between us and you haven't done your part. If you can change your attitude and start treating me, your mother, with love and respect, then I'll be happy to continue paying. If you can't, then believe me Ben, I will stop supporting you. No one treats me like a doormat, even someone who's been through my vagina and who owes their very existence to me. Have you got that, son?'

Ben blushes. He stares at Carol without saying a word. Moira kicks him under the table.

'I got it,' Ben says sullenly. 'I am sorry for being such a jerk, Mum.'

'Say goodbye to the old ways,' Carol says. 'And hello to the new me.'

'If it's all right with you, Carol, I've told Ben he can stay the night with me,' Moira adds. 'I've got to go now so I'll take Ben and his stuff and then put him on the train to Reading tomorrow.'

Ben leaves his dinner untouched and goes upstairs to pack. Carol feels as if she could fly. Moira and Jason stare at her.

'Mum! That was awesome. You showed him,' crows Jason, punching the air.

'Yeah, that sure was some speech, Carol,' Moira says drily. 'Especially that bit about someone who's been through your vagina. Nice touch. I like it. But leaving that aside, well done.'

They have a three-way hug. Carol thanks Moira and says a heartfelt thank you to Great Mother for all the gifts she's given that day.

Chapter 29. Carol

'I did it! I did it on my own!' Carol boasts to Sue when Sue phones later in the week. 'I stood up to Ben. I told him to leave and he did. I was magnificent. Authoritative and calm. Tilda was so proud of me. She did a special ceremony to thank Great Mother with chanting and dancing and ... Oh, there's the doorbell. I've got to go, Sue. That must be Tilda and Jason back from their Nature walk. Bye for now.'

It isn't Tilda and Jason. It's Pete with a large bunch of flowers in his hand. Carol accepts the flowers reluctantly. 'What are these for?'

'I came to apologise for being so insensitive last week. I should never have presumed to talk to Ben without checking with you first. I am really sorry.'

Carol narrows her eyes suspiciously. *What's he up to?* she wonders. *Is he wooing me? Doesn't he know I am no longer single? Moira must have told him by now.*

'You don't have to apologise. It all worked out well.'

'Mum,' Jason cries, running up the front path, his curls bouncing. 'We were out by the lake and we saw bats. They were so-o-o amazing. And before it got dark, we saw a kingfisher's nest and five swans and two herons and a cormorant and some Canada geese. What else, Tilda?'

'Heyyo Pete,' Tilda says, smiling delightedly at him and Carol. She walks over to kiss Carol. 'Beautiful flowers! And we saw ducks, pigeons, owl, woodpecker. No otters.'

They flow into the house, Pete swept along with them.

'And we talked to a lot of trees,' Jason burbles happily. He bangs his head against the door frame a few times.

'Stop! What are you doing?' Carol asks, alarmed.

'Let me guess,' Pete says. 'Are you a woodpecker tapping a tree?' Jason looks pleased.

'Do you ever listen to the trees, Jason, or do you just do the talking?' Carol asks.

'I do the talking. They're interested in what I have to say. They never tell me to stop talking.' He sticks his tongue out at Carol. 'And they always shower me with love.'

Carol pulls Jason into a hug and ruffles his hair fondly. 'That's wonderful, Jason. I wish I could get showered with love when I'm with trees. It doesn't seem to work for me. You see, Pete, Tilda's passion is trees. She's spending a lot of time waking them up and talking to them so we can hear what they have to tell us about our alienation from Nature and what we can do to correct the situation.'

Pete's eyes light up. 'That's amazing,' he cries. 'That's what I'm into now. I was just about to tell you about my latest passion. I've been thinking about going on a trip around Britain to ancient trees, like a pilgrimage. I've got a camper and I was going to go off for a few months and connect with trees. Tilda, do you know about the Tortworth Chestnut Tree? It's twelve hundred years old and it's not far from here. I could take you there.'

'She's already been,' Jason says smugly. 'I drew her a map and she walked to it.'

'Really?' Pete is looking intently at Tilda.

Tilda nods at Pete and turns to Carol. 'Gift from Great Movher,' she winks and wanders out of the living room, humming.

'What does she mean?' Pete asks. 'I'd like to talk to her some more.'

'I don't know where she's gone. I'll go find out.' Carol tracks Tilda to their bedroom where she is getting ready for bed.

'Tilda?' Carol stands at the door, wringing her hands. Her stomach is clenching. 'What did you mean when you said gift from Great Mother?'

Tilda touches Carol's nose and forehead with her own, gives her a kiss and climbs into bed. From under the duvet, she calls, 'Pete will take me home. Wake up trees on way. Goodnight, my precious one.'

Carol's heart nearly stops in shock. Tilda hasn't talked about going home since they returned from Dunster Beach and Carol has put it out of her mind. But it seems that Tilda has been making private arrangements with Great Mother and now Great Mother is providing the practical means for her return.

Carol can see there is no point speaking any more about it with Tilda since she is hiding under the duvet pretending to be asleep. Glumly, Carol goes downstairs where Pete and Jason are in the midst of an animated discussion about – yes, she hears correctly – trees.

'Tilda's gone to bed,' Carol announces in a flat tone of voice. 'I'm feeling tired myself. Let's get together soon. And don't worry about, you know, stepping in with Ben.'

Pete looks concerned. 'Is anything wrong? You look upset.'

'No, I'm fine. Just tired,' Carol says, but the tears spill down her cheeks. Out of the corner of her eye, she notices that Jason is also looking concerned. He comes quietly up to her and puts his arms around her waist.

'Oh, yeah I can see you're fine,' Pete says. 'Maybe I should go.' But he doesn't leave. He remains seated, watching her.

Clinging on to Jason, Carol sobs. She catches her breath and says reluctantly, 'Great Mother sent you to take Tilda home and I don't want her to leave me.'

Jason cuddles Carol. 'Mum, I don't want her to leave either but she has to go. You know that.'

Carol can't stop sobbing. 'No, I don't know that. Why can't she stay for years instead of months? She can always go back to the same time she left. Like in *Back to the Future*, she could set the time machine to whatever time she wants to go back to.'

'She doesn't have a time machine like in *Back to the Future*,' Jason says authoritatively.

'Oh, I get it,' Pete says, stroking his goatee. 'Is she still saying she's from the Neolithic time?'

'Don't you believe it?' Carol asks. Maybe he won't take Tilda back to Newgrange if he thinks she's nuts. The seed of a plan germinates in Carol's mind. Maybe she can find a way to foil Great Mother's plan.

'How should I know? As you said, that's her story and she's been sticking to it. Anyway, I've got an open mind,' Pete says. 'But I would like to talk to her more about ancient trees. I'm getting really excited about my pilgrimage.'

'Just Britain, right? Not Ireland?' Carol asks, in as casual a voice as she can manage. 'I'm sure there are enough ancient trees in Britain that you wouldn't need to go out of your way to Ireland.'

'I'll look into it. I hadn't thought about Ireland,' Pete says cheerfully, rubbing his hands together in delight.

'Don't bother. You don't want to encourage Tilda's delusions, do you?' Carol looks Pete in the eye.

He looks surprised and shrugs. 'I'm happy to go along with her delusions.'

Carol slumps in defeat. It's not going to work. There's no way she can exert her puny will against the combined will of Tilda and Great Mother.

Chapter 30. Carol

Francis loved vhis. We come here many times.' Tilda points to the view of the city, then chants quietly to a hard-boiled egg.

'I didn't know Francis was into walking,' Alison says, opening a thermos of tea. 'Wasn't that one of the things you complained about, Carol, that she wouldn't go out of the house? She never wanted to go for walks.'

'She only walked with Tilda,' Carol says. It's been a month since her breakdown, since she sent her mother away, but she still doesn't feel ready to think about the future and whether she's going to bring her mother back.

They've hiked to the top of a hill. The sound of the motorway traffic drifts up to them. They can see the dense growth of trees escorting the River Frome on its way to join the River Avon, the Mendip Hills rising up in the south, a church steeple pointing to the sky, the distant streets bustling with activity. Weeks of rain have given way to blue skies and shirt-sleeve weather. The thick mud, no longer treacherous and slippery, has dried solid and become walkable. On the trees are the tiniest of buds, like runners on the starting line ready to spring.

'How's she getting on with John and Sheila?' asks Alison.

'I called her last week,' Carol replies. 'But Sheila says she wouldn't come to the phone. So I had to listen to Sheila going on and on about what a pleasure it is to have her mother-in-law living with them, how great it is for the children to be with their Nan. Francis hasn't had a single rage and hasn't gone wandering once since moving in with them. Apparently, she's no trouble at all.' Carol viciously kicks a clod of dried mud.

Alison sighs. 'Carol, Sheila really knows how to press all your buttons, doesn't she? Let me guess: you're feeling judged and guilty and resentful, aren't you?'

Tilda nods in agreement, her lips pursed. Carol bristles. It's true; she is feeling judged and guilty and resentful and those are unacceptable feelings, but the feeling that's even more unacceptable is relief.

'It doesn't matter what I'm feeling,' Carol said, yanking a stinging nettle out of the ground. 'The main thing is that Mum is happy and well looked after.'

Alison and Tilda groan in unison. Alison's hands move towards Carol's throat.

'I could throttle you, Carol,' she yells, dropping her hands to her side just before she reaches her. 'The ONLY thing that matters is what YOU are feeling.'

Carol attacks the stinging nettles with feeling. Alison puts her hands on her hips. 'Carol, it's no wonder you're feeling resentful. Here's a reality check for you: John and Sheila refused to take Francis in when her dementia got so bad she couldn't stay in her own home, even though they have a granny annex and plenty of money to pay for care assistants.'

Carol grimaces, remembering the months of frantic concern about Francis before the incident which forced the move. It wasn't the time her mother had crashed into two cars while parking, or the time she'd put a whole chicken to cook in the dishwasher, or even the times she'd wandered onto the motorway in her nightgown. The incident which Carol could not ignore was when her mother poured herself a glass of undiluted bleach and drank a sip. The burning pain had driven her outside screaming where a neighbour had found her. The neighbour had phoned NHS 111 and made her drink milk. John and Sheila had remained distant and unconcerned, arguing that they were too far away to be of any practical help.

'Carol, you tried to do it on your own without any respite care and you couldn't. No one could have. It's too much. Do you think Sheila is doing any of the looking after herself?'

Carol grumbles. 'No, of course not. They hired a live-in care assistant, an older woman from Ghana named Efua. Efua lives with Francis in the granny annex. The only caring that Sheila does is to let Francis eat dinner with the family once a week when Efua has a night off to spend with her family. John is an important consultant. He doesn't do any hands-on caring.'

Carol notices that Alison is scowling. 'You see, Tilda,' Alison mutters. 'They call her by her first name, Efua, though she is a mature woman with a family of her own. They treat her like that because she's Black.'

'I'm sure they pay her well,' Carol says carefully. 'They're not racist.' Why is she defending John and Sheila when she really wants to moan about them?

'See Sheila and John for who they are, Carol,' Alison says. 'They're not white supremacists but they do have white privilege. Anyway, with you, they're playing a game of one-upmanship. You were playing the dutiful daughter. Remove the masks. Drop the old roles. You must leave all that behind.'

Carol looks at Alison in surprise. Those are the same phrases she'd written in her journal not long before. Where did they come from?

'Look, I'm not a counsellor,' Alison continues. 'I don't know how to help you stop beating yourself up. But I care about you. I want you to be happy. You deserve to be happy. Let me give you a hug, woman.'

Carol lets herself be hugged and gives Alison a hug back. She feels a lot better. As a professional counsellor, Sue would have been more subtle and sensitive, but Alison is more direct and challenging. Carol likes that, some of the time. She can do without having white privilege rubbed in her face but at least she knows where she stands with Alison. Sue can be too soft, too comforting, too understanding.

From her position on the ground, Tilda looks up at Carol and says, 'I miss Francis. She's a good friend. I want to visit her, say goodbye.'

Instantly, Carol's good feelings vanish. She does not want to know what a good friend her mother was to Tilda nor be reminded of Tilda's plans to go home. She feels the tears welling up but is ashamed to admit it. At the same time, she knows she can't hide what she's feeling from Tilda and Alison. The inner struggle is exhausting. She gives up and lets the tears flow and the sobs rack her body.

'I can't stop crying,' she moans. 'Maybe I should take those pills the GP gave me.'

Alison rolls her eyes and glares at Tilda. 'Nice one, Tilda. I just got her calmed down and you go and set her off again.'

Tilda shrugs. They wait for the tears to stop. When they eventually stop, Tilda asks again, 'Will you take me to visit Francis or I go alone?' She looks pointedly at the view and not at Carol.

Carol's satnav is saying no, no, no, ordering her to turn around and go back, but she turns it off. 'I'll take you,' she promises, looking out at the view and not at Tilda. *Damn you, Tilda. Stop pushing me. Don't make me go.*

With a sigh, Tilda stands up, takes Carol's hand and tenderly says, 'Ask Great Movher to help.'

At the mention of Great Mother, Carol starts wailing. 'I don't want Great Mother to take you away. Why can't she let you stay longer, for years, not for months?'

Tilda shrugs. 'Vhen you cry for years, not for monfhs.'

Carol gawps. Tilda spreads her arms wide. 'I am here now. Why you cry now?'

Alison interrupts. 'Has something happened? Have you got a date to go home, Tilda?'

Tilda nods and tells Alison that Pete is going to take her home in his van, visiting trees on the way. Carol is furious. 'No, he won't. He wants to go on his own. It's his passion to go on a pilgrimage to the ancient trees in Britain. He didn't say anything about going to Ireland or taking you.'

'Whoa. What's going on? Are you talking about Moira's friend, Pete, the one she tried to match you up with?' Alison asks. She takes off her jumper and shoves it into her backpack.

'Yes, that one. He came over last night and mentioned this pilgrimage he's planning. Tilda got it into her head that Great

Mother sent him to take her home, but she didn't actually talk to Pete about it.'

Tilda turns Carol to face her and looks searchingly into her eyes. Carol can't sustain the gaze and wriggles free. She wishes she wasn't so transparent.

'We all, we will all go wivh Pete: me, you, Jason,' Tilda says matter-of-factly, as if Carol has no say in the matter. 'Pete wants you to go wivh him, especially you.'

Carol gives her a murderous look. Tilda always sounds so certain. 'How do you know?'

'How you not know?' Tilda replies, then takes a deep breath. 'True, I don't know what will happen. You will die. When? You do not know. Jason will die. When? Do not know. You do not cry every day about when you will die or Jason will die.'

Carol wipes her nose on her sleeve. 'Does Great Mother want me to go to London to see Mum?'

'Ask her,' Tilda says as if it were that simple. Though Carol knows that in Tilda's mind, it is that simple. Tilda is in moment-to-moment communication with Great Mother. They are constantly discussing what's going to happen next. Carol realises that she's jealous of Tilda's relationship with Great Mother. It is getting in the way of her relationship with Carol.

'My satnav says no,' Carol blurts out. She pauses, suddenly feeling doubtful. 'But is that Great Mother speaking to me or some other part of me that's resisting Great Mother?'

'What does your satnav say now? Ask Great Movher again.' Tilda looks excited.

Carol feels like a star pupil about to be given a sticker for finally getting the answer right. She focusses in on her satnav. Hesitantly at first and then more confidently, she searches inside for a feeling connected to the decision not to take Tilda to see her mother. When she's sifted through the mess of shoulds and grievances and self-critical thoughts, she finds a feeling beaming up at her. That feeling is simply relief.

'My satnav says yes,' Carol exclaims in a voice as excited as Tilda's. 'It says I don't have to go back to the way I was doing things.'

'Then it's gift from Great Movher.' Tilda is smiling.

For the first time, Carol notices the cool, fresh breeze, the immensity of the blue sky and the sun glinting on the hills in the distance. The tears, it seems, have dried up. Taking Tilda's and Alison's arms, Carol leads them down to the fishing lake, where they watch a grey heron dive into the water and come up with a fish in its beak.

The relief at not having to see her mother lasts until the next morning when Pete phones. She and Jason have finished eating their usual Sunday breakfast of pancakes with maple syrup. Carol is washing up while Jason and Tilda are settling in the living room with a book.

'Carol, I have a great idea,' Pete announces, his excitement radiating down the phone line. 'You know my plan to go on an ancient tree pilgrimage?'

Carol murmurs, 'Oh no, don't tell me any more.'

But Pete is not paying attention. 'Well, I woke at four this morning with this brilliant idea. I really don't want to do it on my own. Tilda's into the same things as me. You and Jason are too. Why don't all three of you come with me?'

He doesn't wait for an answer. Carol sighs audibly, silently cursing Great Mother for intervening.

'The camper van sleeps three and I have a tent and could sleep outside in the tent. Of course, you'd have to take Jason out of school but I could help with home schooling and he'd learn so much on this trip. And Tilda wants to get back to Ireland. We could take the ferry from Holyhead. What do you think, Carol? Please think about it.'

He skids to a halt and waits. Carol has an image of a puppy wagging its tail and panting, waiting for someone to take it for a walk.

All right, Great Mother. You win, Carol thinks. *You've made your point. Now don't overdo it.*

To Pete, she says, 'Yeah, yeah. Come over tonight and we'll talk about it. Tilda and Jason will be thrilled.'

'And you won't?' Pete sounds anxious.

'I'll explain all tonight. See you later. Bye for now.'

As she hangs up, Carol glances over at Jason reading aloud to Tilda. Tilda is sitting on the floor with her eyes closed, listening intently. Jason is reading with great expression in his voice, sitting on the edge of the sofa as if about to fly off with the words. As Carol listens, she senses the Presence filling the room and expanding until the room is no longer a room but a palace.

'*... my palace opens into the Gardens of the Sun, and there are the fire-fountains which quench the heart's desire in rapture ...*' Jason reads breathlessly. Catching Carol's eye, he says, 'I'm reading *The Dream of Angus Oge* by George William Russell and it's about Newgrange. He wrote it in 1897.'

Carol smiles at him. 'Don't stop,' she whispers.

'*.. a palace high as the stars, with dazzling pillars jewelled like the dawn, and all fashioned out of living and trembling opal.* Is that how the Palace of the Immortals is, Tilda?' he asks, eyes wide with wonder. Tilda nods, though a bit vaguely, Carol thinks. She probably doesn't understand all the words.

'And listen to this bit ... *In days past many a one plucked here the purple flower of magic and the fruit of the tree of life.* Oh Tilda, you must be so excited to be going home. I wish, wish, wish I could go with you.'

He must have noticed Carol's look of panic because he adds quickly, 'Just to visit, Mum, not to stay forever.'

Carol sits next to Tilda on the floor. 'That was Pete. He wants all of us to go with him on his ancient tree pilgrimage and then he'll take you home to Newgrange. He's coming over this evening to talk about it. I guess Great Mother got her way after all.'

'Me too?' Jason asks, leaping around the living room.

'Yes, you too.'

'What your satnav say, Karul?' Tilda asks quietly, her blue eyes pinning Carol to the spot.

'Yeah, well what choice do I have? You and Great Mother have conspired to make this happen. She brought Pete and Jason on board and you've all ganged up against me. But hey, that's fine. I'm OK with it.'

Carol lies back on the floor and says to no one in particular, and to anyone who might be listening, 'But I don't have to like it.'

Chapter 31. Carol

The first planning meeting of the Ancient Tree Pilgrimage Group convenes on 20 April in Carol's kitchen as soon as Jason gets home from school.

Pete takes off his baseball cap and lays a map of Britain on the kitchen table. Three heads pore over the map: Jason's curly top next to Tilda's black locks side by side with Pete's ginger mop, all closely following Pete's finger as he points out the route he has decided on.

Carol leans against the counter, drinking a cup of tea. She's barely containing her irritation. It's all very well to plan the route. It's the practicalities of the journey that preoccupy her; the minor details that determine whether such a journey can take place at all. Minor details like money.

She waits impatiently for the others to complete the pilgrimage on paper. Then she calls the meeting to order.

'Friends,' she says, smiling between gritted teeth. 'Before we launch the pilgrimage, it would be nice to know how we are going to afford it. Pete, you've invited us to come with you on this mad escapade. How is this going to work?'

'No problemo,' Pete says expansively, spreading his arms out wide. 'I gave up work and sold my house over two years ago. I got rid of most of my stuff, my furniture, my books, lots of stuff. Put the rest in my mate's garage. I've been living off that money ever since.'

Carol is amazed and frankly, envious. She's never met anyone so unencumbered; so free. 'Do you still work now?' she asks.

'Sometimes, but only when I feel like it. I left the fire service and went to volunteer in Lesvos for six months. Didn't earn anything there but didn't spend anything either. Since I got back, I've done some on-call work with the emergency services and I teach a bit of first aid.'

Jason's eyes light up. 'You're a firefighter? Wow. I bet that's fun.' He'd been draped over the table, studying the map. At this news, he straightens up and gives all his attention to Pete.

'Yeah, it was a great job. I did it full-time since I was 25. Then I had enough.'

'Did you buy another house?' Carol returns to the practicalities. She hands Jason a peanut butter sandwich.

'Nope. I've had it with home ownership. I've been renting a room in my mate's house. The only big expenditure I've had is my camper van. So I'm good for money for a couple of years at least, maybe more. Depending on how much I spend, of course. But I don't have any expensive habits now that Matthew's finished with uni. I guess it's more complicated for you Carol, isn't it?'

'Uh yeah, you could say that,' Carol grumbles, feeling annoyed that Pete is so carefree and she isn't. Though she has been shedding expensive habits recently, like caring for Francis and paying Ben's university fees. 'I gave up work, or it gave me up, so no money's coming in. I don't know how I'm going to pay my mortgage. Oh God, there's so much I need money for. And Jason's only eleven. I still have some responsibilities, you know.'

'Rent out the house for six months,' Pete says, shrugging. *As if it were that simple,* Carol thinks. 'That cuts out ninety per cent of your money needs.'

Carol gestures around the kitchen. 'Look at all this stuff. What do I do with it all?'

'Just shove it in one room and put a lock on it. Easily done. Or get rid of it.'

Up to this point, Tilda hasn't shown much interest in the conversation. Suddenly she bursts in. 'Darren can live here. He's back on vhe street. He needs a place to live.'

'Who's Darren?' Pete asks.

Carol scowls at Tilda. She taps the table impatiently and speaks to Pete, ignoring Tilda. 'He's a homeless man Tilda befriended. He can't pay rent.'

There is a determined set to Tilda's jaw that Carol hasn't seen before. She repeats, 'Darren can live here. He needs a place to live.

You will have empty house.'

'Does he have any money, Tilda?' Carol narrows her eyes and her voice is sharp.

'No money, Karul,' Tilda says, narrowing her eyes back at Carol. 'You have house. He needs house. He can stay here.'

'In this world, you have to pay for your housing with money,' Carol explains, speaking slowly and deliberately. What more is there to say? She desperately wants to end the conversation but Jason joins in with his usual enthusiasm.

'Mum, why can't Darren live here while we're away? He can stay in my room. I don't mind. That seems fair.'

'Jason, Tilda. This is 2018 and the world we live in runs on money. Darren doesn't have any money. I'm sorry. He deserves better but I can't help him. Can we drop this now please?'

'Give him money,' Tilda says stubbornly.

'Can't you rent out the other rooms to people who pay money and let Darren stay in my room?' Jason suggests through a mouthful of peanut butter sandwich.

'Good idea, Jason,' Tilda smiles at him. 'What do you fhink, Pete?'

Pete has been watching from the sidelines, his eyes moving from one speaker to the next, his chair tilted back. He lets his chair fall forward and takes a deep breath.

'I can see both points of view,' he says carefully.

Carol glares at him, unsympathetically. 'There is only one valid point of view,' she says flatly. 'and it's mine. If I don't pay the mortgage, Jason and I become homeless. What is so difficult to understand about that?' Her voice rises to a squeak of frustration.

'Pete doesn't have house,' Tilda says evenly. 'And he doesn't have stuff. He doesn't need money.'

'Now hold on, Tilda,' Pete interjects. 'I do need some money to live on. But I have plenty of money because I used to own a house. I'm not in the same position as Carol because my son is grown up. It's just me and I have an urge to wander. So I'm happy in my camper van.'

'So you can pay for Karul's house. Vhen Darren can live here,' Tilda says, rubbing her hands together with satisfaction.

'Ha,' Carol exclaims, glad that the spotlight has moved away from her and onto Pete.

Pete strokes his goatee thoughtfully. 'Well, I hadn't thought about that. How much is your mortgage, Carol?'

Carol rolls her eyes and scowls. 'Don't even go there.'

Pete shrugs good-naturedly. 'I'm open to think about it.'

Tilda leans forward, her eyes gleaming. 'Darren has friends. Vhey need place to live too.'

'Tilda!' Carol shouts. She is furious. She looks Tilda in the eye. Tilda looks back. Neither speak or turn away.

'Um, ladies,' Pete says delicately when the stalemate has become uncomfortably long. 'Could we lower the temperature a few degrees, please?' He and Jason exchange uneasy looks.

Without taking her eyes away from Carol's, Tilda says, 'In my land, in my time, we share everyfhing so everyone has all vhey need. You have house, *m'sheens*, a car, many many fhings. You don't need so many fhings. Darren has nofhing. Why not share?'

Carol is breathing heavily. She can't believe she's having this conversation. Since when has it become her responsibility to redistribute her wealth to the poor? How did she become the one with the duty to overturn the status quo and single-handedly create an egalitarian society?

'I did what I could,' Carol retaliates fiercely. 'I shared my house, my life, my things, my time with my mother for three years. And it nearly killed me. But she was my mother. I share with Jason and Ben. They're family. I don't know Darren from Adam. Why would I share with him?'

'You share wivh me,' Tilda says matter-of-factly. 'But I'm not in your family. I was stranger. Now I'm friend. Make Darren friend. Vhen you can share wivh him.'

Carol stares at Tilda, dumbfounded. In that moment, more than anything else she's ever done, she regrets teaching her English.

'Yeah Mum,' Jason joins in. 'You know that poster we have in the living room, the one Sue and Alison brought back from the United Nations for us? It says "do unto others as you would have them do unto you". Well doesn't that mean ...'

'Jason! For heaven's sake, that doesn't mean we have to give our house to some random homeless man.' Carol feels she is losing her grip on reality. 'Pete, help me out here, would you? You are a responsible man of the 21st century. You know how things are done these days.'

Pete looks at Carol apologetically. 'Well, I do know how things are done in this century. And much of what I see, I don't like and want to change. You know what Gandhi said: "Be the change you want to see in the world." That's what I'm trying to do in my life, in my own small way.'

'Are you fucking serious?' Carol shouts. She is teetering on the verge of a relapse. 'You would pay £500 a month for six months for my mortgage so Darren and his mates and their dogs could live it up in my house while Jason and I trail around with you in your bloody pokey camper van?!' She pauses, frowning. 'Make that £1,000 a month minimum. We wouldn't want Darren going without electricity and gas and water.'

Ignoring Carol, Tilda turns to Pete and Jason with a delighted smile. 'Let's meet again in few days,' she says. 'Vhis is good start. I fhink Karul is coming round to vhe idea.'

Pete looks dubious. 'Well, you know her better than I do. If it makes everyone happy, I'm open to considering it further.'

'Not to mention council tax and house insurance and contents insurance and car and TV license and phone and internet. And we'd have to leave him enough for food and alcohol.'

Carol is still muttering to herself at the kitchen table as everyone else slips out for a walk by the river.

Tilda

'My journey home now begins! In three moons, I will return to the Palace of the Immortals.' Tilda calls Crogan and Charmall from the woods above the pond. It is early morning. Shafts of sunlight shoot through the trees. She stops on the path and sings, her arms thrown wide, her head back.

'Let me sing my gratitude to Great Mother,
Let the bluebells carpet the woods in joy.
Let my heart beat a rhythm of
glory in time with the woodpecker.
Let me sing a chorus of leaf and blossom,
of birds at dawn, loud and insistent.
Let me dance with the fresh green leaves of the trees,
with the sparkling celandines and wood anemones.
Let me breathe in the perfume of the wild garlic.
I sing my gratitude to Great Mother.'

'Tell us the story of your journey's beginning, Wise One,' Crogan urges.

'Great Mother saw the suffering of Darren, the lonely, unwell outcast. She heard my pleas on his behalf. It was Her will that he should have a lasting home. I, in my ignorance, attempted to make Carol give him her home but I see now that that would not have been best for him. Yet, I was but a link in the chain of Great Mother's plan.

'I argued with Carol, unleashing her anger. Her anger drove her to seek Alison's counsel. Alison is wise in the ways of helping the cast-out ones. Alison pleaded on Darren's behalf to the outcast helpers. Great Mother opened a space for him in a house where he receives shelter, food and respect. I helped him heal enough to let in the love he so needs.

'Carol's anger drove her to seek people with *muhnee* to stay in "her house". Great Mother guided Pete to find people to stay in Carol's house, people who would pay her the *muhnee* she wants.

This is a time of great displacements of people from places of war and violence to places of safety. A family from a country named Syria have moved in. They told tales of their suffering that made me weep. Pete is giving his *muhnee* to people who pay Carol for the family from Syria to stay in her house.

'Carol is finding it hard to appreciate Great Mother's ways. She held onto her anger towards me for many days. She did not understand how we both played our part beautifully in fulfilling Great Mother's will. Carol struggles to see how perfect the unfolding of Great Mother's plan truly is and how our individual plans amount to nothing if not in alignment with Hers.

'Our preparations are complete.'

Charmall and Crogan send blessings for the journey.

Chapter 32. Carol

Carol jerks awake, her heart beating loudly in her ears. The darkness is suffocating. Where is she? She gropes around the bed. To her right, she feels Tilda's warm, sleeping body curled towards her. To her left, her hand bangs against the cold metal wall of the van. Pete's camper van.

The silence is as total as the darkness. Not even a clock ticking or a fridge humming. No sounds come from outside where Jason is sleeping in the tent with Pete. It's too early for birds.

She tries to lull herself back to sleep, knowing it won't work. The thought of lying awake for hours is intolerable.

'Tilda,' she whimpers. 'Please wake up. I don't like it here.'

Tilda murmurs and reaches over to pat her. One pat is all she gets before her hand drops back down. Desperately, Carol shakes Tilda's shoulder, gently at first, then roughly.

'What?' Tilda grumbles.

'I'm scared.'

'Everyfhing's okay.' Tilda cuddles her close and is asleep again within seconds. Rage and panic bubble up inside Carol. She pushes Tilda away and sits up. She's in a black hole, the darkness surrounding her like a shroud. She fumbles for the light switch. The light casts an eerie glow around the cramped interior of the van. The striped curtains loom against the wall like ghosts. In the shadows, fearsome creatures watch her. The ceiling presses down as if to crush her.

'I don't want to be here,' Carol moans through gritted teeth. 'I want to go home. I can't do this. I hate it.'

Tilda groans and covers her eyes with her arm. 'Go home vhen,' she mutters, her voice hard and clipped.

Shocked, Carol falls silent, her breath coming in shallow gulps. Tilda has never been angry at her before. She has always been calm and unshakeable, no matter how outrageous Carol's moods have been. But it seems Tilda has finally had enough.

'*Please* Tilda,' Carol moans.

Tilda does not respond. Carol is in the grip of something bigger than herself. She sobs desperately, hoping that Tilda's heart will melt, terrified that Tilda will grab the duvet and walk out. Tilda does neither. She sits up abruptly. In a voice stern with authority, she points to the door and says, 'Get out. Face your demons yourself. Go.'

It seems to Carol that Tilda has grown to fill the entire bed and that she has no choice but to leave. Tilda continues pointing until Carol creeps out of the van, collecting her jacket and shoes on the way. Then Tilda turns out the light and lies back down.

Carol sinks onto the low step outside the van, the narrow door shut against her. She rests her head on her knees. *Face my demons!* she thinks despairingly. *I don't want to face my demons. I don't even know what a bloody demon is.*

She turns on her torch and checks her watch. Four o'clock. At five, she is still sitting on the step, hunched over her knees. Her thoughts about demons have not progressed. All she's achieved is an intense feeling of self-pity, an aching back and ice-cold hands. On an endlessly repeating loop, she's been listening to a voice saying, *You are not worthy of Tilda's love. You are pathetic. You can't even stand up to her. Why do you let her treat you like that? No wonder she wants to leave you. You are unlovable.*

She hopes Tilda is feeling guilty for banishing her from the cosy, warm bed inside Pete's cosy, warm, beautifully decorated van. The longer she sits outside, the cosier the inside becomes. Yet, she doesn't dare go back in and risk another encounter with an implacable, merciless Tilda.

At five thirty, the sky begins to lighten. Straightening up, she walks creakily from the caravan site along a path to an open space on top of a hill. Nervously, she looks around for rapists and muggers but there isn't even a dog walker in sight. A half-moon is shining brightly, its shadowed half just about visible, her mind completing the circle. It seems as if the moon is winking at her, trying to catch her eye.

Carol waves. 'Hi Moon. You are a sight for sore eyes.'

Does the moon blush? Carol thinks she seems pleased.

'Moon, I've got these demons in me. They make me scared and full of rage. I want them to go away but Tilda says I should accept them. She says they are here to protect me. Tilda's angry with me for being so needy but she's leaving me. I'm angry at her for leaving. I'm scared of being alone and unloved.'

The moon sends a beam of unconditional love down at her. The demons melt in the beam and are gone. Carol sighs with relief. The demons have lost their power, at least for the moment.

She turns her attention to the drama in the eastern sky. Thin strips of violet and orange clouds reveal the spot where the sun is about to make its grand appearance. Carol holds her breath as the orange orb rises ceremoniously over the horizon. The higher it rises, the brighter it becomes until she can no longer look it in the eye.

Instinctively, she waves her arms in the air and begins chanting 'Ah' and 'Om' with each exhalation. Birds are singing in the trees behind her. She laughs out loud, observing herself conducting the dawn chorus. She is making the sun rise, the birds sing, the clouds burst into purple, the moon expand into its fullness. Her Ah's and Om's amplify over the hill and her heart swells with joy. She is so absorbed in the moment that she doesn't realise she is not alone. Tilda is chanting along beside her.

Suddenly self-conscious, Carol stops in mid-Om. Her initial reaction is to wait to see what kind of mood Tilda is in but she stops herself. She doesn't have to do that anymore. She thanks her demons and scoops up an armful of compassion from the all-accepting moon and an armful of fierce love from the life-affirming sun. She swirls them together and pours the shining mix over her own head and Tilda's until they are both completely submerged. Embracing Tilda, she kisses her tenderly. 'Sweet precious one. I love you. All of me, demons as well.'

Chapter 33. Carol

Why did she agree to an eight-mile hike from the top of a mountain down to the bottom and then up again? The sun had been fierce at dawn. By noon when they began the hike, it was positively ferocious. As she shakes her T-shirt to let the air cool her back, she wonders why she hadn't listened to her inner satnav. From the moment they'd arrived in Bolehill, it had been telling her to drive, not walk, to the ancient yew tree in Bonsall. The tree is in a churchyard, easily accessible by road, not more than a six-minute drive from Black Rock near where they're staying with Pete's mates. But Pete is organising the tree visits and his satnav says walk. As do Pete's mates who scoff at Carol's tentative suggestion of driving. The High Peak Trail is right on their doorstep. Carol feels the disapproval and says no more.

On the way to the yew tree, it helps that the sun is shining, the views are glorious and the route is downhill. Pete and Tilda consult many of the trees on the way. They tut frequently to each other, dismayed by the sad state of the trees in the Forestry Commission woodlands.

After they've eaten their picnic lunch, Carol lies on her back, idly watching a swarm of flies dancing in a column above their heads. Pete offers to share something from a book he's been reading during the trip. Carol would rather zone out but Jason and Tilda are just as eager to listen to Pete as he is to share.

'I was just reading this bit in my book about forests and how a forest is not just a bunch of individual, separate trees. Actually it's one unified being.'

'Is it a green bean or a has been?' Carol asks, kicking Pete lightly with her foot. Silver sparks flicker between them. She likes teasing him.

Pete purses his lips. 'Ha ha,' he says, but continues, his earnestness undiminished. 'The trees look like they're separate because we only see the trunks and crowns, but underneath, in the earth, the roots are all connected to each other. And the trees are not just connected via the roots but through a vast network of fungal mycelia.' Tilda and Jason are nodding as if it all makes sense, though Carol can't believe they know any more about fungal mycelia than she does.

'Well, if an individual tree is diseased or has been chopped down, the other trees nearby send it nutrients through the underground mycelial network. They try to heal it, to help it. They don't cut it off. It just made me think that maybe we can see ourselves that way. I mean us, you know, people.'

Tilda smiles at Pete. Carol can see she's tingling with excitement at Pete's little lecture. Jason is soaking it up, as usual. 'What do you mean, Pete?' he asks, as if spellbound.

Pete leans towards Jason. 'The thing is Jason, we are all connected through an invisible network and we can send love through this network to help individuals. Maybe people do terrible things because they've forgotten about this network. They think they're not part of it. Maybe when we send love to another, it's to remind them who they really are.'

'Yes, very true,' Tilda says. 'Come, let us go on to the tree.' She seems really happy, Carol thinks.

The yew tree is waiting for them, standing on its own in the churchyard. It is very much alive with decaying wood in the crown and on the ground. A new tree has sprouted from within the hollowing trunk. Ivy is growing along its trunk. While the others are exclaiming over it and talking to it, Carol uses the opportunity to take a nap. She'll need all her strength to hike up the hill on the way back.

It is a difficult hike. Carol doggedly keeps up without overt complaint until they reach the end of the journey at Black Rock. Then she throws herself on the ground and closes her eyes. Jason collapses beside her. She shrugs her arms out of her backpack and unties her hiking boots. Jason's curls are plastered to his brow with sweat. Tilda and Pete are walking on ahead, absorbed in conversation. They have already been talking non-stop about trees and forests for several hours, not even slowing their pace on the upward slope. Carol wonders how long it will be before they notice they've lost half the party.

'Mum, get up,' Jason tugs at her arm. 'Pete says we're only five minutes away. We can make it. C'mon.'

'You go ahead,' Carol murmurs sleepily. 'I'll catch up later. I could do with some time alone. Go on. I know the way. I think.'

When Jason leaves with Pete and Tilda, Carol dozes. When she wakes, the sun has already set. There in the sky is the half-moon she met at dawn.

'Hi Moon,' Carol says. She feels comforted by its shining presence. It seems to her as if it is always there looking out for her. Shyly at first, then more confidently, she begins talking to the Moon. 'I don't have to worry that you are going to go off into another dimension. You're on a regular orbit. You know who you are and where you're going. I don't. Everything's happening so fast. So much change. I used to be anchored by my work, by caring for Mum, looking after Jason, worrying about Ben, being responsible for my house. That was my identity. And now, I am stuck in a tiny camper van with Jason and Tilda and a strange man I only recently met.'

Carol wonders what the moon thinks of this confession. She seems to still be listening. Carol decides she can risk saying more.

'Who am I now? That's the question, isn't it? Maybe I'm a person with mental health issues. I've always worked, got a lot of satisfaction from working, from earning my keep. But I literally am not able to work at the moment. My brain is fried. I cannot, I will not work for the drug companies. There must be jobs I can do that don't require any brain power. Like cleaning houses. Care work. Taxi driver. I wake up in the middle of the night in a cold sweat with my stomach cramping wondering how I am going to support myself and Jason.'

The moon is clearly touched by this. As the night deepens, the moon's light has grown brighter. Carol feels a beam of compassion directed at her. She grows bolder.

'Do you know what's really keeping me awake at night, Moon? It's about who I am with Tilda. Being in a relationship with her has brought out two sides of me that are like opposing forces. There's the sexually confident side of me and a fearful, insecure side of me. I feel desire, I enjoy sex. I am fully myself, fully alive when I'm with Tilda. And then I get all fearful, afraid that I'll be alone when she goes home, afraid that I won't be anybody, that I'll cease to exist without Tilda to bring me alive. I feel like I'm a puppet and she's controlling. Does that make sense, Moon?'

'Are you talking to vhe moon, Karul?' Tilda emerges out of the darkness carrying a torch. She sits down beside Carol and puts her arm around her shoulder, giving her a friendly hug. Carol bristles at this blatant display of power over her. Anger and desire and shame well up in her. At that moment, she hates feeling so exposed and weak. She thinks, but doesn't say out loud, *Don't look at me. Don't touch me. Turn away.*

Tilda carefully and slowly takes her arm back and turns so that she is sitting with her back to Carol. Carol catches her breath. Had she spoken aloud without being aware of it? She can feel Tilda reaching out to her, sending her waves of love. But Carol's demon is back, telling her that Tilda is controlling her, hypnotising her even.

'What are you feeling, Karul?'

Carol twists her hands in her lap and speaks reluctantly. 'I want you to stop. You have power over me. Stop controlling me.'

Tilda shakes her head from side to side. Without turning around, she says quietly, 'No, Karul. You are giving me all your power. You stop. Be brave.'

Carol's mind is churning with thoughts she doesn't dare say out loud: *I'm sorry. I didn't mean it. I did mean it. I'm not sorry. Yes, you are controlling me. You are taking my power. I'm not brave. How would you like it if I dominated you?*

Without consciously intending to, she grabs Tilda's hair and pulls her head back roughly. As soon as she's done it, she is overcome with fear. Immediately, Tilda reaches back and grips Carol's hand tightly. The pain causes Carol to let go with a yelp. Carol understands without Tilda saying a word that Tilda would never give her power away. She would not be dominated or controlled. She is not a victim.

Silence grows between them. Tilda quickly gets her breathing under control but Carol's is jagged and becoming more so as the minutes tick by. She desperately wants Tilda to turn around and hold her and just as desperately, she wants Tilda to lose this battle. Tilda waits without speaking. Carol feels waves of love emanating from her and knows she is trying to reach her without words.

Carol looks up at the moon. 'Help me, Moon,' she whispers. 'I'm in a power battle and I'm losing. Help me.'

The answer is sweet and loving. 'Let it go. Take a break. Remember you are pure love. You are as Great Mother created you.'

Does the answer come from the Moon or from Tilda? It doesn't matter. She is suddenly exhausted. It would be wonderful to let it go, have a break. Much more relaxing than engaging in a power battle she can never win. She is beginning to think that winning might not be very satisfying. It would be perpetual war, one battle after another.

She takes a deep breath and pulls Tilda gently towards her, stroking her hair and kissing her ears and shoulders. Tilda leans into her. Carol marvels at Tilda's willingness to trust her when she isn't sure she can trust herself not to lash out again. The silence between them fills with a soft tenderness. It is Tilda who breaks it.

'Let's go to vhe yew tree,' she says, excited, as if the idea has just occurred to her. 'You were sleeping before. Let's go now. In vhe camper van.'

'It's night time,' Carol mutters, reluctant to end the embrace and go haring around the countryside.

'Yew tree is happy to have visitors day or night.' Tilda untangles herself and stands up, pulling Carol with her. Holding hands, they walk along the road to the camper van. Carol is aware that she is no longer in danger of a sudden fit of rage. She feels buoyed up by the Moon's reassuring presence and her trust that Tilda wouldn't let herself be hurt. Even driving the huge camper van on the narrow, winding road and finding her way to the church is not as daunting as it would normally have been.

When they walk into the churchyard, Tilda approaches the tree with reverence. She kneels down to her knees and prostrates herself full length on the ground, chanting joyfully. Carol watches in awe. To her, it is just a very, very old tree, not even a magnificent specimen. But clearly to Tilda, it is a divine Being, a manifestation of Great Mother herself.

'Vis is vhe tree of life and rebirfh,' Tilda explains when she stands up from her prostration. 'It holds all vhe wisdom of vhe world, all vhe lessons, vhe understanding of all vhe ovher trees and of all our ancestors.'

Carol nods. A sense of peace fills her. Her power battles and insecurities and fears evaporate, as if they are nothing more substantial than mist.

'In Palace of vhe Immortals,' Tilda speaks softly, smiling at Carol, her eyes shining, 'I bring vhe spirits of vhe dead to begin vheir journey to anovher world. Vhe Yew is one of vhe guardians of vhe Ovherworld. Vhe Yew Being guides vhe spirits from our world to vhe next.'

'Do you go to the other world with them?' Carol asks tentatively. Death is not something Carol has ever given much thought to, or wanted to. If she does think about it, she imagines a kind of terrifying blank nothingness.

'Yes,' Tilda says, still smiling but now at the yew tree. 'Vhe yew tree gives me strengfh and protection to help vhe spirits on vheir journey and to bring to our world a taste of forever, of no time. I don't know vhe English word.'

'I guess you mean immortality or eternity. Transcendence maybe. I don't know about such things,' Carol says, feeling out of her depth. 'Aren't you frightened of death, Tilda?'

Tilda looks closely at Carol. 'Vhe yew tree Being shows me vhat vhere is no dying, just a change from vhis world to anovher. No need to be afraid.'

'Tilda,' Carol says. 'I don't know what you're talking about but I feel very peaceful here. I'll tuck a bit of the yew tree's peace into my heart.'

'Me too. Vhe Yew tree blesses you wivh peace.'

But love me for love's sake, that evermore
Thou may'st love on, through love's eternity.

By Elizabeth Barrett Browning

Chapter 34. Carol

15th July 2018

Dear Alison and Sue,
    I bet you haven't had a hand-written letter for years. Isn't it old fashioned? Why a letter, you may ask. Well, my phone died and Pete, the Back-to-Nature Man, doesn't have a laptop or a phone. So, I'm writing letters.

I keep thinking back to our time in Dunster Beach last March and feeling overwhelmed with gratitude. I had completely lost the plot and you saved me. I'll never forget what you did for me. I just hope it wasn't too traumatic for you. I'm feeling frustrated with this letter. I can't express what I want to say. Thank you. I love you. That doesn't seem enough but it's the best I can do in a letter. I'm not very good with words. Oops. Scrap that last untrue, self-hating statement. Tilda would never let me get away with that kind of sentiment. She's on a mission to get me to see Love everywhere, in everything and everyone, including in me.

I miss being with you. I feel so far away. I have no idea when we'll get back to Bristol. I'm writing this on the ferry from Holyhead to Dublin. Our merry little band of pilgrims has completed the Ancient Tree Pilgrimage of England and Wales. I don't know how many ancient trees we visited since we started in May. It seems like hundreds but is probably dozens. We've been all over the country. Don't tell Pete or Tilda or even Jason but as far as I'm concerned, when you've seen one tree, you've seen them all. I can't really tell them apart. Still, this is a beautiful country and I love being outside in Nature.

We've had good weather thanks to Great Mother (Tilda's influence!) since Pete and Jason are sleeping outside in a tent while Tilda and I are in the camper van. You know that I've never been into camping but once I got used to it, it's not that bad. I mean, I do have cravings for a proper bed in a room big enough to spread my arms and not touch both walls. But to my surprise, I don't miss my house or my furniture or my kitchen or any of my stuff, or my job, especially not my job. It amazes me that I can just walk away from it all and not feel that I've lost myself. Being on the road has helped me find myself. That sounds crazy, doesn't it?

The thing is that I love being with Tilda, of course, and Pete's okay. He's actually quite fun, a bit earnest for my taste but basically, his heart is in the right place. He's respectful. I like him. The main thing I'm getting from all this mad wandering about is a relationship with Jason. I love spending so much time with my beautiful, amazing son. He is one special boy. I love him so much. I totally missed the first ten years of his life. I'm getting to know him in a way that I never could BT – Before Tilda.

BT – that's how I see my life. BT, then WT – With Tilda, and soon PT – Post Tilda. OMG! Losing Tilda. I can't write too much about it without feeling like my heart is going to break into pieces. She is really leaving me forever. She did say she would only stay for six months and it's been more like nine. It's not long enough. I can't bear it. But she is really going and she is so excited. She came with a mission from Great Mother to wake us, trees as well as people, and she believes she has succeeded. She has certainly woken me up though I keep telling her that I'm only half awake and she should stay another twenty years to have a chance at fully waking me. She thinks I'm being funny. I'm not.

Tomorrow, Pete is dropping me and Tilda at the lodge at Newgrange. He is taking Jason away for a week so Tilda and I can spend our last few days together, just the two of us. Then she is going into the Newgrange monument by herself to travel back to Neolithic times. After that, PT, I have no idea. The future is a blank.

We'll be in Ireland any minute now. I'm determined to be fully awake every moment for the next week. My last days WT. OMG!

Sending you love,
Carol

Chapter 35. Tilda

Dearest Carol, may my words travel over fhousands of years of time and reach you still sparkling wivh love. Our last moment togevher is forever as if etched in stone on my heart. It was night time. Vhe moon was a sliver of gold, vhe stars bright sparks of joy.

We tore ourselves apart from our final embrace. I climbed over vhe entrance stone and was by vhe entryway to vhe Palace of vhe Immortals. I was about to go past vhe gate into vhe chamber, about to leave you forever. You were on vhe ovher side of vhe entrance stone, your hands resting on vhe triple spiral. I was wearing my ceremonial garments I had worn on my journey to you, my necklace of periwinkle shells wrapped around my forehead in a spiral pattern, my moccasins on my feet. You were wearing your special red dress and your favourite tree of life earrings. On your feet were your heavy hiking boots, untied.

You called my name, a song of pure love. I turned. You smiled wivh your whole body and blew me a kiss. It landed on my shoulder and gave me wings to go. I removed vhe gate and went inside.

Now whenever I fhink about true love, I always remember vhat moment.

In vhe time we had been on pilgrimage wivh Pete in his camper van, I saw friendship growing between you and Pete. I fhank Great Movher daily for vis. May it be a source of healing for you and for Pete. It made it easier for me to leave you, knowing you are not alone. Yes, I know you told me on vhe ferry you don't want me to be a matchmaker. You said, 'Pete is not suitable lover material. He is not capable of making love to me in vhe style to which I have become accustomed.' I fhink you can train him to be good lover. But I am not wivh you so I hand it over to Great Movher.

I will never forget waiting for vhe call in vhe lodge in Newgrange. We spent hours every day making love as if we could stock up on love to last our lifetimes. I recorded each moment into my memory – your nose crinkling up when you teased me, vhe taste of your nipple hard against my tongue, vhe smell of your skin after lovemaking, vhe silky smoovhness of your hair, vhe way you gasped when I touched your vagina, vhe weight of your body on mine, vhe way my body responded to your touch. I am a Wisdom Keeper and I remember what I put in my memory.

When Great Movher called me to come, my soul rejoiced. But vhe woman you call Tilda, vhe woman who has been your lover, vhat woman's heart was broken. I started to cry as if I would never stop. I could see in your eyes you were shocked and frightened.

We had become as one being, like a forest is one being wivh tree roots and branches touching, connecting, sending love. An angelic axe had arrived to clear vhe forest we had become. I fell into a dark hole. We wrapped ourselves around each ovher and lay on vhe floor in vhe room in vhe lodge, weeping. I know not for how long. You recovered first and hauled me out of vhe hole. You mopped up our tears and washed our faces.

Wivh sweet grace, you said, 'Enough, my sweetheart. Vhe time for tears is over. Let's go to vhe river, fhank Great Movher for our love which is for eternity and order a takeaway Chinese.'

You led me to vhe river where we prayed togevher. My heartache eased. But vhe fear did not leave. You wanted to walk wivh me to vhe entrance of vhe Palace of vhe Immortals at midnight and say our final goodbye vhere. I was afraid vhat in your grief, you would rush inside where vhe powerful forces created for vhe journey would kill you. My fear and guilt convinced me you wanted to die because I broke your heart. Wivh stern words, I told you to stay in vhe lodge. Karul, I acted wivhout respect for you, for your mastery. I am sorry.

At midnight, I woke and dressed in vhe dark. I knew you were awake, trying to be still. I chanted silently and left vhe lodge. At vhe side of vhe road, I stopped. I remembered vhe car hitting me. I was unable to cross. I chanted louder yet I could not move.

I heard vhe sound of your boots coming slowly towards me. My knees felt weak wivh relief. Wivhout turning around, I reached out one hand. You took my hand in yours. Vhey fit togevher and we became one again. Out of vhe corner of my eye, I saw you had dressed in your special clovhes. Do you know how beautiful you were, how my heart melted at vhe sight of you? How I wish I had stopped chanting long enough to tell you.

From vhe lodge, you and I walked hand in hand across vhe dangerous road. We stopped on vhe bridge over vhe River Boyne. I asked vhe Salmon of Wisdom for vheir blessing for my journey and fhanked vhem when vhey gave it. From vhe river, we walked along vhe roads to vhe Palace. Our hands were trembling where vhey touched.

As we climbed over vhe fence at vhe base of vhe Palace, you looked me in vhe eye and said, 'I read somewhere vhat vhe only whole heart is one vhat has been broken. We're parting wivh whole hearts.'

Vhen we embraced for vhe last time.

Chapter 36. Carol

L ong before the first rays of the dawn sun touch the triple spiral carvings on the entrance stone, the chanting ceases. With her heart thumping and her hands shaking, Carol creeps over the wooden steps and inches along the passageway, feeling her way in the dark by touching the stones on either side. Will she find Tilda's dead body lying in one of the alcoves? Or is there a secret passageway to a hidden back entrance? She turns on her torch as she reaches the chamber and scans every corner and crack. Tilda is definitely not there. If the stones had opened to let Tilda sneak out, they had closed again as tightly as before.

The bubble where she'd placed Tilda's fantastical story of time travel bursts with a sudden loud pop. 'Tilda, where are you?' Carol whispers. She is more frightened than she's ever been in her life.

'Don't be afraid, my precious one. I am home. I love you always.'

The voice is Tilda's and whether it's in the chamber or in her mind, Carol can't tell. She wants to not be afraid. She wants to feel Tilda's love but, in that moment, alone inside the chamber, surrounded only by huge, unyielding stones, she feels nothing but panic. She flees, banging her head as she scurries out.

She is greeted by the dawn sun who puts on a spectacular display for her eyes alone.

'Thank you, Sun,' Carol calls. 'You are beautiful.'

The panic subsides enough for her to register how calming the sound of her voice is. She can't chant the way Tilda chanted but she can sing. Softly at first, then louder, she sings the first song that comes into her head, a Beatles song that her mother had sung in her singing group. '*Nothing you can know that isn't known. Nothing you can see that isn't shown. Nowhere you can be that isn't where you're meant to be. It's easy. All you need is love, love. Love is all you need.*'

She sings her way back to the lodge where she sleeps fitfully. Over the next few days, she is lost in a dense grey fog which lifts occasionally to reveal random, unconnected moments of clarity. Like the moment she wakes to the aroma of freshly baked buttered soda bread left in her room by Roisin, the kind, wild-haired manager of the lodge. Or when she stands on the bridge over the rapidly flowing River Boyne hypnotised by the swirl of the water, passed by crowds of tourists on their way to the Newgrange monument. When she catches the eye of the waxing moon in the night sky. When she holds Jason's head against her chest as he sobs. When Pete's sympathetic smile touches her wounded heart.

As July drifts into August and August into September, the three of them settle into a rhythm. Pete and Jason study the map and work out the routes. Pete does all the driving. Carol sits in the back, staring out the window, sometimes crying quietly, often her mind blank, occasionally peaceful.

Carol wakes each morning with no idea what the day will bring. Without consciously intending to, she discovers Moments. She thinks of these Moments as mysterious treasures hidden in the day. She has no desire to record them in a journal, take photos or put them in bubbles at the back of her mind. Nor does she feel the need to analyse them or express an opinion. Her only task is to uncover them, notice them and let them be.

She feels like a miner gradually discovering that the little nugget of gold she has just uncovered is part of a rich seam. There is the Moment when Pete teaches Jason to make spaghetti bolognese in the camper van; when the three of them play endless games of canasta and scrabble in the holiday park in Donegal; when they sit at a viewpoint on top of bleak Glengesh Pass eating disgusting fish and chips while being eaten by midges; when the three of them dance and clap to trad live music in an Irish theme park village pub.

Driving around Donegal, they stop in a cafe in Ardara on a day so hot that the butter has melted into a yellow puddle in the chipped butter dish. A tiny fan makes a noisy attempt to move the hot air without discernible success. An older woman with sweat-plastered hair slowly peels herself from the fan and comes to their crumb-stained table.

'Can I have a bowl of ice cream?' Jason asks Carol, wiping his damp forehead with the back of his hand.

'Make that two,' Carol says to the waitress. 'Both chocolate.' Carol imagines that the waitress scowls disapprovingly or maybe she is just bad-tempered because of the heat.

'I'll have the soup of the day,' Pete says, pointing to a prominent box in the photocopied menu advertising soup of the day in large letters.

It isn't her imagination. The waitress lowers her pad and pencil and glares at Pete.

'It's fearsome hot to be eating soup,' she says, her scowl deepening. She crosses her arms and stops writing on her pad.

Pete blinks. 'I'd like the soup,' he repeats pleasantly, smiling up at her.

'You can have ice cream,' she says, not smiling.

'I want the soup of the day,' Pete says, crossing his arms, but the waitress has stomped off. She returns five minutes later with three bowls of melted ice cream.

'There's your soup,' she snarls, slamming the bowls on the table.

They manage to drink their ice cream and get out of the cafe before collapsing in fits of giggles. For several days after, one or another will say in a sombre voice, 'It's fearsome hot to be eating soup,' and they all fall about laughing.

That is, until Carol mentions school. They are sitting in the sandy cove in Malin Beg after a long walk down a flight of wooden steps. They have just finished their picnic when Carol drops it into the conversation like it's a bomb about to explode.

'You're supposed to start secondary school any day now. We've got to get back to Bristol.'

'It's fearsome hot to be ...' Jason begins.

'That's enough, Jason. I haven't been paying attention. We've got to go tomorrow.' She feels panicky, incompetent, a bad mother. She knows she should send Jason to school but she can't even begin to imagine how she will make it happen. Jason and Pete have identical glum faces but neither of them argue.

'C'mon you two,' Carol pleads. 'We've got to get back to the real world.' The exhortation exhausts her. She lapses into silence, her thoughts in a turmoil: *I don't want to go back. I want to stay with Pete. It's too soon after Tilda leaving to start another relationship. Why doesn't he say what he wants? Maybe he doesn't want to be with me. Maybe he wants his life back.*

Shoulders hunched, Pete studies the map and works out a route back to England. His compliance with her request convinces Carol that Pete is eager to send them back to Bristol and get on with his life. Why else would he be driving them across Ireland and onto the ferry? Throughout the journey, all three are silent and morose.

Pete's route home takes them through Snowdonia National Park. They stop in a cafe and are settling down to eat lunch when Jason notices a poster in the window for a holiday rental.

'Mum, Pete, look at this,' he calls excitedly. 'We could rent a five-bedroom, two-hundred-year old Welsh stone cottage near Harlech Beach. Can we do it?'

Carol catches a glimpse of Pete's face. He is looking at her with desperate hopefulness. *This is one of my Seam of Gold Moments,* she thinks.

'Mum, I don't want to go to school,' Jason says, his eyes reddening and his voice tight. 'I want to carry on like we've been doing, travelling around in the camper van, just the three of us. You, me and Pete. Please, Mum. Why can't we?'

In that moment, Carol knows without a doubt that that's what Pete wants as well. She puts her head in her hands. The thought of going back to Bristol, to a life of responsibilities, home ownership, a job, Jason at school, city living, a life without Nature, is like a crushing weight, sapping her spirit.

Ask Great Movher. She hears Tilda's voice as loudly and clearly as if she were sitting right next to her. But she doesn't need to ask Great Mother because Great Mother's answer is as loud and clear as Tilda's. It is broadcast direct to her heart which leaps with joy when she thinks of life on the road with Pete and Jason. It is as if she's grown wings and is soaring.

Chapter 37. Carol

If the cottage is free, I'll take that as a sign that Great Mother wants us to carry on together,' Carol says, calling the phone number on the poster. Jason holds his breath and Pete tries to look nonchalant as Carol speaks to the letting agency. Yes, the cottage is free. Yes, they can have it for one month, two months, as long as they like. They move in the next day.

'I'll have this room,' Carol says, choosing the one with the rose patterned bedspread and the view of the sea. 'You boys can fight over the other four bedrooms.' The idea of having a room of her own is blissful, after months in the cramped camper van.

She is about to fling herself on the bed when Jason says, 'Aren't you going to share a bedroom with Pete?'

'That's not really your business now, is it, Jason?' Carol replies sharply. She glances at Pete who raises his eyebrows and looks interested or hopeful or willing to consider the idea. She isn't sure what to make of his expression.

'Well, it is my business, Mum, because if you are going to have sex with Pete, I want my room to be far enough away that I can't hear you shouting like you did with Tilda.'

Carol gasps. 'Did I shout when I was, um, when I was with Tilda?'

Both Pete and Jason nod their heads slowly up and down, with expressions that clearly indicate that she had made a lot of noise.

'The camper van isn't very soundproof, you know,' Pete says delicately. 'We could hear you from the tent.' He looks highly amused. Carol winces. Did she really make that much noise?

'I'm, I'm sorry, Jason,' she exhales slowly. 'I guess I haven't been thinking about how you've been affected, have I?'

'It's okay Mum. At first I thought Tilda was hurting you. That was before we came away with Pete. So I asked her.'

'You couldn't ask me?' Carol whispers. She is not comfortable having this conversation with Jason, especially with Pete standing by.

'No,' Jason replies with a look of surprise. 'Remember when we were in Dunster Beach? You said it was none of my business. Tilda thought it was. She told me all about sex.'

No, surely not. Did she really tell him it was none of his business?

'What exactly did Tilda tell you about sex?' Carol asks, feeling distinctly nervous on top of her embarrassment. What strange notions did Tilda put in her son's head?

'I am eleven and three quarters, you know,' he says huffily. 'I am old enough to know about these things. She told me that sex is something people do for different reasons, like making babies or for fun or even as a way to hurt someone. But it can be a way to show love to someone and then it gives the people a lot of pleasure and some people make a lot of noise when they have that kind of pleasure. And she said that a lot of people in our world have really screwed up ideas about sex and that stops them from getting the pleasure.'

'What kind of ideas?' Pete asks. He's leaning casually against the wall, not looking at Carol.

Jason winds his fingers through his curls. 'I can't remember what she called it – monogy, monopogy. It sounds like monopoly but it means when you only ever have one partner all your life. Or just one partner at a time.'

'Monogamy,' Carol says. 'Yes, Tilda really did not agree with monogamy. That wasn't the way she did things at home in her Neolithic community. Or so she said. When she was here with us, she didn't make love with anyone but me.'

Out of the corner of her eye, she notices that Pete is shifting from foot to foot. Before she can focus on him, Jason starts talking in an excited voice.

'She started learning about sex when she was my age,' he says. 'She learned by playing with other boys and girls about her age, and some adults too, and carried on all her life, making love with the same group of five people – three girls and two boys. Sometimes all five of them would make love in a group. Sometimes she'd pair up with one of the boys, sometimes with one of the girls.'

'Yeah, she told me that too,' Carol says, chewing her lip in worry. 'But Jason, in her time you became an adult when you were twelve or thirteen. Or maybe there was no separation between children and adults. That's a modern way of looking at age. It's really different now. If an eighteen-year-old has sex with an eleven-year-old, it would be seen as sexual abuse, as child molestation. We consider it wrong. Adults go to prison over that kind of thing.'

Jason shrugs. 'I know it's different now. Tilda asked me how I learn about sex and I said we had some lessons at school but when I told her what we did in those lessons, she said that wasn't what she meant. Since you two are home schooling me, we can add that topic to our curriculum, can't we?'

Carol looks closely at Jason. She knows that Tilda had spent considerable time with Jason, teaching him about Nature and Neolithic life and what else? Why wouldn't she include sex in her lessons?

'She didn't give you any um, you know, like hands-on, practical lessons, did she?'

Jason pauses. 'Well, now that you mention it,' he says and bursts out laughing at Carol's shocked expression. 'No, Mum. She said that wasn't her business to do.'

'Um, Carol,' Pete says, still not looking Carol in the eye. 'Could I have a private word with you?'

'Are you going to have sex?' Jason asks eagerly.

'Jason, I'd like to talk to your mother about um, about things that are private, that are not your business. Do you think you could give us some space?'

'No problemo,' Jason says. He winks at Pete and skips outside. They watch from the window as he wanders down to the beach. As soon as he is far enough away, Carol goes into the small back garden where she sits on a bench by a low stone wall.

Pete comes out quietly, hesitantly. She can sense him behind her and his presence feels different, as if something has shifted in the space between them. He rests his hand on her head and slowly strokes her hair, gradually moving down to her shoulder. Carol pats the bench next to her and tugs his hand, inviting him to sit beside her. They are both barely breathing. Carol is intensely aware of where their bodies touch, of the warmth of his skin, of his arm on her shoulder, of desire welling up within her. In all the months they've been travelling together, they've never touched each other or spoken about their feelings for each other.

In that moment, she feels there is something inevitable about to happen, something right, that is meant to be. She smiles at him and says, 'So, what do you want to talk to me about?'

'Sex,' he says softly.

'Oh, that,' Carol says after a brief pause.

'Carol, I need to get this out in the open. I feel we're on the brink of a beautiful relationship and I don't know if you feel the same way. I really want this to work. I, um I don't know the right words to say. I want to say I love you. OK, I'll say it. I just did say it.' He lapses into silence, rubbing his hands together in his lap.

Carol glances at him out of the corner of her eye. For someone on the brink of a beautiful relationship, she thinks he sure looks miserable.

A demon grabs Carol by the throat. She can't speak. She wants to say that she loves him too. But she doesn't say the words. She listens to the demon snarling in her ear, saying things she knows are not true. *You don't want a relationship with a man. It will be just like with Mike. Men don't know anything about making love. Pete's a nice guy but he doesn't have a clue. You'll end up on your own again. He can't meet your needs.* Blah blah blah. She feels like screaming at the demon.

Pete rubs his chin a few more times and says, 'I'm terrified I'll say or do the wrong thing and then you'll ...' It seems like a demon has grabbed him by the throat as well. But Pete pushes the demon aside and goes on, speaking rapidly. 'I don't know why Gillian killed herself. For the last five years, I've gone over and over it in my head trying to figure out what I had or hadn't done.'

Carol bites her lip. She's forgotten about Gillian. How insensitive can she be! She's never asked about Gillian, just put her out of her mind.

'I didn't have a clue that she was so unhappy,' Pete continues. 'What kind of husband lives with his wife for twenty years and doesn't have a clue? She seemed happy enough. Though she did criticise me a lot, especially about my lovemaking.'

Carol's stomach is churning. He is tormenting himself and it's painful to witness. She feels small and useless.

'We had our issues and we bickered sometimes but I just thought it was a normal relationship. Doesn't every couple have some issues? Clearly I was so self-absorbed that I didn't see the signs.'

A surge of protectiveness overwhelms Carol. She can't stand to hear him beating himself up. She wants more than anything to make him feel better.

Pete rushes on, not waiting for Carol to comment. 'I don't want that to happen again. I want to know what's going on with you. I want to be able to trust you to be honest with me.'

Carol takes a deep breath and ignores her demon. 'I'm so so sorry, Pete.' She squeezes his hand. 'I do love you and I want a relationship of love and trust and honesty and all that good stuff. I want it more than anything in the world. And I want it with you. And I don't want it yet because it's too soon after Tilda left. And I'm scared. And I've got a demon in my head telling me it won't work and men don't know how to make love and you'll be just like Mike and ...'

Her words get lost in Pete's mouth as he leans over to kiss her. Carol is flooded with relief and happiness, her demon momentarily vanquished.

'Tilda wanted us to get together, you know,' Pete says, stroking her hair and pulling her closer. 'She spoke to me about it. About what I need to do to be a good lover to you. I had no idea how to make love to a woman until Tilda showed me. What I did with Gillian was not satisfying to her, as she often told me. With Gillian, I felt clumsy, ignorant. I want to do better with you.'

Carol's demon sets off a warning bell in the back of her mind. 'Did Tilda SHOW you how to be a good lover or did she just TELL you?' she asks suspiciously, pulling back from his embrace.

Pete tugs at his goatee. 'Well, it was for your benefit, you know.'

'You fucked her, didn't you? Damn her.' Carol crosses her arms and scowls.

'What do you expect from a Stone Age shaman?' Pete says, shrugging his shoulders. 'They are so uncivilised, no morals. And she was not to be refused. She intimidated me. Don't look at me like that. It's true. I had no choice. Please don't be mad, Carol. Let me show you what I learned and then you can judge whether it was worth it or not. She loved you very much. She did it from love.'

'I am the one to train you. I don't want her meddling in my life, controlling me. She pissed off to Neolithia. She has no right to boss me around from five thousand years ago.'

Pete puts his hand over Carol's mouth. 'She taught me to worship you as the divine feminine incarnate. And she said that if I don't treat you right, she will find a way to come back from wherever and sort me out. She didn't specify exactly how but I don't intend to find out. Still, if you'd rather I assert my rights as the dominant patriarch while you walk five paces behind me, then—'

'Oh shut up,' Carol says, pulling Pete's hand off her mouth. 'Tilda showed me how to make love to you too so don't even think of taking advantage of me. Anyway, she doesn't have to protect me. I can deal with any attempts on your part to dominate me.'

'We'll see about that. So do I get to share a bedroom with you?'

'No way. That's my space. You'll have to bow to the floor and kiss my feet before I let you anywhere near my divine feminine bits.

Hey. What are you doing?'

Pete has leapt off the bench and is on his knees, kneeling in front of Carol and lifting her feet to his mouth to be kissed.

'Now will you let me near your divine feminine bits please?' he asks sombrely. Carol starts giggling. Before she can object, Pete throws her over his shoulder in a fireman's lift.

'I'm going to call Tilda if you don't put me down,' Carol shouts from her upside-down position on Pete's back. She tries to kick but he has a firm grip on her legs.

Pete does not put her down but carries her into the cottage where they come face to face with a stern-faced Jason, his hands on his hips and his eyes narrowed.

'Tilda would not approve,' he says through pursed lips. 'I'm taking the bedroom in the attic.' He marches up the stairs without another look back.

'You are in so much trouble,' Carol says as Pete quickly sets her on her feet. She adjusts her T-shirt and raises her chin in the air. 'But I'll let you get away with it this once because you're just at the beginning of your training to be my lover. Now show me what Tilda taught you. And no more talking.'

Pete follows Carol into her bedroom, looking distinctly unchastened and altogether too pleased with himself. As she closes the door, Carol fires off a quick call to Great Mother. 'I hope you know what you are doing, setting me up with a fireman. I may be out of my depth here. Please help us to find love with each other.'

And so it becomes one of her Seam of Gold Moments.

Chapter 38. Carol

I am the sunlight in the heart, the moonlight in the mind; I am the light at the end of every dream, the voice for ever calling to come away; Come with me, come with me.

The call has become more insistent, harder to bury among the busy doings of the day. Just as it was two years before, Carol hears it in her dreams, in that moment before full consciousness returns. She hears it as she comes out of the shower, as she listens to the latest news of the COVID death toll, as she makes dinner for her household when it is her turn on the rota, as she sits under the sycamore tree in the field behind her house, as she watches Jason and Pete plan their next Extinction Rebellion action.

The call is loud and clear. It is a call that she can't ignore, that she doesn't want to ignore.

'I'm hearing the call again,' she says to Jason when they are walking by the river on their once a day permitted exercise session. 'I don't think I'm supposed to go to Newgrange though; how could I with the lockdown? Still, it must be something to do with Newgrange. It's calling me to come away but to what I don't know.'

'Tilda woke up a lot of the trees around here so why don't you ask one of them?' Jason suggests. He takes his mother's arm and steers her towards a mature tree dangling its branches in the foaming water at the base of the weir. 'Try this chestnut tree.'

'I suppose I could, Jason but I've never really got into talking to trees like you do.' Carol lets herself be led to the tree and looks at it dubiously. To her surprise, she notices a flicker of interest coming from the tree.

'Now Mum, touch the trunk with both hands. Close your eyes and just be with the tree. Start by thanking it. They like to be appreciated. Next ask it, first of all, what you can do for it and secondly, what it has to teach you. Then just listen. The answer may not come immediately. Give it some time. Okay?'

Carol does as she is told, first checking that there are no other people around to see her hugging the tree. The bark is smooth to the touch with rough patches and warmer than she'd expected. She murmurs her thanks and rests her forehead against the trunk. As soon as she closes her eyes, she smells Tilda. Shocked, her eyes fly open and she peers around in all directions. The only person she can see is Jason sitting quietly on a fallen log, gazing into the churning river. Closing her eyes again, she returns her attention to the tree. Instantly, she feels Tilda's presence with her.

'Tilda?' she whispers. 'Are you here in the tree or have I dialled into Neolithic time through this tree?'

Tilda's voice comes through loud and clear into her mind. 'Finally! I've been calling for weeks. Hi Karul. I'm here, my precious one. I've come to be wivh you, to be your spirit guide.'

'Tilda, where are you? I can't see you but somehow I know you're here. I can hear you. How is this possible or should I even ask?' Carol is gripping the tree with both hands. She is bubbling over with excitement, tears of joy welling up.

'Yes, you should ask,' Tilda's voice plays into her mind. 'You can't see me because I don't have a body anymore. I'm pure spirit. Instead of going to all vhe trouble to travel here from anovher time or to be born into anovher body, vis time I am travelling light.'

'I've missed you so much, Tilda. I hated that you left me. I think of you every day.' Carol sighs and leans closer to the tree. Is it her imagination or does the tree embrace her? She allows herself to feel held. At her feet, the river pours itself over the weir, dancing and splashing as it flows ever onward.

'I am here wivh you all vhe time from now. I won't leave you again. Our love is like vhe river, always coming, always going, always here now.' Tilda's voice is soothing, soporific, merging with the sound of the water. Carol wakes suddenly as her head falls forward and hits the hard trunk.

'Ouch,' she says, stepping back from the tree. 'Where is here,

Tilda? Where are you exactly? Are you in this tree?'

'Not in tree. In you. But vhere is not a simple answer to vhat question. I am in several realms at once. All you need to know is I am here for you, wivh you, a part of you. I am your spirit guide, here to help you.'

'That's all very well, Tilda, but I don't want you in my head or in several other dimensions,' Carol says. 'I'd rather have you in the flesh in this time zone, this reality. I want to make love to you with my whole body, not in fantasy. You woke me up to the joy my body can experience. That's what I want. With you in a body.'

Tilda doesn't reply. A silence grows between them. Carol begins to fear that Tilda will withdraw her offer and abandon her again. She rushes back to the tree and knocks on the trunk. A spider scurries out of the way of her fist.

'Tilda, come back. I didn't mean it. You can be my spirit guide. We don't have to have a sexual relationship. Listen, when you left, I thought I could never love another the way I loved you. And that is true. Our love was unique. But I have come to love Pete and it's totally different from the way I loved you. And that's okay. Well, it's more than okay. It's good, very good. It's not as passionate or intense, that's for sure. I mean, he's a man. I know you took it upon yourself to 'train' him which was not your business to do and I'm still cross with you for meddling, but—'

Carol pauses, wondering if she should mention the infidelity at this point. *How does one relate to a spirit guide?* she asks herself. *Probably not a good idea to challenge them.*

'Tilda, are you there or here or wherever? I can hear you breathing. How can I hear you breathing if you don't have a body? The thing is I've got a bit more training to do with Pete. But he's coming along nicely. The main thing is that we're having fun together. And that he knows who's boss. Well, most of the time. Every now and then, I let him throw me over his shoulder so he can play the big he-man fireman. Actually the main thing is I'm not on my own anymore.

Pete isn't about to disappear down some triple spiral worm hole any minute like you were.'

Carol takes a deep breath and tries to slow down the flow of words. How can Tilda be her spirit guide when there are all these issues to resolve between them? Why isn't Tilda answering?

'Pete's promised to stay with me. He loves me and I love him too. I feel safe with him. We work things out together. Like what to do about money or whether to see Mum or even what to have for dinner or who's going to do the washing up. You know what's the best part? With Pete, I have a partner who's at the same level as me in terms of making a loving relationship. Like I said, we're working it out together. I like that. A lot. And it's not just with Pete. With Ben, too. We're getting better at making a loving relationship. He dropped out of uni and is travelling around the world. He's working in Australia now. He calls every now and then to let me know what he's up to. He is getting his life together. He's no longer so hostile.'

'Are you done yet?' Tilda interrupts.

Carol collapses against the tree with relief. 'I thought you'd left me again. Don't do that to me Tilda.'

'I'm here. I heard everyfhing you said. I went away to ask Crogan and Charmall whevher we can have sex when I'm your spirit guide.'

'What?' Carol splutters.

'It's my first time as a spirit guide. I was just told vhat spirit guides don't usually have sex wivh people incarnate but if we want to try, vhen we can.'

'We can do what?' Carol asks. 'Can you borrow a body or would it be more like phone sex?'

'I don't know. It's not my main purpose as a spirit guide but I'm happy to try if you want.'

'Tilda, if this is your first time as a spirit guide, are you getting any supervision?'

'Of course. No one's ever alone here.'

'Do you have a guide book to follow or should I Google it for you? Someone's bound to have written one.'

Tilda giggles. 'No guide book.'

'What about training?'

'Yes, darling, I was trained by my spirit guides, Crogan and Charmall, in Neolivhic time. Now will you let me be your spirit guide, Karul?'

'I haven't finished interviewing you for the post. Other than multi-dimensional spirit sex with a disembodied lover, what do I get out of this arrangement? It sounds like an opportunity for you to boss me around some more. Which you were very good at and which I don't need.'

'Everyone needs guidance from wivhin, from spirit world.'

'I know. You're right. And I do appreciate your guidance. But wouldn't it be better for you to be Jason's spirit guide? He has taken on board everything you taught him. He's out there saving the world from environmental destruction, mass extinction, not to mention a global pandemic.'

Tilda laughs heartily. 'Jason has a host of spirit guides, angels and archangels at vhe highest level guiding him. He has important work to do and he's supported from vhe spirit world.'

'Really? That is so reassuring. Look, I still have issues to work on, Tilda. I know I need your guidance. So, yes, I do accept your offer to be my spirit guide.'

'Come wivh me, Karul. I will take you out of your body. I want to show you somefhing.'

'What is it? Is it safe? Will I be able to get back in my body?' Carol trembles. She isn't ready. This is going in the deep end. She digs her heels in.

'Your body is not safe,' Tilda says gently. 'Your body is fragile like a leaf in autumn. Trust me, Karul. What I will show you is more wonderful vhan any orgasm.'

'Okay. I guess,' Carol whispers.

It seems to Carol that Tilda reaches in and takes hold of her and lifts her effortlessly out of her body. They rise through the branches of the chestnut tree, up above the river, above the city. She can see tiny streets filled with traffic, the tops of miniature houses and buildings, the toy-like motorway cutting a slash across the city. They are soaring higher and higher until they are at the level where airplanes used to fly before they were grounded by the pandemic. And still they ascend, beyond the earth's atmosphere, until they can look at planet Earth hanging in space, a beautiful globe, the oceans patches of deep blue.

'Look Karul. Can you see a vast grid over vhe earfh? It's like a spider web covering vhe earfh all around. It is vhe cosmic web. It comes from Great Movher. She asks vhe Archangels to watch over our planet. Vhese are times of great change, Karul. Vhe cosmic web holds vhe earfh steady as vhe energy shifts.

'Do you see vhe lights wivhin it? Vhe cosmic web is lit by vhe love and light spreading from our hearts. Vhe cosmic web holds us and it is our work to hold vhe cosmic web and make it strong.'

As Tilda describes the cosmic web, it comes into focus in Carol's mind. She can clearly see spots of light shining throughout the cosmic web with lines of light crisscrossing the grid from the spots.

'Your spot is on vhe grid Karul. Can you find it?'

To Carol's surprise, she easily finds her place on the cosmic web.

'Now send love from your heart to vhe people you love along vhe web.'

Carol brings Jason to her mind and sends him a beam of love. She laughs with delight as a spot of light flares up on the web. She does the same with Pete, with her mother, with Ben, with each of her friends, and with Darren. Each time, a spot on the web flares up and shines brighter.

'Tilda, can I do it with people who are dead?'

'Yes, my precious one.'

Carol finds her father's point on the web and lights it up. A thrill passes through her.

'Where's your spot, Tilda? I want to light you up.' Carol feels she is fizzing with joy. 'Is this what you meant by being more wonderful than any orgasm of the body?'

'We're just at vhe start. Now send to places where people are suffering, where is war and violence, disease and fear, where people have lost hope.'

Carol is not surprised how much of the planetary web is alight. But it saddens her to see the scale of suffering.

'I suppose we can, or should, use the cosmic web of light to send blessings to people who cause suffering like Donald Trump and the man with the swastika tattoo who attacked you,' she says, slowly processing the ever-changing vision before her.

'Very important, yes. And to all leaders in vhe world.'

Tilda continues her instructions. Together they light up the web, directing beams of light and love to all human beings, then to all the animals, to all the plants and to the rocks and minerals, to all beings of past and future. Carol is entranced by the way the web sparkles and shines in a dazzling display of colours and shapes as she and Tilda broadcast to different beings.

'In Neolivhic times, vhere were forests all over Movher Earfh, connected by vhe tree roots, trees talking to trees, trees talking to all Beings. People destroyed vhe forests since vhat time. Two years ago, I came to help wake up vhe trees, especially vhe ancient trees like vhe Tortworfh Chestnut Tree and vhe ovher trees we met wivh Pete. When vhe trees are awake, we can connect vhe trees to vhe web of light. Vat's how we can save Movher Earfh from destruction and return Her to balance. We have to honour vhe trees and follow vhere guidance. Vhat is our work, Karul, my precious one. Now back to your body.'

'Not yet, please,' Carol begs. 'I want to stay here forever.'

Tilda just laughs. The descent seems far too abrupt, much quicker than the way up. As she re-inhabits her body, waiting patiently by the chestnut tree, Carol feels the grid of light come alive within her. Each cell of her body, each organ, each molecule is vibrating, communicating, glowing.

'... and there was everywhere a wandering ecstasy of sound: light and sound were one; light had a voice, and the music hung glittering in the air.'
from *The Dream of Angus Oge* by George William Russell, 1897

ACKNOWLEDGEMENTS

I am grateful to the many spiritual and personal growth teachings and practices that I have explored throughout my life and which have found their way into the story, particularly but not only: Rabbi Shefa Gold's Kol Zimra programme of sacred Hebrew chanting, the Grandmothers' Teachings on the Net of Light and A Course in Miracles.

Many books and articles have helped me in my understanding of Neolithic archaeology, society and spirituality, including:

The True Hero's Journey in Fairy Tales and Stone Circles by Andrea Hofman, 2018

Voices Out of Stone – Magic and Mystery in Megalithic Brittany by Natasha Hoffman and Carolyn North, 2010

Newgrange and the New Science - Exploring the Subtle Energies of Ireland's Ancient Neolithic Monument by Kieran Comerford, 2012

Wisdomkeepers of Stonehenge – the Living Libraries and Healers of Megalithic Culture by Graham Phillips, 2019

First Light: The Origins of Newgrange, by Robert Hensey, Oxbow Books, 2015

Animism, Ancestors and Adjusted Styles of Communication: Hidden Art in Irish Passage Tombs by Robert J. Wallis, in Archaeological Imaginations of Religion, edited by Thomas Meier and Petra Tillessen, Budapest, 2014

We Have Never Been Material by Andrew Cochrane, Journal of Iberian Archaeology 9/10, p137-57, 2007

My thanks go to Fiona Hamilton and Melanie Faith for mentoring and feedback in the writing stage; to Jennifer Kaye Davies for proofreading; to Jacqueline Abromeit for the cover design; and to my family, particularly Maria Kennedy and Shanteya, for their invaluable help and support.

ABOUT THE AUTHOR

Lisa Saffron was born in Berkeley, California in 1952 and moved to England in the 1970s. She's been a writer since childhood, writing poetry, novels and non-fiction. A visit to the five-thousand-year-old Newgrange monument in Ireland sparked the idea to write a novel exploring what people today can learn from the wisdom of the ancient stone building societies. The story grew out of her lifelong exploration of spiritual and personal growth teachings. During her life, she's led workshops on compassionate listening, carried out research into environmental health, founded PinkParents, a charity for lesbian and gay parents, and been a foster carer. She lives in Bristol with her two grandchildren, her partner and her guru - Maggie, the cat.